CW01429941

ACKNOW___

For years I've day dreamed about what I'd write in this part of my book if I ever published it and now I have the chance to actually sit down and write it, it's a very surreal feeling.

This book has been a huge part of my life and my imagination for such a long time and there have been many people who have read it when it was just printed off my pc, hole punched and put in a Little Miss Naughty folder and had editing notes along side the paragraphs. So thanks to Helen Long, Julie Brannagan, Gayle Grisdale and Tracy Evans.

I have been lucky enough to have great work colleagues who have encouraged me with my writing and listen to my ramblings about characters and plot changes. So to my lovely friends on TEAM AGENCY, you're all sound!

This book probably wouldn't have seen the light of day without the support and advice of a great friend who introduced me to the authonomy website, Christine Thom (she's a fab writer...so watch this space). Thanks Chris, you are a total star, love you lots.

I have met some fab people on the authonomy website and would like to thank the lovely Lynne and Frances for really getting behind Betrayal and supporting it. I'd like to say I'm sorry the book made you cry, but I'm not really! Your reactions made my day.

Finally, the last and biggest thanks go to my family, Mark and my girls Rebekah and Faye You've let me follow my dream and I love you with all my heart. Thanks for believing!

**Become a fan of "Bev Dulson (books)" on Facebook
for updates on this book and my next one …
Love Overboard!**

PROLOGUE

A TIME FOR REFLECTION: NEW YEARS EVE 1999

The dawn of the new Millennium and the start of new beginnings. Summer was amongst the crowds in Times Square, New York City, surrounded by her friends. Jez stood behind her, his arms wrapped around her waist, pulling her close to keep her warm. The tip of her nose was bright red from the cold December air. A new century, time to put the past behind her and look forward to her future with Jez. He had proposed on Christmas Eve. She had known from the start that Jez was 'The One.' She had accepted his proposal without hesitation and was now in a place where she could forget the past, banish the bad memories from her everyday life and maybe finally accept that the truth may never be known. Maybe it was even better that way. Jez bent down towards her, kissing her cheek she turned her face towards him and brushed his lips with her own.

"Love you babe."

Why did she fill her thoughts with the past when she had a much nicer future, her and Jez's future to think of? New Years resolution? Forget what has been and think of what will be.

****

Amber stood a few feet away from her best friend, Summer She watched Summer and Jez cuddled up together, laughing and kissing in their own little private world. She glanced across at her boyfriend Matt, who although standing next to her might as well have been on the other side of Manhattan for the amount of intimacy there was between them. He'd hardly muttered a word all evening, no change there then. She didn't know why she'd expected New Year to be any different. She already knew that the kiss she'd receive at midnight would be a peck on the cheek, if she was lucky. Why did she stay in such a passionless, lifeless relationship? She knew the answer to that straight away. She could never have a normal relationship, not after what she'd done. No sparkling rock on her finger like Jez had given Summer. Still she was a woman of the nineties, well almost noughties. Who needed guys any way? She moved from one foot to the other and rubbed her hands together in an attempt to keep warm. The past was something that should be well and truly left where it was. However she was smart enough to know that the repercussions of your actions could last a life time. She preferred to think about here and now. Matt may not light her fire, but her lover certainly did! New Years resolution? Keep her lover and live up to the noughties!

****

Christmas and New Year were Jackson's favourite time of year, lots of parties, lots of alcohol and lots of getting laid. Times Square at New Year you just couldn't beat it. He high fived a guy who was walking past him.
"Hey man!"
There was nowhere else he'd rather be and here he was with his friends close by, Summer and Jez in their loved up bubble oblivious too everyone and everything around them, Amber and Matt where behind him with their invisible mile between them. He could never figure that relationship out. Next to him were Claudia and his room mate CJ. Life was kinda cool at the moment he tended not to dwell on the past, sure there were things he'd done that he wished he hadn't. Some things he couldn't even tell his close friends, but hey he lived for the moment and to hell with the consequences. His laid back Caribbean attitude meant he was always chilled. If he didn't treat life like that then he'd end up like Matt - boring! His New Years resolution? Keep life

cool man.

****

Matt couldn't wait to leave this ridiculous place, he couldn't think of anywhere worse to spend New Year, waiting for that God damn ball to drop. Out of the corner of his eye he could see his sister, Summer with that jerk Jez. He couldn't believe she was actually going to marry him. His girlfriend Amber was standing next to him. Girlfriend? What a farce! What was he doing with a sex mad, self obsessed bitch like her? He really didn't know. He glanced at his watch twenty minutes to mid night, he wondered if he could slip away. He needed to get to his office. No one knew if the millennium bug would have an impact or not. He couldn't afford to lose any important data. He took his job as an accountant very seriously and he wanted to make sure all his clients' files remained intact. Yeah, he'd slip away as soon as possible. His resolution? Start the New Year as he meant to go on, in the office.

****

Jez rested his head on Summer's shoulder, moving closer to her. He couldn't believe how much he loved her. He never imagined he could feel like this, she was amazing and she was all his. Everything he did was for her. She'd had a really rough time over the past few years; he just wanted to make her happy. He'd never had a family; he grew up in foster homes. Never knowing what it would be like to be loved or to show love and now that he was experiencing it he was never gonna let it go, not ever. Summer was the most important part of his life and he would do anything to protect her. Help her forget the bad times. He'd always found blanking things out was effective, but he knew Summer couldn't do that. For now; he couldn't think of a better place to celebrate New Year than with his arms around the most beautiful and amazing woman in the world. New Years resolution? Make Summer his wife.

****

Claudia stood in between CJ and Jackson. She felt safe with these guys, she was wary of men after what happened to her. She glanced over at CJ and not for the first time noticing how attractive he was. She loved the way his hair curled slightly at the nape of his neck; did he even know it did that? She liked knowing something about him that he didn't. She also happened to be in love with him, she just needed to find the courage to tell him that. Jackson made her laugh so much. He was always such good company. They were her knights in shining armour. They had saved her from a serious assault that she'd never quite been able to get over. Romantically all her hopes were pinned on CJ. She looked over to Summer and Jez, they were so much in love, would she and CJ ever have that? He didn't have a clue how she felt. She'd never found the right moment to tell him. They were best of friends, but more than anything she wanted them to be a couple. People at work called her the ice maiden behind her back. In truth she was saving herself for the man she loved. New Years resolution? Lay her heart on the line and reveal her true feelings to CJ, it couldn't be that bad - could it?

****

CJ was enjoying the carnival atmosphere, tapping his feet to the music and moving his shoulders in time to the beat. He loved it when he was in a situation like this when people you'd never met before just came up and hugged you and wished you well. If only life could always be like that. Claudia seemed quiet tonight. He caught her attention.

"You ok?" he mouthed. She nodded, smiling at him.

Out of the group of friends he was closest to Jackson and Claudia. He and Claudia were the quiet ones of the group and similar in personality; they could talk for hours on any given subject. However, no matter how close he was to her he could never tell her his secret. Only one other living soul knew and he couldn't tell anyone else. It was better that they didn't know. Secrets and lies, life seemed to be full of them. He looked round at his friends, did they all have skeletons in the closet or did they know everything about each other? He supposed there were parts of themselves' that they kept hidden just like he did. Did they really know each other at all? New Years resolution? Keep hiding those secrets... at all costs.

CHAPTER ONE

Summer Stevens lay in bed; it was now the year 2000, Y2K, the Millennium. Whatever people called this particular New Year or however they celebrated it, one thing would remain the same, the hangover. Despite feeling like the party was still going on in her head, she had woken up with a warm glow radiating around her body. The reason for that emotion lay next to her, snoring away. Jez Walsh, her fiancé since Christmas Eve. No man could ever compare to Jez, she adored him and knew she was so lucky to have found him, although how they met wasn't exactly romantic...

Summer was in the back seat of her dad's car. Her mom and Dad were in the front chatting about their next business trip; her mom had the journal out on her knee checking off appointments. It seemed to Summer that their marriage was more of a business partnership.

"So we're due in Washington next Wednesday for your meeting with the President. I need to make sure I've picked up a birthday present for the First Lady before we go." Eleanor Stevens made notes in her journal.
"What did we get her last year?"
"A Wedgewood dinner service. I had it shipped in from England especially."

Summer sighed, she was sure the White House already came equipped with plates.
"I was thinking Waterford crystal this year, although it may be too late. It will have to come from Ireland. Or possibly Egyptian sheets."

George Stevens chuckled. "What to buy the woman who has everything."

"Maybe she'd prefer something just for herself mom," Summer began. "I'm sure she'd love to curl up on the sofa watching Friends DVD's in a nice new pair of PJ's."

"Oh honey, it's not that simple."

She noticed her dad glancing at her from the rear view mirror as if he'd forgotten she was there, nothing unusual about that.

"I've made an itinerary of everything..."

The car jolted.

"What the..." Her dad looked in the mirror as the car shuddered, it was hit again. Summer tried to look out of the back window but all she could see was headlights dazzling her. Her dad was trying to swerve out of the way.

"George! George!" Her mom was screaming.

She heard an almighty bang and then everything went black.

The fire truck from Ladder fourteen was first on the scene.

"Dante, Walsh and Adams go check out the car." The fire captain yelled as he began to direct the cars out of the way so that the EMT's could get through. The traffic on Brooklyn Bridge was almost at a standstill by now.

The fire fighters ran towards the car, they could see the hood had been pushed almost into the front seats of the car.

"Jeez, this looks bad."

Summer thought something was wrong with her vision when she opened her eyes, everything was flashing blue and red. She didn't know where she was. She tried to move but her legs were jammed and the whole of the left side of her body ached. As her eyes became used to the lights she could see her dad slumped

over the steering wheel. She couldn't see her mom.
"Mom...dad..."
Nobody answered.
She screamed.

"You guys check out the front passenger seats I'll check out the back," Jez Walsh shouted to his colleagues.
He'd already seen that the people in the front seats were in a bad way, but his attention was focused on the girl sitting in the back was becoming increasingly distressed. He clambered into the back of the car.

"Hey, it's ok. We'll get you out. You're gonna be just fine," Jez tried to position himself so that she couldn't see what was happening in the front. She looked scared to death. "Where are you hurt?"
"My, my legs are stuck and my side... my mom... my dad..."
"Honey, it's ok," he reached out for her hand. "What's your name?"
"Summer," she whispered.
"Ok Summer, I'm Jez and I'm gonna help you get out. Can you move your toes?"

She nodded her head. He could tell that from the force of the impact the passenger seat had trapped her. There was no way she was going to be able to get out until her parents had been freed. He looked up out of the window. The power tools were being off loaded from the truck. It wasn't going to be pretty.

"Looks like we're gonna be here for a while Summer. My guys need to get your mom out first and then we can move this seat."
His radio crackled, the EMT's wanted him to get his butt out of the car so they could administer treatment.
"The medical guys wanna get in here and check you out. Is that

ok Summer?"
She shook her head. "Please don't leave me, I'm scared. Please stay Jez."

Maybe it was the way she said his name. Maybe it was the look in those beautiful green eyes of hers, but he didn't want to leave her either.
He nodded and reached for his radio. "That's a negative captain. Passenger is stable, but trapped in the back until front seat can be moved. She still needs assistance from me," Jez hoped to God that his captain would realize that she was about to witness her parents being cut from this wreck.
"Affirmative, Walsh. Medics on standby if situation worsens; keep me up dated."
She smiled up at him. "Thank you."
"Hey no worries; I'm more than happy to sit here with you."

She shivered. He reached out and stroked her bare arm; she looked straight into his eyes. Just for a moment, they weren't in that car. They were a million miles away. He couldn't describe the feeling that just hit him, but he knew she felt it too.

"You're cold," he whispered. He wriggled out of his fire coat and wrapped it round her. She winced as she moved forward.
"Are you sure you don't want me to get a medic, get something for the pain?"
"No, please just stay. What's happening with my mom and dad?" she thought she could hear her mom moaning.
Jez glanced over his shoulder. He could see they were just about ready with the power tools.

"Ok Summer, this is what's gonna happen. The medics can't help your mom an dad yet; the car needs to be cut open to get them out," he could see the fear flash across her face. "It's ok; it's the *quickest way to get them out. The noise will be loud, but I'm not going any where. I'm staying right here with you. You won't be alone."*

Summer looked out of the window; she could see the fire fighters and what looked like a chain saw. It looked like something out of a horror film.
"Summer, Summer!"
She snapped her head back towards Jez.
"Listen to me honey."
His face was only inches away from hers, all she could see was him.
"Right, it's gonna get real loud in about thirty seconds so listen up. I want you to just look right here," he pointed to his eyes, "Don't look anywhere else. If it gets too noisy, then...just move you head here," he moved his hand down to his chest. "I'll do my best to keep the noise out."
She nodded, already looking into his eyes.
He could get lost in those eyes. Get a grip Walsh, start being professional. He ordered himself.

Summer's bottom lip was starting to tremble, she was petrified. He didn't wait for the machines to start. He just pulled her to him, gently, so as not to hurt her and wrapped his arms around her, protecting her. The noise of the machine's cutting through metal was horrific. This was the first time he'd heard the noise from the inside. It wasn't nice. Summer was shaking in his arms. He tried to pull her as close as possible to drown out what he could. It seemed to be taking forever, but he knew in reality it was pretty quick. This was what they were trained for. Once the machines had stopped he lifted Summer's head up gently.

"Summer it's over; we'll get you out in no time."
"Mom and dad...are they ok?"

He could see her dad being placed on a gurney, it didn't look good. They were still trying to get her mom out.

"I really don't know, but they're in the best hands now Summer..."

"Thank you."

"What for?" he couldn't stop looking into those eyes.

"For not leaving."

"Hey. I told you, I wasn't going anywhere."

They eventually freed Summer from the wreckage. He was still by her side as she was wheeled towards the ambulance rig.

The medics lifted the stretcher into the rig, alarm crossed her face.

"Are you going?" She looked panic stricken.

"Hell. No. I told you I'd stick around," Jez looked over to the other fire fighters.

"Dante! Tell the captain I'll meet you all back at the fire house."

The hospital was only two blocks away from the ladder fourteen base. The captain would probably go ballistic with him...but sometimes you had to break the rules.

The accident that had left her just bruised and battered had killed both her parents. She couldn't understand how she had escaped so lightly and they hadn't. The nurses told her that a fire fighter had been ringing up to enquire how she was and he'd sent some flowers. Jez. Summer recalled how tenderly he'd held her hand and hadn't let go. How he'd told her to look into his eyes and she never wanted to stop... How this total stranger had been there for her at the worst moment in her life.

The following day Jez turned up at the hospital, she felt the connection with him immediately. He sat at her bedside for hours, listening as the grief poured out. She asked him what he was doing there. He told her that he hadn't been able to stop thinking about her. That was where their relationship had begun. By day one of being together they had already been through so much that the strong intense bond between them just kept getting stronger. Without the support from Jez and Matt, she'd never have gotten through it all in one piece. She hoped she would never have to face anything like that again, but knowing what she knew now, that was wishful thinking…

Fate worked in mysterious ways, the accident that took her parents lives had bought her soul mate into her life. He was physically attractive; he kept himself in shape at the gym at the fire house, she loved it when he wrapped his strong muscular arms around her. His dark hair was cropped and he had the bluest eyes she'd ever seen. His infectious grin always made her smile and he was the most amazing guy she had ever met. He totally captivated her, there were no sides to him; what you saw was what you got and what you got was pretty damn good.

Summer had complete faith in their relationship, it was so strong that it had even withstood the trauma of that awful vacation two year's previously. The events of that trip had changed her life and her friend's lives for good - and not for the better. Her mind drifted back to that ill-fated morning, the memory of the lifeless body was too much to bear. She blinked quickly to try and erase the horrid pictures from her mind. Jez turned over in his sleep and draped an arm across her body, his snoring had stopped and he was now breathing quietly. She wondered if he ever had dreams of what happened like she did. Did little things trigger off bad memories like it did with her? Did he ever wonder who the killer was? Did he ever think she did it? She shook her head as if to shake the depressing thoughts away. She decided a nice strong cup of coffee would sort her head out. She leaned across and gently kissed Jez, he stirred slightly. She quietly slipped out of bed.

Matt Stevens stood in the kitchen of the Penthouse apartment that he shared with his sister. He was making bacon and eggs, the perfect cure for a hangover. The apartment had belonged to his mom and dad, he and Summer had inherited it. Their parents had left them well provided for, as a high profile political couple money was never an issue. However the main bulk of the money, to be distributed between them was kept in a trust fund until Summer reached her twenty fifth birthday. Therefore his girlfriend Amber and Jez the Jerk also lived in the apartment to help with the bills.

Matt didn't really see eye to eye with Jez and disliked having to live under the same roof as him, but even he could see that it would be unfair for Amber to move in and not let Summer ask Jez to do the same. In hindsight, it might not have been a good idea to take that extra step with Amber. They were going through a rocky patch and at times he really needed his own space. Sometimes he thought the only reason they were still together was the fact that Amber liked living in a prestigious part of New York, she was that type of girl. The toast popped up out of the toaster just as Summer appeared.

"Any coffee yet?"
"Coming right up."
"How come you're up so early? It's New Years' Day," she asked.
"Y'know me, I can get by on a few hours sleep. D'you want any breakfast?"
She sat down and began flicking through the morning papers. "If there's any going, look at all these pictures of people celebrating the new millennium all over the world."
"People party at New Year, every year. The way the media are going on, you'd think there had never been a New Year's Eve

before."

"You can be so cynical at times Matt," she scolded him.

Matt was twenty six, three years her senior. He was average build, average height, Mr. Average as Amber often referred to him. His short brown hair was slightly darker than Summer's hair, although she cheated and had caramel highlights put in every eight weeks. His eyes were brown, hers were green. If you looked at a family photo Matt was a younger version of their dad and their mom had looked so youthful that she was often mistaken for Summer's older sister. Matt placed a plate in front of Summer.

"Mm, this looks good."

"I suppose Jez is still in bed?"

She nodded.

"He's so lazy."

"Matt, leave him alone, it's New Years Day for God sake. We didn't get in till the early hours. He's entitled to a lie in. Where's Amber? Out jogging in Central Park?" Summer added sarcastically.

"She's in bed. Point taken."

"I wish you'd make more of an effort with Jez. I just can't understand what you've got against him," she sighed.

"It's nothing in particular; I just don't like the guy. You can do so much better than him."

"Jez and I have been together for three years, we're engaged for God sake! He's everything I want, He's never cheated on me, would never be violent towards me. He'd never do anything to hurt me and if that's not enough he got me out of the car crash. Exactly how high are your standards Matt?"

"It's not that I'm not grateful to him for helping you through the accident, but that's his job."

"His job was to get me out of the car; he didn't have to visit me in hospital."

"I don't know; maybe we just have a clash in personalities and as far as I'm concerned no guy is good enough for my little sister."

"Matt, I'm twenty three. I'm not so little anymore. I'm perfectly capable of looking after myself."

"I know. But since mom and dad have gone, it's my job to look after you."

Summer couldn't respond, the thought of the car crash and her parents death coupled together with the awful images of Colorado that morning were getting to her. Sometimes it all just felt too much. Matt reached across the breakfast bar and squeezed her hand. Nothing tore him apart more than seeing the look of pain flash across her face whenever their parents' death was mentioned. He knew she felt guilty that she was the only one who survived. The last couple of years had taken its toll on Summer, first the car accident and then what had taken place in Colorado.

Marcus' death was shrouded in mystery, nobody apart from the group of friends who had gone on that vacation to Colorado knew about his untimely demise. Nobody else knew for the simple fact that whoever killed Marcus was one of them. They had no choice but to conceal his death to avoid anyone going to jail and to try and get on with their lives the best they could, some managed it better than others. There was no one to miss Marcus, he had no job, no room mate and his parents had emigrated to Australia six months prior to his death. Due to a disagreement they made it clear to Marcus that as far as they were concerned they no longer had a son. Well that was certainly true now.

In fact the only relatives Marcus still had contact with were himself and Summer. As far as Matt knew Marcus' parents had never tried to make contact with him and were unaware of his death. Whenever Matt's mind took him back to the days of Marcus' death the thing that worried him most was Marcus' parents trying to make amends with their way ward son. It was a possible time bomb just waiting to go off, then the whole situation would explode right when they least expected it.

Summer went back into the bedroom; she could hear the shower running in the en-suite bathroom. She flopped down on the bed. She loved her bedroom. The walls were chocolate and mocha coloured, giving the room a really warm cozy feel to it. She often lit candles to give it a more romantic feel. She and Jez had decorated it themselves and loved snuggling up in there in the cold winter months. The room also had patio doors that opened out onto a small balcony, separate to the main balcony attached to the penthouse. It gave them a bit of privacy and it was one of their favourite places to sit on the long hazy summer nights. The comforting feel of the room couldn't dispel the anxiety she was feeling right now, she was almost close to tears.

Over eighteen months had passed and Summer still hadn't forgotten, she could never forget. She was just glad she had Jez to keep her sane. She sighed deeply. Who would have thought when they flew out to Colorado that by their return flight to JFK that their whole world would have changed forever. Her mind wandered back to that outward flight.

She and Jez sat together, watching the in flight movie. For the life of her she couldn't remember what it was but she supposed that wasn't important. They were both too excited about their first vacation together to take too much notice of the movie anyway. They spent ages talking about the skiing they would be doing, the cozy nights in front of the log fire; it was supposed to have been perfect.

Matt sat in the row in front with Jackson D'arby and CJ, part of the group of friends who were traveling with them. The three of them were loudly discussing who the best player in the NBA was. As they had already consumed half of the planes' alcohol supply, that debate had the possibility to go on for hours.

Amber Gordon and Claudia Michaels, Summer's best friends sat in front of the guy's with Marcus. The girl's were flicking through Cosmo, trying to avoid having to make conversation with Marcus, even though at the time he was Amber's boyfriend. Amber and Marcus were an even stranger combination than Amber and Matt. They were the most miss-matched couple ever. They were constantly putting each other down and seemed to enjoy it. It was their favourite pastime. They didn't even look right together. Amber always looked chic and sophisticated in the latest Donna Karan. Her shoulder length blonde hair was always sleek, smooth and never out of place. Her complexion was perfect and her make up always looked like it had been applied in a beauty salon and was never ever smudged. In fact she looked like she'd just stepped out of the pages of Cosmo herself.

Marcus on the other hand had a permanent disheveled look with designer - or so he thought - stubble. He had this misconception that he was some kind of Adonis. His hair was shoulder length and a dirty blonde colour. He thought he looked like some mean and moody film star. She recalled how Marcus had unsuccessfully tried to chat up the air stewardess, asking her if she would help him join the mile high club. This infuriated Amber. Summer often wondered why Amber put up with him. She was gorgeous by anybody's standards, with curves in all the right places. She could have anyone she wanted, so why she chose Marcus was probably just as big a mystery as who killed him.

From the bed Summer watched Jez wander out of the bathroom, he was naked except for a towel wrapped around his waist. Tiny droplets of water slid down his muscular shoulders and toned chest, his hair was still damp. He looked so God damn sexy. She felt a rush of desire flood through her body. She saw his eyes drop taking in every inch of her body.

Jez watched her look appreciatively over his own body, her eyes resting on where his own arousal was apparent. He moved closer to her, letting the towel drop away from his body. She looked so irresistible lying there on the bed gazing at him with that sexy look in her eyes. He lay down next to her and gently rolled her onto her back.

"Hey you," he whispered as he kissed her lips softly. The eagerness of her kiss turned him on even more. He slipped his hand under the soft satin negligee and let his hand run across her smooth skin, moving up towards her breasts, letting his fingers brush against her nipples. He pushed the thin material over her head, exposing the fullness of her breasts to him. He lowered his head to kiss them. She responded with a moan of pleasure as she arched her back to push herself closer to him. He gently ran his tongue over her nipple, feeling it instantly harden. She reached out to touch him. He kissed her with more urgency enjoying the feel of her touch. He let his hands roam all over her body, her breathing became faster, her moans more frequent, his name on her lips. He couldn't wait to be inside her, but he wanted to pleasure her first. He began to kiss his way down her body; he slid his hands underneath her butt and raised her up closer to his face using his tongue to bring her to the brink.

When he knew she could take no more he positioned himself on top of her and eased himself inside her. He watched her breasts move against him as her body jerked with pleasure. She wrapped her legs around him pulling him even closer to her. They collapsed in each others arms and lay entwined on the bed. He held her close enjoying the feel of her naked body against his. He could feel her heart racing.

"Happy New Year babe," he whispered.

"What a way to start," she sighed happily.

CHAPTER TWO

Summer and Jez spent the majority of New Years Day lazing around the apartment watching TV. Neither of them had felt like moving. Summer had been out on their private balcony earlier on looking over the City, New York certainly looked like it was suffering from the after effects of the night before. After spending all morning curled up in bed together, they were now snuggled up on the sofa.

"We figured you two would still be chillin," Amber announced as she walked into the living area. "We rented a movie if you wanna watch it with us." She finished as she took her coat off.
"What d'ya get?" Jez asked.
"Mission impossible," Amber replied.

So with nothing better to do the four of them sat watching the movie. Matt couldn't get into it. The movie had been Amber's choice, she'd already seen it before but apparently Tom Cruise really did it for her. Whatever 'it' was he could only pity Tom Cruise. Anyway, Amber was the least of his concerns at the moment.

He was worried about Summer. He had always been protective of his little sister, more so since the death of their parent's. They had no other family close by, so really they just had each other and he would always look out for her. He knew how emotional and fragile she was after their parent's death, it had affected her deeply.

Marcus' 'accident' hadn't helped matters. He knew the events in Colorado still preyed heavily on her mind. He tried not to think about it, in fact he had almost totally blocked it out of his mind. He and Amber had never spoken about it, the subject of Marcus and Amber's relationship hadn't been discussed either. He didn't even know how Amber felt about the whole Marcus situation. In hindsight, judging by the way his relationship with Amber was on a downward spiral, it was probably a conversation they should have had.

Despite his problems with Amber, Summer was causing him to have a sense of unease at the moment. She hadn't been herself for a while, she thought very deeply about things and being the type of person she was, she wouldn't rest until she knew the truth about what really happened to Marcus. What would be the consequence of that happening? Trying not to think about that he turned his attention to why Summer seemed so pre occupied by Marcus. He supposed it should be easy to understand why it was on Summer's mind, after all Marcus was their cousin, they may not have liked him very much. He had done some terrible things to all of them, people who were supposed to be his friends. He was a ruthless person, the type of guy who took pleasure in other people's misfortunes. He would actively look for ways to cause chaos and problems. He was a nasty piece of work, but he was still family and blood is thicker than water. His dad had always instilled in him that it was important on the face of things to show a united front. As the senator of New York City this was vital to George Stevens. It wasn't politics that got you votes it was good old fashioned family values. George Stevens along with his glamorous wife Eleanor Stevens always portrayed themselves as perfect parents. They were present at both his and Summer's graduations, along with the relevant members of the press, never one to miss an opportunity.

Matt wasn't bitter, he didn't know any different. He'd never been on fishing trips with his dad, sat up and had a beer late at night watching the Super bowl highlights, he was used to it. What did annoy him was the pedestal Summer had put their dad on, he could do no wrong in her eyes. If he promised to be home early and he got in after she had gone to bed, it was ok 'coz she knew how busy he was. If he was away on business and hadn't called, it was ok 'coz sometimes his cell wouldn't have a signal. It was all ok 'coz the minute he walked through the door she would be making him coffee, asking him about his trips, not seeming to mind that he never once asked her about her life. Yeah on the face of it, they looked just like one big happy family just like his dad wanted. He supposed he should be grateful to Jez for making Summer happy, but he just had a niggling feeling about him that just wouldn't go away. He'd never liked any of her boyfriends, but that was his job as her big brother. Jez was different though he was way too smooth. Matt watched him out of the corner of his eye. Summer was curled up against Jez, he was stroking her hair. They were always so touchy feely with each other and it was blatantly obvious how much in love they were it was quite nauseating at times but Matt couldn't trust Jez not to break Summer's heart.

Later that same night Summer was looking through some papers she needed for work. She kept a file in her bedroom with all kinds of documents, letters, bits and bobs. As she was looking through the file she came across a photo of Marcus.
"What's that doing there?"
His smiling face was staring up at her, that menacing smile that seemed so familiar, too familiar. Gingerly she picked it up, almost afraid to. The look in those eyes, those steely blue eyes sent a shiver down her spine. She was convinced that there had been pure evil in him, but then wouldn't that make the person who murdered him just as evil? No she couldn't think like that. None of her friends were evil and the killer was someone close to her, Matt, Amber, Claudia, Jackson, CJ and of course Jez. She

loved then all and whatever had driven one of them to kill had to have been a moment of madness. She had to believe that it wasn't premeditated; to discover that it had been planned would be even worse than finding out who killed him in the first place. No, none of her friends could be compared to Marcus.

There were countless incidents of where Marcus had used an unfortunate situation for his own personal gain. He had done it to her. She was seventeen and was at Marcus' twenty first birthday party. She had been dating a guy called Brad for a few months; he was the coolest guy in school, the guy who every girl wanted to date. For a while they were the golden couple. She was the captain of the cheerleading squad and he was a quarter back and the star of the football team. They were even homecoming king and queen at their senior prom. He had been putting pressure on her to sleep with him, she wasn't sure about it. She liked him a lot, but deep down she knew she didn't love him and she also knew that when he told he loved her it was just to try and get her into bed. She had discussed the matter with Amber. They were supposed to be studying for an English quiz, somehow the matter of whether she should sleep with Brad or not seemed slightly more important.

"Don't be such a wuss Summer, just get on with it, it's only sex. You don't have to be in love with the guy."

"I know that, but I'm just not sure…"

Amber laughed. "You don't have to wait for your wedding night these days y'know."

"I want to, but, well… shouldn't I feel more excited about it? Shouldn't I have butterflies in my stomach at the thought of Brad touching me?"

"It's not like a freakin Disney film y'know. It's wham bam, thank you ma'am, if you're lucky. Why d'you think I go for older guys?"

"If it's that bad, what's the point then?"

"To get it over and done with, you don't want your virginity hanging round your neck. Just get drunk, it'll be fine." Amber had her first sexual experience at fifteen so she felt like a bit of an expert on the subject.

So that was exactly what Summer did, a few Vodka's at the party built up her confidence enough so that when Brad led her off to one of the bedrooms she knew that tonight was the night. Despite the fact that she'd lost her virginity that night, it hadn't been anything particularly memorable, she didn't know what she'd gotten all stressed out for, and in fact it was practically over before it had begun. Both of them pretending they knew what they were doing when neither of them had a clue. It was nothing like her experiences with Jez, he could make her body respond with the merest touch of his lips on hers. She had gotten sidetracked. Jez always did that to her. Anyway, there she was sprawled on the bed, very worse for wear, Brad on top of her, when in walked Marcus with some blonde bimbo in tow. He obviously had the same idea. Of all the people to catch her at it, why did it have to be Marcus? He wasted no time in telling her that Matt wouldn't be too pleased to know his little sister was in the next room doing stuff she shouldn't be and as she was a minor it really was his duty to tell her mom and dad what she had been up to. She couldn't believe her bad luck.

Marcus reminded her that his silence could be bought. She had spent the next few months giving him almost all of her allowance. It was only when Amber and Claudia became suspicious that she had no money and no boyfriend - she'd stopped seeing Brad, it would've only given Marcus more ammunition, that Marcus' little blackmailing scheme came to an abrupt end. The girls persuaded her to tell Matt what was happening, which she did. He was angry at first but then just relieved that she hadn't gotten herself pregnant or anything. He was however going ballistic at Marcus' behaviour, he promptly stormed off to see him. Matt never told her what he'd said to Marcus, but she knew one thing he never asked her for another dime again.

Summer still had the photo of Marcus in her hand, she crumpled it up and out of nowhere tears fell. She couldn't understand why she felt so upset about his death or why she was letting it get to her when she disliked him so much. The world was probably much better off without Marcus in it. Jez walked into the bedroom, she tried to hide her tears, but he could tell straight away that she was upset. His eyes focused on the scrunched up photo. He bent down and gently took it from her hands, he took one look at it and tossed it straight into the trash can. He moved to the bed, sitting down next to her. He wrapped his arms around her and pulled her close to him. She rested her head on his chest as she quietly sobbed. He stroked her hair gently.

"It's alright babe, ssh it's ok," he whispered.
"Jez, I'm so confused, I can't get him out of my head, the person who killed him is one of us, someone we love and trust is a murderer. How can they live with themselves?"
"Don't think about it, it's over. It's finished."
She moved her head up to face him. "You're wrong, it's not over, and it won't be over till I know who killed him."
Jez took her face in his hands, he gently brushed the tears away from her cheeks with his thumb, and he kissed her lips softly.
"What's important is here and now, me and you … I'll get you through this I promise," he whispered. "I love you so much."
"Not as much as I love you."

They lay together on the bed, her head resting on his chest, protected by his arm pulling her closer to him; his other arm was wrapped around her body holding her like he was never going to let her go. He lifted his hand to her cheek and stroked it till she fell asleep. He wanted to help her so much, to take away the pain. She felt so vulnerable to him, so innocent. He'd noticed it straight away, when she was trapped inside the car. He couldn't explain how he'd felt that night, he'd never experienced anything like it before but it was like a thunderbolt. It became his whole focus to get this girl out of the car and make sure she was alright. Ok so that was his job, but the feelings behind it were driven by an emotion that he'd never felt before. This girl, Summer, had struck a chord in him. Despite this sense of vulnerability she had been amazingly brave as she watched her parents being cut free and struggled with her own injuries. He knew he couldn't leave her and when she's asked him to stay he knew he had no alternative. He didn't know what she'd done to him but it felt pretty darn good. After he eventually left the hospital he couldn't sleep that night. He couldn't get her out of his mind, not that he wanted to. He plucked up the courage to go and see her. Now here he was three years later holding the girl of his dreams in his arms. She still gave him that stomach flipping feeling, she was the one for him, and he'd known that on that cold dark rainy night on Brooklyn Bridge. He sighed deeply as he closed his eyes. He drifted off into a troubled sleep, with nightmarish dreams about the equally nightmarish vacation in Colorado.

The alarm clock buzzed at seven o'clock. Summer reached over and pressed the snooze button. She moved closer to Jez and snuggled into him, he stroked her arm lightly. He was half asleep. She thought back to last night. She was angry at herself for getting upset over that stupid photo of Marcus. She felt like she was losing her mind and had no control over her thoughts. She had even begun to wonder if she had actually killed Marcus and somehow lost all memory of it. She'd read that happened to people sometimes when something so traumatic occurred and the person couldn't deal with it so they just forgot it. She doubted it was as easy as it sounded but if that was the case it would certainly explain her inability to move on. In fact if she was completely honest with herself she was more obsessed with the whole situation than ever. The only way she could move on was to find out what really happened that night eighteen months ago.

Amber Gordon sat at her usual table in the coffee house near her office waiting for Summer. She sat by the window, people watching. She ran her own very successful interior design business. She had lots of famous clients and had spent the morning with a soap actress who thought she deserved an Oscar, a politician with very wandering hands and a doped up rock star. At least she had something to look forward to this afternoon; she had a special appointment with her man of the moment. That was the bonus of being the boss; she could lock her office, draw the blinds and have an hour or so of fun. She took her career seriously but a girl's gotta have fun too! She knew her staff were aware of what she was up to, but that was part of the thrill. She checked her watch; Summer was running late, still she was in no rush to get back to the office her 'appointment' wasn't for another two hours.

Amber gazed into her skinny latte as she absentmindedly stirred it. She had a million thoughts running through her head and it wasn't about colour schemes or fabrics. She was concerned about Summer's bizarre behaviour recently. Of course she knew exactly what was behind it all or rather, who was behind it. Then there was Matt, their relationship wasn't exactly wonderful at the moment. She supposed she was getting bored of him, he wasn't exciting enough for her, in fact he was pretty dull really. Mr. Average. The guys she usually went for were anything but dull. That was the attraction with Marcus, so he was a jerk, but he certainly wasn't boring. Matt needed to be the one in control, he wanted someone submissive. Someone who didn't know their own mind and could be easily led, not someone like her. She didn't need a man to rely on, she depended on herself and no one else she played by her own rules. Not even Summer knew everything there was to know about her, most things, but not everything. She had secrets that she couldn't even tell Summer, many of them about Marcus. Their relationship had been a rollercoaster ride. Probably the only good part had been the sex, which had been pretty mind blowing. Marcus was also the controlling type but in a different way to Matt. He was aggressive and while their sex life had been explosive, so were their rows, things got thrown and on more than occasion he had become violent. He always hit her where it wouldn't show. She had been too proud to admit this to anyone, she was Amber Gordon, Miss Independent and in control. He may have over powered her physically, but mentally she was tougher. She out smarted him in the end. When would guys realize she was the one calling the shots, always. Marcus had learnt that the hard way.

"Sorry I'm late; I got held up with one of the DJ's." Summer apologized as she sat down opposite Amber, she worked for NYCFM as a researcher. She really enjoyed her job in fact it didn't feel like work, it was so much fun. She got to meet all kinds of famous people while she was researching the items for the programmes.

"I tried to get in touch with Claudia to see if she could join us, but her secretary said she was in meetings all day," Summer added.
"The perils of being a top lawyer hey. How's your morning been?"
"Hectic as usual, I feel like I've done a weeks work in one

morning," she sighed. The waitress came over and she ordered a frappucino.

"You look tired," Amber commented, a note of concern in her voice.

"I haven't been sleeping well," she admitted.

"Anything wrong?" Amber asked innocently.

"No, just the usual stuff."

"Wanna talk about it?"

"Honestly Amber, it's nothing."

"Summer we've been friends forever; I know when something's bugging you. Now quit with the bullshit and spill."

"It's Marcus," she whispered.

"Figured as much. Why are you wasting your time thinking about that asshole?"

"I can't stop thinking about his murder. Don't you ever want to know who killed him and why?"

"Some things are better left unknown," she replied slowly.

"You must think about it. Doesn't it keep you awake at night?"

"Honey the only thing that keeps me awake at night is a good session."

Summer pulled a face.

"Look Summer, just drop it and forget about him. Matt's driving me crazy with his "brotherly" duty to be concerned about you. For all our sakes and your own sanity, leave it in the past where it belongs. Marcus is better off dead anyway."

"Oh my God Amber, how can you of all people say that? You were his girlfriend when he died."

Yeah well we all make mistakes. There are things you couldn't even begin to imagine that went on between us two..." She stopped at that, she really didn't want to get into this any further.

"Things that you could kill him for?"

"Oh for God sake Summer. I was foolish enough to think I could tame his wild ways that maybe underneath all the arrogance, selfishness and downright nastiness, there may have been a decent guy there. All I'm guilty off is being a poor judge of character."

With that being the final word on the matter, she changed the subject to the sale that had just started in Saks. Summer was only half listening. She couldn't do what Amber, Matt and Jez had asked, she could never forget about Marcus. The nightmares were still too real. She couldn't let go of the past there was still too many unanswered questions.

Jez arrived home earlier than usual, he walked down the hall of the apartment into the kitchen. Matt was at the breakfast bar, working on his laptop. Great Jez thought to himself.

"Hey," Jez muttered as he went over to the fridge to grab an OJ. Matt didn't even look up to acknowledge him.

Jerk. "D'you wanna drink?" Jez asked.

"Nope."

An exciting conversation as usual, they could just about manage to be civil to one another. He could do without all the hassle of this animosity between them. As Summer's brother, Jez hoped to get on with him, for Summer's sake if nothing else. Matt was having none of it. He knew Matt thought of him as all brawn and no brains and didn't think much of his job as a fire fighter. He could never understand the mentality behind that. Matt was a freakin accountant, Jez saved lives, go figure. He was sick to death of Matt and his inflated ego. He would love to tell him exactly what he thought of him, but he knew he had to keep the peace, he didn't want to add to Summer's problems. He hoped things would improve once they were married. Matt would have to accept him then. For the time being he was just going to have to give as good as he got, whilst trying to keep the situation relatively calm. Jez picked up his drink and walked out of the kitchen aware of Matt's glares.

CHAPTER THREE

Claudia Michaels quickly ran her fingers through her long auburn hair to give it a tousled look. She applied her lip gloss just as quickly. She was running late, but she still had a spare minute to check her emails, see if there was anything important she needed to look at for tomorrow. She clicked on her inbox. Two new messages, one off Doug Harper her old MD, she'd read that when she needed cheering up. The other was from Leyton Carter, a lawyer from a rival firm. He knew of her reputation for successful convictions for domestic violence cases, for which she was known as an expert and he often asked for her advice on some of his own cases. One of the reasons she was so passionate about violence against women was because she never reported her own assault, something she had always regretted.

So by fighting other women's corners it took away some of the guilt she felt about letting him get away with it, although he didn't get away with it in the end, did he? She clicked to open the email, she scanned it quickly. He was asking her if she was free one night and would she like to go out for a bite to eat sometime? She dumped the message in the trash. He was a really nice guy and she was a little bit flattered by the attention he gave her. He'd asked her out a few times, maybe if she didn't feel so involved with CJ she might have given him a chance, as it was all her romantic thoughts were about CJ. She clicked her PC off and sighed, she was tired after being in meetings all day with the other partners. They had been discussing a merger with another firm. There was a lot of unsettlement amongst the staff as they were concerned that the proposed merger could mean redundancies. In today's talks Claudia had managed to secure all the jobs in her department. A less focused person may not have managed it, but when it came to business she knew exactly what she was doing. She was proud of her achievement. She picked up her Adidas sports bag and headed out of her office, her secretary's desk was empty, Gloria was long since gone.

Claudia strode across the open plan office towards the elevators, she was aware of the looks she was getting from some of her colleagues who were also working late. At twenty five, Claudia was the youngest partner of Robert James & Co. the law firm for which she worked. She joined the company straight from High School, working in the typing pool at the bottom of the ladder. It was through sheer hard work and determination that she was where she was today, plus the fact that the MD at the time Doug Harper had taken a personal interest in her. He could see her potential and took her under his wing, much to the annoyance of the senior partners. Claudia felt like she was constantly battling to prove herself to them, but she wouldn't let them get in her way, she had ambition. As soon as she'd been employed by the company she got her head down and got on with her job. She had no time for office gossip, which usually meant she was the subject of it. Such as the time of her promotion to office manager some years ago, she heard the whispers about the weird girl from typing who was now a manager. How on earth had that happened?

The general consensus was that she was sleeping her way to the top. Doug had taught her a long time ago to ignore idle gossip; it was usually caused by jealousy. He was a wise man and she respected him deeply, they had formed a great friendship over the years, there had never been anything sexual between them. Although he was nearing sixty he took good care of himself, worked out regularly. He was a good catch for someone; he was rich, handsome, distinguished and powerful. He had confided to Claudia that he was lonely; most women were only after his money. He had proposed to Claudia, offering her a life of luxury.

She had declined. A life of luxury was not what she wanted, well not without earning it first. She had worked too hard, come too far to give it all up to be someone's trophy wife. Doug had understood her reasons, but they still went out regularly for dinner and she often escorted him to the theatre or Gala events. Her refusal of his proposal hadn't affected their friendship at all; he even said it only made him respect her even more. He had been her only friend in the whole God damn company.

Claudia had missed him when he retired and moved out to the Bahamas. They e-mailed each other regularly and she knew that whenever she needed a vacation there was always a place waiting for her in the Bahamas. She should've gone there eighteen months ago instead of Colorado. She was still known as Doug Harper's protégé in business circles and his bit on the side in the gossip columns.   She'd earned a reputation as a hard nosed, cold hearted business woman, respected but people were wary of her. Just as Doug had predicted all those years ago people were jealous of her success. She was the least liked partner, despite that unbeknown to the staff she was the only one on their side, trying to make sure they got a good deal. Like today for instance, the staff would never be made aware that it was she who had safe guarded their jobs. Not that she really minded, she was there to do a job, not to win any popularity contests. She knew she had to have her wits about her, there were far too many people waiting to see her fail and no matter what, she had to keep portraying herself as the strong, cold woman she appeared to be, even if nothing could be further from the truth. Like Doug she was lonely. The irony wasn't lost on her.

Jackson and CJ arrived at Matt and Summer's apartment laden down with pizzas.
"We come bearing gifts." Jackson announced as he walked

through the door and along the hall.

"You guys are lifesavers." Matt got up from the sofa and took some of the boxes from CJ.

"Hope you've got fat free pizza in there somewhere," Amber grinned at Jackson.

"For you darling, of course I have," he replied. "Where is the gorgeous Summer?"

"Out on the balcony," Jez answered.

"Well go and get her I've got chicken and sweet corn with extra cheese just for her," Jackson ordered. In the next breath he began talking about a group of tourists he had on his tour today. He was a guide at the Statue of Liberty. He always had amusing stories to tell. Jackson was bi-sexual and overtly camp. The tourists either loved him or loathed him. He'd nearly had the sack about a million times for upsetting some old dear from England or some up tight couple from Canada. He always managed to land on his feet, whatever the situation. Jackson had come over from St Thomas with his family when he was a child, but he'd brought enough of his chilled out attitude with him to last a life time. He never took anything seriously. His job as a tour guide was the fifth in as many years. He said life was too short to be stuck in some boring nine to five, and he wanted to have fun in life. CJ was Jackson's quieter room mate; they got on really well despite their diverse personalities. CJ deserved a medal for sharing an apartment with Jackson, but it worked for them. The only problem being that with Jackson's overt camp ness, people automatically assumed that they were a couple.

Jez had to climb through a window to get to the main balcony. Summer was leaning against the wall gazing out at the twinkling lights of the City. It looked fantastic all lit up. By day they had views of the world financial centres tall skyscrapers, the Empire State building, across Central Park and right over to the Hudson. At night Summer described the City as being like a Christmas tree with all the different coloured lights. Jez sat on the window ledge, watching her deep in thought. The evening breeze blew her hair, she had his jacket on. She looked so beautiful, but then she always did. Even when she thought she looked awful in something, all Jez could see was beauty. He couldn't believe how lucky he was, she was incredible, the best thing to ever happen to him. He would never understand how someone like her had fallen for a guy like him, but he was glad she had.

Jez hadn't had the best start in life. His parents had left him at a children's home when he was a few months old, he'd been shunted around kids homes for most of his childhood. As he started to get older he realised his chances of adoption and finding a family were getting slimmer by the day. Nobody wanted a kid with baggage and an attitude, they wanted newborns, babies they could instil their own beliefs onto, not some kid who already had a mind of his own. He'd felt so rejected not just by his own parents, but the couples who came to choose a child and didn't pick him. The day he'd left the children's home he'd been given a letter along with his belongings, unbeknown to him, that letter had also travelled with him to the various homes. The letter had been left with him all those years ago. Jez had sat on a bench in Central Park, reading the letter from his father. It explained that he had been the product of an affair; his mother had dumped him on his father's doorstep and disappeared. It was too much of a burden for his father's wife to bring up his illegitimate child. He was a constant reminder of her husband's infidelity. At the end of the letter, his father asked for his forgiveness and hoped he understood why they couldn't keep him. It was the best thing for all of them and he was sure that a couple who desperately wanted a child would give him a happy life.

"Yeah, right." The letter had been signed, dad. No name, no

address, nothing to tell him who his father was. Jez didn't care. He screwed up the letter and threw it into the nearest trash can. He only had one person he could rely on and that was himself. He got up off the bench, walked to the nearest Fire house and joined up. He shared a run down apartment in the Bronx with three of the guys. His experience had left him cynical. He had no interest in finding love, sure he was into girls, but he wasn't in it for the long haul. As soon as they showed any signs of getting serious he was outta there. That was until he met Summer, she had turned his world upside down for the better, she melted his heart, made him realise he was punishing himself. She loved him unconditionally. He had finally found someone who could love him and it felt good, real good. He couldn't wait to marry her, have a family with her, a family he never thought he would have. He got off the window ledge and strolled up behind her, she was still unaware that he'd been watching her. He put his arms around her and rested his chin on her shoulder. She didn't even flinch.

"Hey gorgeous, whatcha thinking?" he asked.
"Just about our future."
"Tell me."
"When we get married we can't live here with Matt and Amber, I was thinking we could move upstate. We need somewhere with a garden, for the kids."
"Kids? How many?"
"Two, a boy and a girl."
He could hear the smile in her voice.
"What are we calling these children of ours?"
"Jordan for a boy…"
"…Summer for a girl, any daughter of ours is bound to be as beautiful as their mother."
"I think we need to talk about girls names." She laughed as she turned to face him; he encircled her in his arms.

"It doesn't matter what we call them or where we live, its love and security that counts and our kids are sure as hell gonna have all the love in the world."

Summer knew he was talking from experience and could tell he was trying to hide the pain in his voice.

"I just imagine our home, with us and our kids and I can't wait until it's real." She smiled up at him.

"It won't be long babe, but right now I can't think of anything better than being here with you and holding you in my arms. You know what else?"

"What?" she whispered.

"I'm starving and Jackson and CJ have brought pizza. C'mon Stevens."

When Claudia finally arrived at Summer's apartment everyone was just chilling out eating pizza.

"Hey guys, hope there is enough for me?" She asked as she pulled up a chair and sat down next to CJ. He grinned at her and handed her a glass of wine.

"Saved this for you."

"Thanks, you read my mind." she replied gratefully. A nice glass of wine or two was just what she needed after a long day at the office. She glanced around the room, everyone seemed to be talking at once and laughing at one of Jackson's crazy stories, everyone that was, except Summer. She looked miles away. Claudia could guess exactly where she was and who she was thinking about. She had spoken to Amber that afternoon and she had told her that Summer was stressing out over Marcus. She looked around the room again; it was weird to think that someone in this room had killed another person. She shivered slightly. She'd leave the thinking about it to Summer. Claudia was quite happy to leave Marcus in the past; he was no great loss to her.

Summer's mind had shifted from the cozy scene in the apartment, to the Swiss style lodge in Colorado. The lodge itself was amazing. It was stylish and spacious but still had that secluded log cabin feel about it. There was plenty of room for the eight of them. The bedrooms all contained pine furniture, with the master bedroom having a four poster bed and an en suite with a huge Jacuzzi bath. This had been her and Jez's room, Amber had said it was too nice for Marcus and the others were all single. The main living area and kitchen were open plan; the central piece was a huge log fire which they all appreciated after a long day on the slopes. There was another bedroom off the main living area; this belonged to Amber and Marcus. There were another three bedrooms upstairs, Matt and Claudia had a bedroom each, Jackson and CJ shared the last bedroom. She had totally fallen in love with the place; she loved opening the drapes in the morning and taking in the picturesque view of the snow covered mountains all around them. The air smelt fresh and clean, such a nice change from the hustle and bustle of the City. The snow was as white as she had ever seen it, the picture had been perfect, well until they found Marcus' lifeless body, tarnishing the image of the cabin. The dream that was Colorado had, in the blink of an eye turned into a very real nightmare, a nightmare that she couldn't escape from.

"Earth to Summer," Jez almost shouted.
"What?" She asked suddenly transported from her thoughts and back to the present.
"We were deciding whether we should go for a drink or catch a movie."
"I was thinking about going to the gym," she replied. She had nervous energy to burn off.
"Look at the weather babe, it's far too cold to be jumping around in a leotard, no matter how sexy you might look," Jez laughed.
Summer wandered over to the window, the clouds were so big

and ominous, moving rapidly. The weather had changed dramatically since she was out on the balcony before. It looked like the heavens were going to open at any moment. She hadn't seen a sky like that since the Saturday in Colorado, the night before they discovered Marcus' body. She felt a chill go down her spine, she automatically wrapped the sweater she was wearing tighter around her body. She supposed, in hindsight the storm should have pre warned her, an omen that something bad was about to happen. Right at that moment she had a strange sense of foreboding, things were going to get worse before they got better. She felt the blood rush to her head.

"I'm going to lie down," she whispered.

"I'll come with you babe." Jez got up to follow her.

"No Jez. I want to be on my own," she snapped.

Jez's face clouded over with concern as he watched her storm across the apartment, into their bedroom and slamming the door behind her.

"What the hell have you done to Summer?" Matt shouted across the room at Jez.

"I haven't done anything, why do you presume that because she's upset it's my fault? I'm just as worried about her as you are."

"Well something's upset her."

"No shit Sherlock! She's been like this for weeks."

"So what are you gonna do about it?" Matt demanded.

"Be as supportive as I can be and not cause her any more hassle like wasting my time with you."

"I'm only trying to look after my little sister."

"Oh my God, have you heard yourself? She's not five, she's a grown woman for God sake."

"She's still my sister and if you ever hurt her I swear to God I'll kill you."

Everyone turned to look at Matt, not quite sure they'd heard him right.

"Listen Matt, I don't know what your freakin problem is, but I love Summer more than anything. I'd do anything to protect her from being hurt. It drives me crazy to see her like this, not knowing what to do and it doesn't help with you being a total pain in the butt."

"You listen to me Jez…" Matt began, but he was interrupted by Amber.

"Leave him alone Matt, this is stupid. We can't start fighting between ourselves. We all know Summer seems a little pre occupied by Marcus at the moment. We have to stick together, if we don't it wont just be Summer who falls apart it will be all of us. Can't you see that the only reason this whole Marcus thing didn't crack us up in the first place was because we stuck together, if we'd have gone our separate ways after Colorado, we'd probably be in a mental institute by now."

"Amber's right Matt. Arguing will get you nowhere, Summer's obviously having a bad time at the moment, like Jez says, and we need to be there for her," CJ added.

Matt sighed heavily. "I know, I know. I can't help it if I think he's a jerk though can I?"

"Right back at ya, buddy," Jez replied sarcastically.

The atmosphere was slightly subdued in the apartment after Matt's outburst. Everyone appeared to be interested in the documentary they were watching on the Discovery channel. Claudia kept glancing over at CJ who seemed equally engrossed in the TV and totally unaware that she was watching him. She might as well have been non existent as far as CJ was concerned. She had held a torch for him for so long. There was a time when she thought that they may have had a future together. Claudia and CJ had always been very close, as close as friends could be. Out of the circle of friends, they had very similar characteristics, both were pretty quiet although assertive when it came to their work and careers. CJ was a lab technician working on vaccines. It was just when it came to the group, there were bigger personalities and egos competing with each other. CJ was really shy around women and even though Claudia had dropped plenty of hints, friendship was as far as it went. It probably didn't help that when it came to relationships Claudia wasn't that experienced either. She'd been far too busy with her career to give her love life a second thought.

There had been this one time, with CJ, strangely enough whilst they were on vacation in Colorado. She was in her room at the log cabin, to escape Summer and Jez in their loved up world. She wasn't envious of her friends she just wished she could have that with CJ. She had flirted so much with him but he was oblivious. Or maybe she was just crap at flirting. She had tried so many times to pluck up the courage and tell him how she felt but deep down she was scared of losing his friendship. Despite her tough in control persona, she was scared of rejection.

Thinking back to that particular night, made her stomach flip. She was sitting on her bed looking over some case notes. She was listening to her favourite music, Bon Jovi on the CD player in the room. She was so lost in her notes and listening to Jon Bon Jovi's sexy gravely voice belting out about unrequited love, yep been there, done that, wearing the T shirt, that she didn't hear the knock at the door. CJ's head appeared around the door. Her heart almost skipped a beat, she mentally checked that she looked ok, her make up was what was ever left after applying it this morning, she'd shoved her hair up in a loose scrunchie, so that probably looked messy and she was in her PJ's. Still PJ's could be sexy, maybe.

"Good I'm glad you're still up."
"Why? What's up?" She asked putting her notes down, taking

her glasses off and leant against the wall.

"Nothing, just fancied a chat," he replied. He plonked himself down on the bed. "What ya doin?"

"Oh just looking over some case notes."

"Jeez, on vacation? How dedicated are you!"

She shrugged her shoulders.

"What's it about anyway?"

"A single mom getting beaten up by her ex. I need to make sure this case is watertight so the bastard doesn't get off on a technicality."

"You're really into all that feminist stuff aren't you?"

"As the great Jon Bon Jovi once said – In a world that gives you nothing, we need something to believe in," she grinned.

"Whoa, a rock chick, feminist hot shot lawyer, you don't come across them everyday."

"Just don't tell them at work that I'm a rock chick, I have a sophisticated image to keep up!"

"So, no time for office romances then?"

"Nope. None at all," she smiled sadly.

CJ caught the look of sadness that flickered across her face. "You've got no time but you'd like to make time?" He tilted his head to one side, she watched his blonde hair flop into his eyes and he absent mindedly ran his hand through it to push it back into place.

"Yeah. I suppose I would. I've spent years developing my career, working long hours, but I'm getting kinda fed up of coming home to an empty apartment," she sighed.

"Got your sights on anyone?"

She nodded her head slowly.

"Go on spill," he encouraged.

"Well, the thing is, this guy, I've tried to tell him how I feel, but he doesn't seem to get the hint." She admitted hoping that this was a big enough hint. Jeez, why didn't any one give you an instruction book for these things?

"That's men for you, wouldn't know a hint if it jumped up and bit you in the ass."

There was her answer.

"So you think I should just come right out and tell him?"

"Yeah, otherwise you'll be dropping hints forever. Who in their right mind is gonna knock you back sweetheart?"

"I don't know CJ. I'm scared he'll turn me down. I have never failed at anything I've done, I don't think I could handle the rejection."

"Hey honey," he began as he moved closer and put his arm around her. "If he says no that's his problem, not yours, he would be mad to turn you down."

Claudia tilted her face upwards towards his to answer him, as she did so; she found her lips only inches away from his and her eyes were gazing straight into his dazzling blue eyes. She knew she shouldn't and she tried really hard to fight the urge, but she had to give into her feelings, she had imagined being in this situation so many times, she had wanted him for so long. She hardly had to move to kiss his lips. She kissed him lightly on the lips. CJ pulled away, he had a strange unreadable look on his face just as she was about to back off, he grabbed her and kissed her. If only she'd had the guts to do this ages ago. He ran his fingers through her long auburn hair, the scrunchie falling out of her hair. She mimicked his movements. Just like she had fantasised so many times before, CJ made love to her, she couldn't believe it was really happening. It was over quicker than she expected, she didn't mind. Next time would be better.

There never was a next time. He'd never once spoken to her about what happened between them. Claudia glanced over to him, lounging on Summer's sofa. He was unaware that she'd been staring at him for a few minutes. He never even knew that the guy she had been talking about was him, he hadn't even realised that night was her first time. CJ was right about one thing, men are stupid.

CJ was conscious that Claudia was looking at him. He was trying to look calm, show no sings of the upheaval   he felt inside. Everything was going crazy, everyone kept losing their tempers with each other. Summer was totally all over the place, Matt kept freaking out. Something was gonna give soon, he just knew it. There were too many secrets, he could tell everyone was holding back. They called themselves friends, but they didn't know each other at all. They certainly didn't know the real him, not even Claudia knew.

Summer lay on her bed, she was annoyed with herself for freaking out on Jez before, and he hadn't done anything to deserve that. She was letting this whole Marcus thing take over her life. Why couldn't she just let it go? The other's had, so why couldn't she? Marcus was her cousin, she had a right to know who killed him, she reflected. Maybe Matt was quite happy to bury his head in the sand and not give a damn about what happened to him, but she wasn't prepared to do that. How could she just accept someone's murder and get on with her life? She ran through the list of suspects and their motives in her head.

Amber's reason for possibly killing Marcus could well be down to having walked in on Marcus in bed with one of the ski instructors, some blonde bimbo with plastic boobs. Amber had gone ballistic and they had one of their worst fights ever that night. She wasn't the type of person to let her guy get away with cheating and she would be out for revenge. Although they were arguing in their room, because it was downstairs, the whole cabin heard every word and how Amber had shouted numerous times that she would kill him. She'd made that threat, was she prepared to carry it out? Marcus had been killed three nights later. Wouldn't Amber have just done it there and then? Wasn't that how crimes of passion happened? The killer loses their head for one mad moment and kills their lover; they don't wait for three whole days do they?

Amber wasn't the only one with a grudge to bear on that vacation. Marcus had come back to the cabin worse for wear one night, he was a heavy drinker and violent with it. Everyone was in bed except her, she'd slipped out of bed quietly so as not to disturb Jez. There had been a bad storm and she hadn't been able to sleep properly. The worst of it seemed to be over, so she'd got up and headed to the kitchen to make a warm drink. As she sat at the kitchen table Marcus stumbled through the door, slurring his words and using the door frame to stop him from falling over. Although the majority of the storm had now passed, it was still windy and his hair had been blown all over the place.

"Marcus, are you drunk?"
He staggered forward this time using the wall to keep him upright, swaying slightly. He slowly clapped his hands and had a stupid grin on his face.
"Clever girl, there's me thinking you were just some dumb chick."
"Apparently not," she mumbled.
"What? What did you say? Speak up," he shouted.
"Nothing, it wasn't important."
She hated how Marcus always made her feel slightly scared when she was on her own with him. He was so out of control at times that you never knew what he was going to do next.
"It must've been important for you to speak to me, Miss High n Mighty goody two shoes, thinks she's too good to speak to the likes of me."
He began to move towards her, still swaying. She could smell the alcohol on him before he'd even reached her. "Let me

remind you princess, we share the same blood, you might wish I'd just disappear, leave you and your precious friends, but I will always be here, always."

By this time he was right behind her, his cheek almost touching hers. She felt her heart racing, she had to get away from him. She pushed her chair back to try and unbalance him and headed for the door, but he was unmoveable in his drunk heavy state. He blocked her and slammed her into the wall. She cried out in pain.

"Not leaving already princess?" He stopped any escape with his body. His face was right up close to hers, the smell of rum was making her feel sick. "Y'know princess, it's a shame me and you are related 'coz I reckon Jez has some real fun with you, I know you're not as innocent as you make out. Wouldn't mind a piece of that action."

She spat in his face. "You are one, vile, disgusting….bastard."

"Ooooh strong words princess."

She pushed against him with all her mite. He shoved her hard against the wall, bringing his arm up he whacked her across the face. The blow was so strong, she slid down the wall to the floor. For a few seconds she felt dazed. She knew she had to get away from him. She tried to crawl across the floor, but she felt his weight push her down hard. Her nose hit the concrete floor. She felt the bile rise in her throat as she realised there was no way she could escape. Whatever he was going to do to her, she had no way of stopping. She looked around to see if there was anything she could protect herself with, but there was nothing within reach. He yanked her up by her hair; she could feel blood trickle down her face.

"Son of a bitch."

Jez. Thank God. She flopped back down to the floor as Jez heaved Marcus off her.

"What the hell do you think you're doin?" He slammed Marcus up against the wall, grabbing his shirt with both hands.

"Get off me," Marcus demanded.

"Wanna fight? C'mon then, I'm all yours," Jez shouted as he slung a right hook at him.

Marcus tried to wriggle out of Jez's grip, but Jez was too strong.

"You don't wanna fight me huh? Just like picking on women? Think that makes you some big ass man? You aint no man Marcus, you're a joke, scum." Jez pulled Marcus closer. "You go anywhere near Summer again and I swear I'll kill you, that aint no threat Marcus it's a God Damn promise." His voice was barely above a whisper, but he spoke with conviction. He loosened his grip and flung Marcus towards the door. "Now get outta my sight."

Summer was slumped on the floor. He bent down to help her up.

"You ok babe?"

She nodded her head slowly. "He just went crazy, I don't even know what's just happened." As she spoke he tilted her head slightly towards the light.

"I don't think your nose is broken. I'll get you cleaned up.

"Jez I was so scared, I really thought he was gonna kill me. I don't know what would've happened if you hadn't stopped him."

He held her close. "I'll always be here to protect you, no one will ever hurt you, not while I'm around. That jerk will pay for this."

Two days later they found Marcus' dead body.

Summer sighed deeply. She'd forgotten how petrified she's been that night. For all she knew Jez may have saved her life yet again that night. The worst part was that as far as she could recollect she hadn't provoked him, he'd just turned on her for no reason. She also knew that if she had managed to get hold of something, it might very well have been her who had committed murder. Marcus had warned her that he would always be there and it was true that until she found out who killed him she could never escape him. There was something deep inside her that told her she had to unlock the mystery, if she didn't it would take over her life and she didn't want that. She had a wedding to start planning. She would start by apologising to Jez, the last person she wanted to take any of this out on was him.

Jez sat alone on the sofa in the living room. He was channel surfing, but he wasn't really paying much attention to what was on TV. Summer was still in the bedroom, Matt and Amber had disappeared into theirs, although he could hear raised voices, they were obviously arguing again. The others had gone for a drink at the bar at the end of the block; he couldn't blame them for trying to escape the tense atmosphere in the penthouse tonight. He was becoming more and more worried about Summer. Matt wasn't much use, all he did was criticise him and imply that it was his fault that Summer was unhappy. How could Matt not see how he felt about Summer, how much he loved her. Matt's behaviour was probably making her feel worse, he reasoned. Summer was the type of person who wanted everyone to get on with each other, in all honesty he was fed up of trying to be friendly to Matt. However it was that trait that made him feel like he had to protect Summer from bad things. She wanted everyone to live in perfect harmony and when things went wrong she took it as a personal failure, just like Marcus' death.

He knew Summer blamed herself. He sighed, he wanted his bubbly, happy fiancée back she had become so withdrawn and he didn't know what to do to make everything ok again. She was the most important person in his life, she meant everything to him. Whenever he wasn't with her he would only have to whisper her name to bring a smile to his face. He never thought he'd ever fall in love with someone and especially to have fallen this hard.

She was so perfect; there was nothing about her that he would change. Even her name was perfect. Summer. Everybody loves summer, makes them feel good, summer makes people happy. People love the warm summer sunshine.

Her parents' must've known what a sunny personality she was gonna have, that's why they called her Summer. At least that's what the Summer he knew and loved was like, but lately she she'd lost some of her sparkle. He'd get her over this obsession with Marcus, they were a team. They'd get through this together, they always did. He smiled to himself, Jeez, if the guys at the firehouse knew how he thought sometimes he'd never hear the end of it. He'd just likened his fiancée to a warm summer's day, if his nickname, Romeo wasn't bad enough, they'd start calling him Shakespeare as well! Then again, he'd shout from the top of a skyscraper, right across the City if he had to, just to say he loved her. She brought out a soppy romantic side out in him; a side he never knew existed until he met her.

Jez knew straight away that she was special, he wasn't just interested in getting her into bed, he wanted to get to know her as a person and he wanted to treat her right. By the time she had recovered physically from the car crash and they'd started dating properly, it had been a good few months before they had slept together. By which point he wanted her so badly and he knew he had fallen for her big time. He had booked them into a suite at the Plaza. They ordered room service, he had no plans to leave the room all night. He could picture her lying on the bed in the white fluffy hotel robe after being in the bath. Her hair piled loosely on top of her head, strands of hair framing her face. She looked so beautiful that night. She had no make up on, wasn't dressed up but he had never wanted anyone so much as he did in that moment in time. It wasn't just how gorgeous she looked, it was the person she was, the person she made him feel he could be. They drank champagne and talked for a while and then he made love to her. When he thought about it, that was the first time he'd ever made love. With other women it was just sex. With Summer it was amazing, it wasn't just physical it was emotional. God he loved that girl.

Summer must've been completely tuned into what he was thinking; he looked up and saw her leaning against the door frame. She took his breath away, all she had on was one of his oversized shirts, her long dark hair was tousled, her bare legs long and silky. His body ached for her. God the things she did to him drove him crazy.

Where's everybody gone?"
"Matt and Amber are in their room and the other guys have gone out for a drink."
She walked towards him; he didn't take his eyes off her. She straddled him.
"Babe, I'm sorry about before," she whispered. He moved his hands around her body and placed them on her butt.
"You ok now? You looked like you'd seen a ghost before."
"Maybe I had," She mumbled.
"Marcus?"
She nodded. "One of our friends killed him. I need answers."
"Babe. I know it's hard for you, I mean Marcus was your cousin but you have to let it go. Would it really make you feel better if you knew? It wouldn't change anything, Marcus is dead."
"I know, I know, nothing will bring him back and as awful as it sounds, I wouldn't want him back. He was pure evil. I just can't stop thinking about it. I need to know what happened, was it an accident or did someone plan to kill him? At least if I knew the truth I wouldn't be looking at everyone as if they were a killer," she sighed.

"Even me?"

"Don't ask me that Jez, I don't know if it was you, you don't know if it was me. All I know is I trust you with my life, whenever I've needed you you've been there. You're my soul mate we were meant to meet that night on the bridge and we're meant to be together."

"Hey, I aint got no halo, I'm just here to love you and take care of you. You are everything to me, in fact I could probably never put into words how much I love you, but you do know don't you?"

"Course I know. It's you and me together forever."

"Listen I know 110% that you didn't kill Marcus."

"How?" She could barely get the word out; did he know something she didn't?

"You are the most gentle and caring person I know. You'd condemn yourself to a lifetime of guilt if you ran over a cat. You are the last person I'd suspect."

"They always say it's the last person you suspect."

"I know you, inside out. The one person I'm sure of is you."

She leant forward to kiss him. She didn't like the way this conversation was heading. Could she be as sure of him? His mouth covered hers as he kissed her with a deep sensual kiss. Who was she kidding, of course she could. This was Jez, her Jez. He broke away from her.

"I know were having a serious talk, but do you know how sexy you look dressed like that, sitting across me? I am so turned on."

"That was kinda the idea," she smiled.

"I want you. Right now," he whispered. He went to pull her closer to him, but she was too quick, she jumped off him.

"Gotta catch me first." She laughed and ran across the room. He ran after her and wrapped his arms around her waist, pulling her to the floor as he caught her up, she was laughing too much to resist.

"You didn't run very fast."

"Maybe I wanted you to catch me quicker," she said through her laughter.

He loved her laugh, it made him feel warm inside. He positioned himself on top of her, bent his head down and brushed her lips with his own. She pulled at his shirt revealing his washboard stomach. As he slipped his hand underneath her shirt and up her body he realised she was naked underneath it. He groaned her name.

She pulled away slightly. "We better go into the bedroom; we don't want the other two to catch us."

"Mm, I suppose you're right." He jumped up and scooped her into his arms.

Amber marched out of the bedroom.

"If you think I'm listening to your sanctimonious crap you can think again." Amber screamed as she stormed across the apartment. Matt appeared at the bedroom door.

"Where the hell are you going?"

"As far away from you as possible, jerk."

"Amber, don't you dare storm out on me."

"Oh go to hell." She slammed the front door behind her.

Mat looked at Amber's retreating back then to Summer and Jez. He glared at Jez seeing him standing there holding his sister, both in a state of undress. He turned on his heel and slammed the bedroom door shut.

"Too late, we got caught," Jez laughed as he carried her towards the bedroom.

CHAPTER FOUR

Jackson and CJ were drinking JD and coke, Claudia drank white wine, they were sitting in a bar a few blocks away from the penthouse.

"Tell you what guys, I was glad to get out of that atmosphere tonight." Jackson said as he downed his drink in one go.

"Messing with your karma was it?" Claudia laughed.

"It's no joke, something's going down and it aint nice," he added.

"Summer'll be ok; she's just a bit down at the moment," Claudia sighed.

"It's not just Summer though is it? Matt totally lost it tonight; he didn't need to go off at Jez like that," CJ commented.

"I'm telling y'all, it's all gonna blow soon and I don't think we're gonna have to wait that long till it happens." Jackson beckoned the waiter over an ordered another drink as he spoke.

"I think you're wrong. We've managed to get through nearly two years with the Marcus thing hanging over us. The time to find out has well and truly passed," Claudia interjected.

"Some people go through their whole lives with skeletons in their closets," CJ murmured to no one in particular.

"I think we were all crazy in the first place thinking it was a good idea to cover up a murder," Claudia whispered.

"You gotta get on with life, I feel for Summer, she's obviously struggling trying to hold everything together, but I didn't waste any time worrying about Marcus when he was alive and I sure as hell aint gonna waste anytime worrying about him now he's gone," Jackson shrugged.

"Maybe she did it; maybe that's why it's stressed her out so much," CJ suggested. Claudia nodded in agreement.

"Y'all crazy, Summer's obsessed by it 'coz that's the type of person she is. She worries if she has nothing to worry about. Nah Summer is probably the only one of us who I have never suspected. She's had a lot to deal with guys; it stands to reason she may be feeling a bit unstable."

"You think she's mad?"

"Not mad, we just need to keep an eye on her, she may be in danger of going over the edge."

"Jeez, this is depressing," CJ sighed.

"You're right." The waiter brought Jackson his JD and coke. He drank it down in one again and stood up. "C'mon guys, there's more booze at our apartment, lets head over there."

Amber pressed the buzzer to Jackson and CJ's apartment.

"D'arby and Jensen residence."

"Hey Jackson it's me. Can I come up?"

"Sure thing honey." He pressed the button to open the door.

Five minutes later Amber was on the sofa, glass in hand, ranting about Matt to Jackson and CJ. Claudia was asleep on the sofa.

"Jeez, she had too much to drink?" Amber asked as she noticed the two empty wine bottles on the floor.

CJ nodded. "She only had one when we were in the bar, but we haven't been back here long as she's polished off two bottles."

Amber began to relay her argument with Matt to the guys. "I don't know where it's all gone wrong, we never speak unless it's to argue, he never touches me, let alone have sex with me. He's a frigid bastard."

"Or gay," Jackson added. CJ shot him a look.

"Ignore him," CJ began as he rolled his eyes at Jackson. "Doesn't he want to sort it out?"

"He's too pre occupied with his job. He wants to be the best accountant there ever was, sad bastard. He sits their in his dad's study like some freakin' English Lord of the manor, he'd rather check his figures over than my figure. I mean for Christ sake, what's that all about? What man in their right mind would turn me down? I'm an independent woman, I have my own very successful business, I don't need a man BUT I do have physical needs."

"Everyone has physical needs darling, look at me, I have the best of both worlds. I can't understand people who are celibate they miss out on so much fun."

"I think Matt's taken a vow of celibacy, it's been ages. He should be grateful that he's got someone like me. I've got a body women would pay thousands for in surgery, but does he appreciate it? Does he hell!"

"Your self confidence is one of the things I love about you Amber. Besides it doesn't have to be down to you, maybe he hasn't got much confidence in the bedroom department."

"I think it's more to do with the fact that I'm assertive, he doesn't like being dominated, but I'm just not the submissive type. To top it all when I stormed out on Matt, would you believe it but there's our very own Romeo and Juliet, Jez and Summer half naked in the living room, just to rub salt in the wound."

"Yeah but those two are always at it, they constantly have this glow about them and you just know what they've been up to," Jackson laughed.

"Jez and Summer are the exception to the rule, they are so annoyingly, perfectly happy. Let's face it though, who would begrudge Summer's happiness after all she's been through," CJ added.

"You see, that's the thing. I'm not jealous of Summer, I'm glad she's happy, but I don't want a relationship that's all lovey dovey. I'm not ready to settle down, I just want regular sex!"

"Talk it through with him; it's always the best way to solve problems."

"Ever the sensible guy CJ."

"Or the alternative is to find a guy who floats your boat," Jackson suggested.

"It's not quite that simple," She muttered. "Listen, can I stay here tonight I need a decent nights sleep before I face Matt again."

"Course you can babe. You take my room; I'll crash on the sofa,"

Jackson replied and winked at her.

"Thanks guys, what would I do without you?" She stood up and gave them both a kiss on the cheek and headed off towards Jackson's bedroom.

"I think I should get this sleepy head home."

CJ sat in the cab on the way to Claudia's apartment. She was slumped against him, her long red hair sprawled all over his chest. She was half asleep. The cab driver had already warned him that if she was sick he'd not only have to pay for the damage but clean it up as well.

He sighed deeply; the ten minute journey was taking forever as the cab crawled along. Every hour was rush hour in New York. Being stuck in traffic was not helping his mood. He was feeling frustrated and not happy at all with the way things were going at the moment. Tonight had been a perfect example of how crazy everything had gotten. Matt and Jez's argument, Summer's obsession with Marcus, Claudia's drinking. He didn't know what concerned him the most. Matt and Jez were big enough to sort each other out, but Summer was very fragile and Claudia, what was happening to her? What was making her drink so much? They were really close friends and he should be able to ask her what the matter was, but he was scared of the answer. Scared that maybe it was his fault. He knew he'd treated her badly that night; he shouldn't have just gotten up and left her to wake up alone. He should've talked to her, not just ignored the fact that they had just slept together.

The cab jerked, her head fell into his lap, he gently lifted her head up and rested it against his shoulder. There were too many secrets and lies between them all. If there was one person he wanted to be truthful with it was Claudia. The dark cloud he carried with him was too heavy, he couldn't carry on living like this. Maybe it was time it to tell the truth. He knew if he came clean he ran the risk of hurting people, but it was a chance he had to take. The cab eventually pulled up outside Claudia's apartment. He paid the driver and managed to get Claudia out of the cab and carried her into her building. It was going to be fun trying to get her settled. He was worried about her; maybe he should sleep on the sofa tonight. He didn't really want to leave her or maybe once she was asleep she'd be ok and she'd just sleep it off. He had no doubt that she'd gone to sleep in worse states than this.

"You took your time."

"I had to help CJ get Claudia into a cab, no easy task when she's drunk. I had to make sure they were safely out of the way. We don't want anyone to know about our clandestine meetings do we?" Jackson replied.

"Well, I suppose you're worth waiting for."

"Considering you're sex starved at the moment, anyone would be worth waiting for."

"I'm not sex starved it's only been two days since our last meeting."

"Yeah, I totally love that you have your own office," he grinned at the memory.

"One of the perks of running your own company."

"Poor Matt, he doesn't know what he's missing."

"Yeah right, probably hasn't even noticed I'm gone. Don't even think about trying to make me feel guilty, you're as much into this as I am and Matt's supposed to be your best friend," Amber protested.

"All's fair in love and sex," he laughed.

"Love? The only person you've ever loved is yourself."

"I could say the same about you Amber Gordon."

"Will you quit talking and get that sexy ass of yours over here; a girl could die of boredom."

"The one thing you aint gonna be honey is bored."

Claudia sat alone in her apartment, it was gone two am. She'd woken up, sprawled over her bed about half an hour ago. She just about made it to the bathroom before she threw up. She couldn't even remember how she got in such a state that she'd been sick. She recalled being in a bar with Jackson and CJ, how she got home she didn't know. She had a shower after being sick and now she was wide awake. She sat on the sofa, a half empty bottle of wine on the table, which would make her feel drowsy soon. It didn't even cross her mind that if she hadn't been drinking in the first place, she'd still be asleep. She reached over and filled up her glass. She got up and wandered over to the window and sat on the ledge. She watched the city moving below her; it looked like she wasn't the only one up in the middle of the night. It made her feel slightly less lonely, because when all was said and done, that's what she was. Sure, she had her friends, but she craved to have someone special in her life. She wanted intimacy, romance, passion and most of all love. She wanted to come home from work after a stressful day and have someone to help her relax rather than going to the fridge and opening endless bottles of wine. She wanted nice romantic nights in by the fire, cuddling up in bed after hours of making love and waking up to that someone special every morning.

She thought CJ was the one to give her all that. They had so much in common, always seemed to be on the same wavelength even as far as finishing off each others sentences, CJ mostly got over shadowed by Jackson who was such an extrovert and attention seeker. CJ preferred to be on the side lines, he was a people watcher and if there was ever a heated discussion going on, which between their group of friends there usually was, he would listen and then he'd just say one thing and that one comment would make so much sense. It was blatantly obvious to her that CJ just wanted to be friends. He never made any reference to their one night together. He didn't seem to be interested in anyone else, what was so bad about her that he couldn't take a chance on her? She thought about Leyton Carter, the guy she knew through work. She'd never even meet him, but they'd gotten to know each other pretty well through emails and phone conversations. They had acquired a mutual respect for each other, but had become friendly enough that he felt comfortable reminding her at the end of his emails that she still hadn't taken him up on the offer of a drink. She couldn't, not when CJ was the only guy she was interested in and until he actually came out with the words and told her otherwise she would hang on for him. Maybe love and happy endings only happened to the Summer and Jez's of this world. Marcus had seen to it that every relationship she had would be tainted by what he did to her. She sighed heavily and got up off the ledge and headed towards the bedroom. She had an early breakfast meeting and she didn't want to have more bags than Macy's under her eyes.

Across the city, Matt was working in his father's study. He glanced at the clock on his desk, it read 2.15am, and he still had loads of work to get through. He'd been working solidly since Amber stormed out at least her disappearance meant he could work uninterrupted, well apart from the noises coming from his little sisters' bedroom earlier. It was hard to cope with the fact that his kid sister had a sex life, especially with that jerk Jez. He picked up on the photo on the desk of his family. It was taken on Summer's graduation day. He still found it hard to believe that his parent's were gone. He kept his dad's study exactly as it was and even now he still expected to walk into it and see his father working well into the night, he was certainly his father's son. His parent's had lived and breathed politics. It was widely thought that his father would run for President when the next Presidents term was over. In fact one of the headlines at the time of his death had been "The Best President We Never Had." It had been hard when they died, not as hard as it might have been. They weren't a regular family, sure his mom and dad loved him and Summer but they spent that much time in Washington and travelling the country that they just got used to them not being round and when they were at the New York suite his dad was usually locked in the study and his mom would betaking Summer on shopping trips. In fact, on the night of the accident it was rare for so many of the family to be together.

His mom and Summer had been shopping; his dad had a meeting in the City so they'd agreed to meet up at the Four Seasons for dinner. It was on their way home that they'd been involved in that fateful accident. One of the worse parts had been getting Summer over the survivor's guilt. He wanted to be the one she turned to, but Summer had met her knight in shining armour and turned to Jez, even more so after Marcus' death. He made a promise to his parents at their funeral that he would take care of Summer, but Jez wouldn't let him. Of course, there was also the other event from that night that, a secret that had died along with Marcus and that only he knew, something he could never tell anyone. He sighed and glanced around the room, his concentration broken. There were boxes neatly stacked in the corner from his dad's Washington office. He hadn't had time to look through them or was it more the fact that he wasn't ready to look through them yet? He took his glasses off and rubbed his eyes, his mind had totally strayed from work and now he was thinking about things that should stayed locked away in his mind.

Amber was fast asleep in Jackson's bed. She was in a deep sleep and didn't hear Jackson get out of bed. He reached the bedroom door and opened it gently, the light from the hall way shone into the room, he turned and looked at Amber. She really was beautiful when she was asleep, she was stunning anyway but when she was asleep she looked peaceful. Her usual hard exterior was gone. A wave of regret flooded over him, they both knew what they were doing but he wasn't being exactly truthful with her. They were just having fun, she didn't need to know everything, but standing here in the dead of night, watching her he felt like it was all getting too serious. He had a horrible feeling that someone was gonna get hurt. He wanted to get back into bed with her and hold her while she slept, but he knew he couldn't. He knew she was battling with demons, just like he was. He'd heard her talk in her sleep. Surely Matt must've heard her; he couldn't be that much of an idiot. She had the same dream almost every time and he knew Amber's nightmare was real. He turned his back on her hating himself for doing it. The last thing she needed was people turning away from her, she needed her friends and some friends they all were, too busy wrapped up in the secrets they were all trying to keep from each other. He shut the door and crept quietly back to the sofa. The last thing he needed was CJ hearing him.

CJ lay in bed, he hadn't been to sleep yet, he was worried that he had done the wrong thing leaving Claudia like that. Still, it wouldn't be the first time he'd abandoned her. He'd heard what Amber and Jackson had been up to and he'd heard Jackson creep out of the room to go back to the sofa, obviously so CJ wouldn't find out about them. CJ wouldn't mention anything to him; he was used to Jackson and his ways. Besides they were going to great lengths to keep it a secret from him and the other guys, well Matt. God, the shit would hit the fan then. Anyway, if there was one thing he was good at it was keeping secrets. He turned on his side and closed his eyes. Maybe he was getting fed up of the secrets, maybe it was time to start telling the truth.

Summer lay in the comfort of Jez's arms, they were in the spoons position, they always slept as close to each other as possible. She was dreaming about Marcus, that she'd killed him. She became restless in her sleep and woke for a second, she felt Jez's strong arms around her and drifted off back to sleep, this time she dreamt of Jez and everything was all ok.

Jez didn't dream or if he did he never remembered them. All he knew was he fell asleep with Summer in his arms and he woke in the morning with her still in his arms and that was just the way he liked it.

Amber was in the elevator going back up to the penthouse. She had woken up alone that morning, as she knew she would. Jackson must've left sometime during the night and back to the sofa. They couldn't risk CJ finding out about their little fling. She and Jackson had been over friendly for a few months now and although she didn't feel guilty about cheating on Matt she would feel bad if it ruined Matt and Jackson's friendship. If it hadn't have been Jackson it would've been some other sexy guy. If that made her a bad person, then so be it. She even quite fancied getting Jez into bed, what with that sexy body and fire fighters uniform, but Summer was the one person who Amber truly cared about and she would never do anything to hurt her. She knew how content Summer was with Jez and if anyone deserved to be happy it was Summer. Amber, well she deserved everything she got didn't she? As she had left Jackson and CJ's apartment this morning Jackson whispered to her that he'd make an appointment at her office. God, Jackson thought he was doing her a favour, men never realised that it was her in control, she used them. At least that's what she kept telling herself.

The elevator pinged as Amber reached the top floor of the apartment block and the penthouse suite. She put the key in the door and sighed as she pushed it open, time to face the music.

She found Summer and Jez in the kitchen, he was feeding her bagels and she was laughing. God, sometimes those two made her sick, they were so bloody happy together. As she dropped her bag onto the floor, Matt walked into the kitchen. They both stopped and stared at each other, she was aware of Summer and Jez looking from one to the other.

"Hey," he finally said.

"Hey," she echoed.

"Where did you stay last night?"

"On Jackson and CJ's sofa." – Lie

"I er missed you."

"Me too." – Lie.

"Look Amber, I gotta go to work, we'll talk tonight." He grabbed a bagel from the table and headed out towards the hall way. He hadn't even kissed her goodbye, but what did she care?

"Whatever." She replied to the door that had just closed behind her. She looked at Summer and Jez, yeah they should look guilty sitting there looking all loved up. Without speaking she headed off towards her bedroom to get ready for work. After all she had a lunchtime meeting to prepare for.

Jackson and CJ were having breakfast.

"I was doing some thinking last night."

"Oh yeah, what about?" Jackson asked.

"I was thinking about Summer and how stressed she seems to be over Marcus and I got to thinking about how Marcus kept threatening to reveal my secret to everyone and how scared I was of everyone finding out and I've reached a point in my life where I'm not scared anymore. The longer I hide this, the more Marcus has won and I won't give him the satisfaction," CJ breathed heavily. "So, I thought that as we are all together tomorrow night for my birthday, it seems as good a time as any to tell them."

"You're sure about this?"

"Too right."

"You gonna tell them every' ting?"

"Yeah it's about time I got all this out in the open."

"Well, just make sure y'all get your presents first."

"Gotta get my priorities right, hey Jackson?" He grabbed an apple from the fruit bowl. "Love to stay and chat but I gotta get to work." He reached for his jacket. "Oh, by the way, was Amber ok this morning?" he asked innocently.

Jackson nodded. "A good night sleep did her the world of good."

"I bet it did." He couldn't help raise an eyebrow. "See you tonight."

Jackson drank his coffee to avoid answering. Well, it certainly seemed like things were about to get interesting, once you opened a can of worms, the whole freakin lot fell out. Still, what could he do about it?

It was Friday night; Summer was in her bedroom applying her make up. Amber and Claudia were perched on the edge of her bed, all dressed up and ready to go out for CJ's birthday. Claudia had bought CJ a limited edition DVD of his favourite movie, which incidentally was also her favourite - another thing they had in common. She hoped CJ would understand the significance, but she doubted it. He'd been too busy showing off a pair of sneakers that Jackson had bought him when she gave him his present. He'd hardly even given it a second glance when he opened it. God he was a jerk sometimes. What did she have to do to get him interested in her? She thought back to the morning after that night in Colorado, she had been ecstatic, but he quickly quashed her new found joy. He thanked her for keeping him company the previous night, he said he'd had a row with Marcus and he just needed someone to talk to. He never mentioned it again and she didn't have the guts to. She often wondered what he and Marcus had argued about, it had obviously affected CJ big time. All things seemed to lead back to

Marcus, would he ever go away?

"Don't you think Marcus hangs around like a bad smell?" Claudia asked idly.

Summer dropped her hairbrush at the mention of Marcus' name.

"Marcus is dead Claudia, did you forget that?" Amber asked.

"I know he's dead, I mean his memory, doesn't anyone feel like his aura is still around?"

"Well, if anyone was the kinda guy to come back and haunt you it would be Marcus, no question about it," Amber reflected.

"No, I know what Claudia means," Summer interjected as she recovered her composure. "He's everywhere; I can't get him out of my head."

"Oh c'mon guys, I don't know what all the fuss is about. Marcus was a serious asshole. He was only ever interested in what he could get for himself. He's dead. There is nothing we can do about, he's better off that way and were better off without him."

"Amber! Poor Marcus is dead!" Summer replied.

"Yeah poor Marcus, what about poor Claudia, he tried to rape her. I'm telling you, he is in the best place for him."

Claudia lowered her head; Amber immediately knew she'd gone too far. "Claudia, I'm sorry. I didn't mean to bring up all that shit. I know it was a hard time for you."

"Yeah, it was. I'm just glad Jackson and CJ got there when they did otherwise it could have been much worse," Claudia replied quietly.

Summer shuddered at the thought. Six months before the trip to Colorado, Marcus had tried to rape Claudia. She had just rented a new apartment and was having a party to celebrate. Summer remembered Claudia showing Marcus around the apartment, and then all hell seemed to break loose. CJ and Jackson had been in the hall way and somehow heard Claudia's screams above the music and found her on her bedroom floor, Marcus on top of her, pining her to the floor. Her clothes were torn away from her body. She was desperately trying to fight him off. The guys pulled him off her, Jackson punching him to the floor. Claudia had flung herself into CJ's arms, grateful for being saved. He'd held her close trying to cover her up. Marcus had denied that he'd tried to rape her; he said she'd been begging for it. Summer could never understand why Claudia hadn't gone to the cops. She was a lawyer; she was in the best position possible to get him found guilty of attacking her. She always maintained that she was too ashamed to report it and too scared of what Marcus might do next if she did.

"I know you all think I killed him. Believe me, I thought about it often enough," Claudia whispered.

"It could've been any of us, well; obviously it was one of us. For all you know it could've been me," Amber suggested.

"Or me," Summer added.

Amber burst out laughing. "Oh come on Summer, you're the only one that nobody suspects. You'd never be capable of killing someone."

"I'd never have thought that any of my friends were capable of murder, but one of you obviously is," Summer snapped.

"Look, lets just change the subject," Claudia pleaded.

Summer was annoyed, even though Amber was her best friend; she hated how she sometimes patronised her. Amber upset people on a regular basis by her out spoken ways. One day, Summer promised herself, she would stand up for herself rather than let people walk all over her. She knew she relied too much on Jez, but he was always there for her no matter what.

Claudia felt quite depressed after Amber had brought up the whole subject of the attack. Thank God CJ had been there to rescue her. Even now she found it hard to trust men, CJ being the exception to the rule. All she wanted was to be with him.

Claudia and Amber had left Summer to finish getting ready. She spritzed herself with her perfume and had a final glance in the mirror before heading out of the bedroom to find Jez. He was watching TV as he waited for her. As she walked into the room he looked her up and down admiringly. She looked gorgeous. She had a long black dress on that he knew for a fact she never wore underwear with, something to do with VPL. Whatever VPL was he was glad it existed! He stood up and pulled her close to him.

"You look beautiful, can't we skip the meal and go straight to dessert," he murmured as he kissed her neck.

"How about we have dinner, and then come back for dessert?"

He moved his lips to her mouth and as he kissed her he gently ran his fingertips from the nape of her neck, down her bare back and gently squeezed her bum.

"I love this dress," he murmured into her hair.

"Why?"

"Cos I know that underneath this very thin material you are naked, you drive me wild woman, I won't be able to concentrate on my food tonight," he grinned.

"Sure you will. Now go and grab a cab, I'll meet you in the lobby, I forgot my purse."

Summer headed back towards the bedroom, she was surprised to hear voices out on the balcony, she thought everyone else had gone. She was about to call out when she stopped in her tracks as she realised what she was listening to.

"Are you sure you're ready? It's a big confession," Jackson asked.

"Ready as I'll ever be. I need this over and done with. I'm another year older, I don't want my birthday's to keep passing me by and I'm living a lie."

"Well, I'm sure you know what you're doing, but if you change your mind and can't go through with it, you know your secrets safe with me."

"No. I have to do it, by the end of tonight, everyone will know

the truth."
Summer stifled a gasp. She couldn't believe it, CJ killed Marcus. She ran out of the penthouse, she didn't want them to know she'd over heard anything.

Claudia sat in the cab on the way to the restaurant with Jackson and CJ. She'd been hoping to get five minutes alone with CJ but Jackson had insisted on coming with them. Claudia had no chance of anything happening with Jackson around. She liked Jackson although at times they clashed over her feminist issues, but as a person she liked him, even if he was loud and over bearing she knew he would never mean anyone any harm. He was safe and that's what was important to her.

"You're quiet tonight Claudia," Jackson commented.
"I'm fine," she replied as she glanced over at CJ, they locked eyes for a second. God those eyes, a memory flashed across her mind, CJ above her, gazing at her with his bluey grey eyes. She wished for the millionth time that she could tell him how she felt; tell him he was her one true love. CJ and Jackson were singing along to the radio, much to the cab drivers annoyance. Despite herself Claudia couldn't help but laugh. They pulled up outside the restaurant; CJ helped her out of the cab. As they walked towards the entrance he slung his arm across her shoulders.
"Thanks for the present honey."
"You're welcome."
She couldn't help but lean in closer to him. That would have to do for now.

Sitting round the table at the restaurant Summer was quietly surveying the scene before her and trying to get her head around what was happening. She didn't feel the relief she thought she'd feel, the truth in fact was that she felt sad. She couldn't think of any other way to describe it. Yeah the nightmare was almost over, but at what cost? Jez sat next to her; not very clever planning meant that Matt was on the other side of him. They were arguing about baseball. Those two were incapable of having a civilised conversation. Jez's hand was resting on her thigh, every now and then he'd run his hand up and down her leg. Sex was the furthest thing from her mind now. Claudia was unsuccessfully trying to flirt with CJ, she wouldn't be so interested when she found out he was a killer, she'd be in total shock. That was the thing that was bugging her, mild mannered CJ a killer? It didn't fit. What the hell had Marcus done to CJ?

Amber was sitting in between Matt and Jackson. She and Matt still hadn't sorted out their argument from the other night; they were barely on speaking terms. Amber glanced around the table and not for the first time was shocked at how pale Summer had gone in stark contrast to how she'd looked earlier in the evening back at the penthouse. Amber was in no doubt that the apparent change in her friends behaviour was all to do with Marcus, she was going to have to speak to her again, this couldn't carry on. She felt Jackson rest his hand on her knee. Jeez, that guy never gave up. She was getting a bit bored with him now; he was taking up too much of her valuable time. She took a sip of her vodka. Just this afternoon he'd come to her office without an appointment. She was in the middle of some important designs. He pulled the blinds then pulled her onto the desk. Obviously she wasn't going to say no, she loved the fact that they were doing something risky and also he was an expert and skilled lover. Matt was even duller sexually in comparison – one position rules! How boring, but what did she expect he was an accountant.

Summer was still trying to analyse the whole situation as she looked round at each of her friends. Amber and Matt were sitting together, but they may as well have been sitting on separate tables for the amount of contact there was between them. They were a strange couple, looks wise they were a great match, but in personality they were poles apart. It must have been a case of opposites attract when they first got together, although judging by the amount of rows they were having lately that attraction looked to be wearing thin. Amber always picked guys who didn't seem her type, the worst being Marcus. God Marcus, yet again, he was back in her thoughts. She just couldn't work out everyone's motives and get them straight in her head. Amber was fuming with him for cheating on her with the bimbo ski instructor. Did she kill in a crime of passion? Claudia had nearly been raped by him, so her motive was clear. What about everyone else?

All she could do was speculate at their reasons. There was an under lying issue between Matt and Marcus something had gone on between them, what she didn't know but the signs were there. There had been a huge row at her parents funeral, Matt had literally thrown Marcus out of the wake and by the time the trip to Colorado came around the tension between the two had reached boiling point. As for Jez and Jackson what ever motive they may have had was a complete mystery to her. Unwillingly she began to contemplate Jez's reasons, it was no secret that he disliked Marcus, most people did, in fact it would be hard to find someone who actually liked him. The night that Jez had walked in on Marcus attacking Summer he had gone ballistic, she had never seen Jez so mad. Could he have killed Marcus over that? Summer knew that the usually laid back, chilled Jackson was getting increasingly pissed at Marcus making an issue out of his sexuality. Jackson had always been open about his sexuality and everyone accepted him for who he was, everyone bar Marcus and maybe he'd just pushed Jackson too far. She shrugged her shoulders then quickly glanced around remembering where she was. This was all so stupid. Why would Jez kill someone because they'd hit her? Why would Jackson kill someone because they couldn't accept his sexuality, Jackson wouldn't care. Why would Amber kill because she'd been cheated on? Her style would be just to do it right back! What about her? Did she really kill Marcus and block it out? She looked at her friends again, all laughing and joking, her friends, not killers. She took a sip of her wine and her eyes rested on CJ, but one of them had killed and now she knew who it was. She didn't need to keep torturing herself with different scenarios. The weird thing was CJ was the only one who didn't seem to have a motive. Whatever CJ's reason it sounded like he was going to reveal all tonight.

After the meal they were chilling out in the living room of the penthouse suite. The guys were drinking beer and the girls were working their way through a second bottle of wine. Summer was feeling restless, waiting for the big announcement.
"You're such a fidget tonight babe," Jez commented.
"Sorry," she mumbled.
He leaned over. Moved a strand of hair behind her ear and kissed her neck.
"Get a room guys," Amber shouted out.
"Just might do that, c'mon babe, you promised me dessert," Jez stood up and held his hand out to Summer.

CJ stood up and cleared his throat. "Actually guys, before you go off and er, do whatever, I er, I wanted to tell you something."
He was suddenly very aware that all eyes were on him. These are my friends, they wont judge me. He told himself. He moved over to by the fireplace so he could see everyone, se their faces, their reactions. He took a deep breath.

"This isn't easy for me…" he began. "In fact it's the hardest thing I've ever had to do. I've wanted to come clean for so long. You are my closest friends, I should've been able to tell you from the start, but I could never find the right moment, the right words, the right anything..."

He looked at Jackson for encouragement, he slowly nodded his head, CJ continued. "I can't go on living a lie, I feel like I've deceived you everyday and now it's time to tell the truth," he paused. Everyone was enthralled by what he was saying, Summer looked like she'd seen a ghost and Claudia... Oh God, Claudia... He realised he hadn't spoken for a few moments. He tried to gather his thoughts, he'd come this far, couldn't stop now.

"I didn't expect it to happen, but it just did and there was nothing I could do about it," he hesitated again.

Summer couldn't take her eyes off him, willing him to say it, to say he killed Marcus. Then it would all be over.

"Please don't judge me, I'm still the same CJ, still your friend, just like Jackson is and I hope that the fact that we're, that we're having a relationship wont change that."

There! He'd done it, after all these years he'd finally come out, the relief was intense.

Summer couldn't believe it, CJ didn't kill Marcus, the killer was still unknown, still sitting here amongst them.

CJ looked round trying to gauge everyone's reactions, Jez began to say something, but he was distracted by Summer.

Summer felt like the room was spinning, she couldn't hear what was being said, all she knew was it wasn't over, she had to get away. As she stood up, her legs gave way underneath her and she slumped towards the floor, the next thing she knew everything had gone black. Jez reacted quickly and caught her before she hit the floor.

CJ looked to Claudia, with tears streaming down her eyes she just shook her head at him and ran from the penthouse.

What had he done?

CHAPTER FIVE

Amber was fuming, how dare Jackson use her like that? What a bastard, not only was he sleeping with her behind Matt's back but he was also deceiving CJ. She thought she'd been the one playing games when all along it was him and if it was one thing she hated it was someone thinking they'd got the better of her. She was sitting silently on the sofa waiting to erupt. Jez was carrying Summer into their bedroom, Matt had his back to her reassuring CJ he'd done the right thing so she could quite freely glare at Jackson. He raised an eyebrow at her and turned towards the kitchen.

She got up and followed him across the room and into the kitchen. He was leaning against one of the work tops, arms folded and a grin on his face. She carried on glaring at him for a moment or so, while at the same time taking in just how sexy he looked just then, with his trademark 501's and plain white T-shirt which on anyone else would look plain and boring on him it looked amazing. His jeans hugged his ass perfectly, his tight top showing off his well defined body and the whiteness of the shirt enhanced his coco coloured skin, his hair was always in neat corn rows. Tonight for the meal he had worn a fitted black leather jacket over his usual attire and he looked like a rock star, yep he was the type of guy who could carry a look like that off and yep he was sexy and boy did he know it. He was still grinning at her waiting for her to speak. She hoped she looked mad and that her face wasn't betraying her thoughts.

"You jerk."
"I can see why that took you a good couple of minutes to come up with."
She shook her head at him. "How could you do that?"

"Amber, honey, you know I sleep with guys."

"That's not the problem Jackson; you deceived me, Matt and CJ!"

"Oh I see, so I'm getting the blame now am I? It might have slipped your mind little miss innocent but you were a willing partner to our special friendship."

Amber wasn't sure if it was the situation making her mad or the fact that Jackson was so damn chilled about it. She bit her lip as she tried to get her head together.

"I was always good at pushing your buttons darling."

"I'll treat that with the contempt it deserves. You may not give a damn, but I do. CJ stood up there tonight to tell us he was gay and that took some guts and along you've been cheating on him. How can I look him in the face?"

"The same way you look at Matt."

"That is totally different and you know it. As far as I was concerned this was between me, you and Matt..."

"Oh, I'd love a threesome."

"Will you just shut the fuck up and let me finish."

She was aware her voice was getting louder, she didn't want to alert the others, she also knew she had him rattled. For a split second his smile faltered and that was all she needed to get herself together, she was back in control.

"What I do in my relationship with Matt is down to me, but I happen to like CJ a lot and I would never have got involved with you if I'd have known about you and him."

"Yes you would, you can't help yourself."

Now it was her turn to laugh. "Oh Jackson, you really do think so highly of yourself, there are a million Jackson's out there and you were just the most convenient. I'll move onto bigger and better things."

"You wish baby, you aint never gonna get bigger and better than me."

"Let's face it, we had fun and now that's it, but you were way out of line."

She knew she'd hit him where it hurt with the bigger and better comment, even if she was lying, but hey he didn't know that! She was used to lies, lived a lie everyday.

"Ok, we'll call it quits, but anytime you want me honey, it's fine with me."

"Whatever Jackson, whatever."

She turned on her heel, her hair swinging behind her, her hips swaying as she walked out of the kitchen.

"You've got one great ass." He called after her.

"Go to hell."

She didn't look back.

Claudia sat alone in her apartment, glass of wine in hand, empty bottle on the floor. She couldn't stop crying. Her heart was broken into a million pieces, he'd slept with her and all along he knew he was gay. That night had meant so much to her and it had meant nothing to him, she meant nothing to him. He was supposed to be her friend, how could he treat her with so little respect? He knew what she'd gone through with Marcus and even though she'd been scared to death by Marcus, what CJ had done somehow seemed worse. Marcus' pain had just been physical. She drank her wine down in one go and seeing the bottle was empty she went over to the fridge for another bottle. She was crying so hard that she didn't even try to wipe the tears away. How was she going to get on with her life? She had truly believed that if she was patient she would eventually end up with CJ. Now she had to start each day without a purpose. She felt like she was falling apart. Hard nosed business woman? More like vulnerable needy Claudia. The doorbell disturbed her from her thoughts.

Matt sat propped up on the bed working on some accounts, a

little bedtime reading. After the revelation of that evening the guys had long since gone home. Summer hadn't emerged from her room and Jez hadn't thought to let him know how she was. She had looked pale all evening and he was getting even more worried about her. Amber had told him to stay out of it. He sighed as he looked up from his work and watched Amber as she carried on with her nightly rigmarole of removing her make up and using her vast supply of face creams. She was so proud of her appearance and if she ever got a wrinkle, well, he didn't want to be around when that happened.

"I can't believe CJ and Jackson." She didn't even look at him as she spoke, just continued to cleanse her face.

"I had my suspicions actually," Matt replied.

"You knew and you didn't tell me?" She spun round to face him. Now he had her attention.

"Amber, I didn't know. I just had inkling and I certainly wasn't going to gossip about it."

"Well I suppose if it Jackson wasn't CJ's partner it'd be you."

"What's that supposed to mean?"

"You know exactly, when was the last time we had sex?"

"Oh for God sake Amber, not that again."

"Matt I have needs."

"It's always about you isn't it? Well why don't you just go and find someone who will give you what you want."

"D'you know what Matt, I might just do that. You're a total jerk and I don't know why I bother with you." She grabbed her jacket and make up bag. "Don't wait up." She called on her way out.

"I won't," he muttered to himself as the door closed.

God she had the ability to make him feel so freakin worthless and inadequate. There was only one other person who could do that to him and that was Marcus. He often wondered if Amber and Marcus would have stayed together if he hadn't died, they were made for each other. He rested his chin on his hand and stared at nothing in particular. He ran that though through his head again, it wasn't really fair to tarnish Amber with the same brush, yeah she was a bitch but she wasn't evil. Nope, there was only one Marcus and thank God he was dead. One less psycho on the streets, which was the best word to describe his cousin because it was only a matter of time before his jokes went too far, but in the event of his death, his fun backfired on him.

Matt hated having secrets from Summer, but he could never tell her the truth about what really happened the night their parents were killed. Marcus was the drunk driver that ran their parents off the road and Matt knew this because he was with him. Matt had only gotten into the car with him in the first place to try and stop him from driving. Marcus began showing off, driving real fast and all over the place, by the time they reached Brooklyn Bridge Matt had been desperately trying to grab the wheel from him. It was then Marcus spotted his aunt and uncle's car he was trying to get them off the road. Matt could still hear him laughing now, thinking it was so funny. He eventually got control of the wheel, but it was too late the car ploughed into the side of the car. The next thing he remembered was finding himself a few miles down the road on his own; Marcus had dumped the car and left him. His parents were dead, his sister deeply affected by the crash and he had his own secret guilt and Marcus, well as usual he got away with it. Marcus had dared to turn up at his parents wake and Matt had told him he was going to go to the police. Marcus had told him he couldn't, he was also in the car with him and he would be an accessory to his own parent's murder. Matt had been so angry he threw Marcus out of the wake. So once again, Marcus had won the battle but he sure as hell didn't win the war.

Claudia opened the door to CJ. God she really didn't need this right now.

"Can I come in?"

"Why?"

"We need to talk, I need to explain," he pleaded.

"You need to talk, you need to explain. *I* don't want to listen."

"Claudia, please…"

Hating herself for being so weak she moved aside to let him into the apartment. The first thing he noticed was the empty wine bottles on the floor. It finally struck him that he really was the reason behind Claudia's drinking.

"I'm so sorry; I never meant to hurt you." His voice was barely above a whisper.

"Bit late for that CJ."

"You're right it is too late, I shoulda told you that morning, no scratch that, I shoulda been honest from the start, then you wouldn't have to go through this. It just got harder and harder to tell you and the more time went on the more I just buried my head in the sand. I kinda hoped you'd just forgotten about it. Your friendship is too important to me to lose."

"Don't make me laugh, if my friendship meant so much, why didn't you give a damn about my feelings?"

"Like I said before, what happened that night never shoulda happened. I felt confused. I thought I was gay, but I wasn't sure. Jackson and I had only been together a few weeks and he wasn't convinced. He thought I was confusing friendship with love…"

That last comment hung in the air and stung Claudia.

"…I'd never been with a man or a woman properly by that point, so I thought if I slept with a woman it would confirm my sexuality and it did. The only problem was…. I never meant it to be you," he sighed.

"Great, that's just great." She was standing in front of him, her arms folded across her chest, putting up as many barriers as she could.

"So I was just some experiment was I? You treated me like some cheap whore, difference being I have feelings. Didn't you know how I felt about you? God dammit I loved you."
She was desperately trying to keep the flood of tears from falling as she yelled at him.
"Claudia, don't say that, you weren't an experiment, it just happened. I've felt so guilty about it and I certainly never meant to make you feel like you were a..." he couldn't finish the sentence.

"Whore is the word you are looking for." She stared him straight in the eye, he broke away first and hung his head in shame.
"Say it!" she screamed.
He shook his head. "I'm sorry." He raised his head slightly; she could see the tears in his eyes. He reached out to touch her, she immediately recoiled. He dropped his hands to his side. "How can I make things right?"
"You can't. I haven't been on a date for two years. I've been celibate since you. All because I held onto that one night, hoping that we could turn it into more."
"Claudia, if I wasn't gay, you would be my ideal woman. Please don't take this whole mess as a reflection on you; you were just in the wrong place at the wrong time. I meant what I said that night, any guy would be lucky to have you".
"Yeah, any guy except you. So did you actually mean anything you said that night?"
"I would never lie to you," he mumbled.
"I suppose technically that's correct, with holding information could be perceived as not lying."
He knew he was losing her; she was speaking to him like he was a client. They stared at each other again. This time Claudia broke away first. She moved to the door and opened it.
"Get out of my apartment."
He did as she asked, he wasn't going to be able to get through to

her tonight. He just hoped to God she had no alcohol left. She slammed the door shut behind him and slid down the back door to the floor, her head in her hands, tears now flowing freely.

Summer lay in a troubled sleep. She was dreaming. She was back in the log cabin. She was out in the back where the hot tub was. Marcus was already in it, a bottle of bud in one hand a cigarette in the other.

"You wanna know who killed me dontcha princess?"
Summer nodded her head. She was freezing standing outside in just her bikini, but she was too scared to get into the hot tub.

"Well princess, who shall we start with? Jackson? Mr Cool, is it possible he coulda killed me? Well princess anythin is possible." He started to laugh, his blue eyes flashing with evil. Summer could only stand there rooted to the spot.

"What about Matt? You might not know what his motive is but I sure as hell do. Maybe it's your knight in shining armour Jez, he hated it when I put my hands on his precious little angel. He would do anything to protect your honour," he mocked.

She still couldn't move. Marcus carried on regardless. Ok. So, Jackson, Matt and Jez we haven't really got anywhere there have we? Now Amber and Claudia, those two can hold a grudge or two can't they?" He Carried on, not giving her chance to speak.

"Amber, well, she's every guy's fantasy, but that girls gotta heart of stone. It was only gonna end in tears between us. She hates losing and with me as her competition she was way behind. When she found me with that ski bimbo she knew she couldn't beat me, I was always one step ahead. The only way she could win was if I was, shall we say, out of the picture. A crime of passion would suit someone like Amber right down to the ground."

"Claudia is the opposite, her heart is made of glass, she's too fragile but she sure as hell hates me enough to kill me. Says I ruined her life, that girl needs to pull herself together. So really when you think about it, she probably wanted to kill me, but didn't have the guts and was hoping that someone would do it for her... a bit like when CJ rescued her from the big bad evil Marcus. Which leads us nicely into why CJ would kill me, one to protect our little Claudia or two, maybe because I knew he was gay and you know how much fun I woulda found that to tell you guys."

"Right. Enough. No more speculation, you want the truth princess you got it. Who is the one person no one suspects? Sweet, innocent, pure as the driven snow, princess Summer. Yep. You got it, it was you all along. The perfect crime, nobody would even think twice about suspecting you. You even discovered the body, what a shock that must've been. Yeah right."
He started laughing again; he got out of the hot tub and moved closer.
"It was you," he sneered. He was coming closer and closer.
"No. Stop," she mouthed.
"It was you."
"Stop."
He pushed her against the wall. "Revenge is sweet princess."
She felt along the wall in the hope of finding something to defend herself with.
She found a dressing gown hanging up, she pulled the cord from it, before she knew what she was doing, she'd wrapped it around his neck and pulled hard, her eyes closed too scared to look. She opened her eyes and saw him, wide eyed fall into the hot tub.
She screamed.

She sat bolt upright in bed. She immediately felt Jez's arms around her.

"I killed him," she sobbed. "I did it." She let herself fall into the safety of Jez's embrace.

"Baby, you passed out, it was only a dream. It wasn't real. He's gone. You didn't kill him," Jez spoke softly.

She felt her body begin to tense up as she shouted. "How do you know it wasn't me? How do I know it wasn't you? For all you know you could be about to marry a murderer. It could be any of us. It *was* one of us."

Jez shook her gently, she began to relax a little and let herself be comforted by him. "Summer, calm down. I know it wasn't you – I know because I know YOU. Marcus is gone; he can't get to you anymore."

"Yes he can Don't you see that's the whole point, he's gone but he's got the last laugh – typical Marcus. I'm getting to the point where every time I look at my friends I'm wondering which one killed him and I can't move on till I know."

"Why is it so important?"

"I need to know for my own sanity, so I can stop looking at the people I love as cold blooded killers."

"Listen baby, you gotta accept that we may never know what happened that night. So rather than try, learn to live with the reality. We've got a wedding to start planning, a whole future ahead of us. Let's try and leave Marcus in the past. Please babe, I want my bubbly happy Summer back. Please."

She looked deeply into his eyes and could see the pain in them, the anguish of trying to hold her together.

"Oh Jez, I'm so sorry. I know I've been so down lately and I shouldn't feel like this not when I've got you. You're everything to me."

"I love you more than you'll ever know Summer and I'm here for you always." He gently stroked her cheek.

"Always?"

"Always," he promised as he pulled her close. She sighed as she snuggled closer to him and slowly drifted back off to sleep.

Claudia was having yet another sleepless night. It was times like this when she hated living alone. She had been staring up at the bedroom ceiling for what seemed like hours. She didn't even remember getting into bed after CJ had gone. She desperately needed someone to talk to. Normally she'd call CJ but he was the problem. She thought about sending an email to Doug, but she knew what his suggestion would be and as much as she loved him it was purely platonic, on her behalf anyway. A sad smile appeared on her face. Was that what life was all about? She wanted CJ, he didn't want her. Doug wanted her, she didn't want him. Would she ever meet someone who wanted her as much as she wanted them? She couldn't even think straight, so trying to get her feelings down in an email would be damn near impossible.

Claudia had felt so many emotions after the night she spent with CJ, feelings she'd never experienced before and now all she felt was used. He'd slept with her just to confirm his sexuality. She would never understand how he could do that to her, they were supposed to be friends. He had know how low she'd gotten after Marcus and how untrusting of men she'd become and then CJ went and did something a million times worse. She turned on her side and glanced at the photo of CJ on the bedside table, it had been there for the last two years. She picked up the vodka bottle next to her and gulped some down. She reached out and knocked the photo of the table. How dare he think he could just apologise and everything would be ok? She took another drink of the vodka and dropped the bottle to the floor. She eventually fell into an alcohol induced sleep.

CHAPTER SIX

The next morning Summer sat on the sofa drinking a cup of coffee idly flicking through a magazine. Matt came out of the kitchen and sat down on one of the lazy boy chairs.

"That was some announcement last night."
"Yeah, what I can remember of it." She had actually forgotten the revelations of the previous night until Jez reminded her this morning, he wondered why it had such an affect on her. She'd just told him that maybe she was off colour or something. She felt a bit stupid admitting that she thought CJ was going to reveal himself as the killer.

"What happened last night? Did you have too much to drink? I was worried about you."
"Something like that," she sighed.
"You're ok now though?" he asked concerned.
Summer nodded her head.
"I would've checked on you last night but Jez wouldn't let me see you…" He let the sentence drift off when he saw the look on Summer's face. He decided to change the subject.
"So, what about CJ then? I did have my suspicions."
"Me too," she mumbled, only about the wrong thing she added silently. The conversation she'd overheard between CJ and Jackson had nothing to do with Marcus.

The front door slammed shut. Matt immediately folded his arms across his chest and a scowled appeared on his face. Amber walked into the room.
"You hung over? You look like shit? Amber asked Summer.
"Jeez, do you always have to be so blunt?" Summer replied.
"You don't look to hot yourself – where have you been all

night?" Matt asked.

"You almost sound like you care. If you really want to know, I've been out with some of the guys from work and had a great time."

Summer jumped up. "I'll leave you guys to it; I'm off for a shower." The last thing she wanted was to be caught up in the middle of one of their fights.

"Do you think Summer's ok?" Amber asked as she watched her friend disappear into her room.

"I think she's just hung over."

"No you fool, in general. She just seems to be getting quieter and more withdrawn. Not like the Summer we know. Still at least she's not sexually frustrated, so she obviously hasn't got the same problem as me."

Matt narrowed his eyes and glared at her. "You know what Amber, I'm sick of this. Summer is depressed and all you can think about is whether you're getting it or not and I very much doubt that you are going without!"

She raised an eyebrow at him. This was the first time he'd ever accused her in so many words of cheating. Why didn't she just tell him it was over and be done with it?

"Summer is your best friend," Matt carried on. "Why don't you try thinking about her for a change? See if you can get through to her."

"I've got no chance; even Jez is struggling at the moment."

"Is golden boys' halo slipping?" he replied sarcastically.

"Matt. Stop being a jerk."

He held his hands up. "Hey, I can't help it if I don't like the guy."

"I know exactly why you don't like him."

"Oh yeah?"

"You don't like the fact that Summer is dependant on some one other than you. I mean, you practically brought her up. I remember when we were still at high school; it was always you who helped her with her homework, made sure she had enough money for lunch and stuff. She looked up to you and you loved it. When your parents died, you assumed she'd turn to you, but she didn't did she? Summer found Jez, he helped her through it and he was there for her when Marcus died. She didn't need your support anymore. Now you feel like Jez is pushing you out of her life."

"Tell me about it."

"Don't be jealous, don't try and compete. You will always be Summer's brother, you will always be important to her, but you have to accept that your role has changed. If you keep resenting Jez, you'll be the one that pushes her away."

"I just want to make sure she doesn't get hurt."

"You'll never be able to do that, everybody hurts – even cold hearted bitches." With that she walked away.

As much as Matt hated to admit it, Amber was right. He despised the fact that she could obviously read him as well as those trashy novels she read. He ran his hand through his hand and plonked himself back down on the lazy boy. He'd always felt protective of Summer, she never got the attention she deserved from their parents, they were just too busy. As he was older, he could cope with the rejection but he tried to shield Summer from it. She seemed so vulnerable and he knew how fragile she could be, she was the type of person who wore her heart on her sleeve. Now that the oh so perfect Jez was looking even more of a permanent fixture he felt excluded, not that he'd ever tell Summer that, she'd never leave him out on purpose and it would upset her if she knew he felt like that. She liked to keep everyone happy. He sighed deeply.

Happy was not a word he could associate with Summer at the moment. He'd never seen his sister so down and he knew it was probably all due to Marcus. Even when he was dead that son of a bitch still seemed to cause trouble. Matt constantly questioned his decision not to tell Summer what happened the night their parents were killed and he still didn't know if he'd done the right thing not telling her. The trouble was, the time to tell her had long since passed. He should've told her at the time but she had her own issues to deal with. He'd been living in fear of Marcus some how pinning the blame on him. He was certainly more than capable of that, hell; the guy had just killed his own flesh and blood and had no conscience about it. Marcus was a loose cannon. If Summer ever found out the part her own brother had played in their parents' death she never would forgive him. He had to be stopped. God now he was starting to obsess about it all. Couldn't Summer just accept that Marcus was dead, the killer wasn't suddenly going to own up now, almost two years had passed. He wished they'd never gone to Colorado. No matter what any one said, they'd all come back from that vacation a completely different person. There were too many horrible memories to try and forget. He'd tried to block it all out and mostly he succeeded, however it didn't take long for those memories to come flooding back and once they reappeared in his mind they were back with a vengeance.

Matt remembered being woken up by a scream, a scream like he'd never heard before. It took him a few moments to get his bearings; once he did he sprang out of bed and ran in the direction of the noise. He could see Amber running through the lounge towards the kitchen, he followed. They carried on running until they reached the door that lead out onto the decking and the hot tub. Summer was sobbing, her whole body shaking. Jez had his arms round her and she had buried her head into his chest. Jackson was standing in front of Summer as if to shield her. He heard footsteps behind him and assumed it was CJ and Claudia.

"What's going on?" Amber spoke.

Matt moved forward and side stepped Jackson that was when he saw what all the screaming was about. Marcus face down in the hot tub and by the look of it, it was Summer who found him.

"Get him out quick, call 911." CJ shouted as he appeared next to Matt.

"Too late, he's dead," Jackson told him matter of factly.

"How d'you know?" CJ jumped into the tub and tried to pull Marcus out, he couldn't do it on his own. Jackson bent down and reached out to try and pull Marcus out while CJ pushed him. As they pulled Marcus' body out of the water, a dressing gown cord, hidden by his long hair, fell from his neck, revealing a red mark on his skin.

"Holy shit!" Jackson stepped back in shock; the body fell back into the water.

They all exchanged a worried look. Matt remembered the bottles of bud and champagne on the floor. He assumed, as they all had up until this moment that he'd drunk too much and fallen asleep or passed out in the tub and drowned. That wasn't the case, someone had strangled him, killed him. CJ climbed out of the tub, leaving Marcus still in there.

"Did anyone call 911?" CJ asked as he ran his fingers through his wet hair and tried to shake off the excess water off. No one replied.

"Good. Summer did you find the body?" CJ asked.

Summer couldn't move away from Jez, she didn't want to look. Jez nodded at CJ.

"Summer, I know it's hard but did you open the door to come in here or was it already open?" CJ probed further.

Everyone looked at each other, wondering what CJ was getting at and thinking he had lost the plot. Jez gently lifted Summer's face so all that she could see was his face. Tears were streaming down her cheeks.

"It was open," her voice was barely audible.

"Right guys, looks like we got ourselves a situation. One of us killed Marcus."

Matt looked around and suddenly realised what he meant. Although the hot tub was out on deck it was protected so that no one could get in, so whoever killed Marcus came in through the door and left by the door, back through the kitchen and into the log cabin. A quick inspection of the cabin followed to check there was no sign of a break in. All doors and windows were locked from the inside. CJ's assumption was right; who ever killed Marcus was still in the cabin.

They couldn't call the cops and they certainly couldn't leave the body where it was. CJ seemed to be the one taking control of the situation. He told them all to keep focused; the sensible thing would be to call the police. But if they all stuck together they could get through this. Basically they were protecting the killer. If the police were called, someone would go to jail, possibly even death row. There were no accusations, no demands, just an unreal reaction to cover it up. Whether that decision was right or wrong, they'd made it and they all had to live with it.

Matt often wondered if covering up one person's crime was worth ruining seven other lives (eight if you counted Marcus). Jackson suggested burying the body, but CJ pointed out that in the cold climate they were in there would be a chance that the body may be preserved for longer, providing evidence and DNA if ever discovered. It had shocked Matt at the time how clinical CJ had been, but he was a scientist so it was probably easier for him to differentiate between life and death.

It was decided that the only way was to burn the body. Jez and Jackson got Marcus' body out of the tub and wrapped him in sheets. CJ and he had built a bonfire and the body was placed between the logs, and then covered with leaves to make it look like they were burning trash and in effect, depending upon your opinion, they where, human trash. As the leaves and logs burnt the sheets caught fire, the pyre slowly burning Marcus' body. The smell was vile. Matt felt physically sick. Summer and Claudia actually did throw up. The other guys all turned a funny shade of green. Amber, well, she just looked the same as always, cool and calm despite the fact that her boyfriend had just been murdered. She didn't even bat an eyelid, he was sure that girl didn't have a heart.

What attracted Matt to Amber was one of life's little mysteries. She wasn't his usual type. Yeah she was pretty, stunning in fact. There was something about her that made guys look twice, but once you got passed the looks, she was like an empty shell. It never crossed his mind as to what made her like that. His thoughts wandered back to Marcus' funeral. No matter who was guilty of murder they were all guilty of covering it up. When the fire had finally burnt itself out and the ashes cooled they scrapped up the remains of the charred bones and deposited them in the lake, all evidence now gone.

For the remaining few days of the trip Summer stuck to Jez like superglue. Maybe that was where his dislike or Jez began. Matt wanted to be the one to comfort Summer but all she wanted was Jez. He had a really bad feeling about the situation and he had an inkling that things were about to get a whole lot worse and he just knew Summer was going to be in the middle of it.

Amber sat at her dressing table, rubbing various age defying, wrinkle free creams into her face. Matt was really pissing her off.

What she was still doing with that doofus she couldn't answer. He was a boring as hell. She slammed the tub she had hold of down onto the table. She was mad with herself, she never should've come out with that cold hearted bitches comment, she'd said too much. Her best defence in life was never to let anyone get too close, but that didn't mean she'd never been hurt. She could never have normal relationship, her past had put paid to that.

Marcus had once told her that they were two of a kind and were meant to be together, not in a nice romantic way that Jez might say to Summer, it wasn't a compliment. What he actually meant was they were both out for what they could get and didn't consider other people's feelings. Marcus said they truly understood each other because they both had the same goals in life, to look out for number one.

A memory started to form in her mind, she normally tried to fight them but today she didn't have the energy. She could see Marcus sitting on a rocking chair on the veranda of the log cabin, his legs propped up on the railings, a cowboy hat on his head, a cigarette hanging from his mouth. He really thought he was something, like Brad Pitt, difference being, Brad Pitt was something. Marcus turned his head toward her when he heard the door open. She was still fuming over the incident with the ski bimbo and had finally decided that enough was enough.

"Well if it isn't my beloved," Marcus sneered at her. Amber didn't reply, she just wandered over to him, pulling her coat tighter as the cold air hit her. She leaned against the rail of the veranda to face him.
"We gotta talk Marcus."
He tilted his head slightly and grinned at her from under his hat.
"We don't need words baby."

She looked at him and wondered how she had ended up like this, one dead beat boyfriend after another. This dead beat being the worse of a bad lot, but she knew why and so did Marcus. Things were never gonna change for her.

"I've had enough of your games. I've had enough of you Marcus, we're finished."

He laughed. "Oh c'mon sugar, you aint still pissed at me are you? The ski girl was just a bit of fun. You aint tellin' me that you're a saint, I know you're not."

"I'm tired of you. I can do better than you."

"Aint that the truth honey, you are one hot chick. But hey, we both know that no guys ever gonna marry you don't we. We both know that's the real truth sugar." He stood up and was inches away from her face. Amber pushed him away, she was determined that this was it.

"Sugar, you know me an you are good together, you understand me we are the same kinda people." He grabbed her and kissed her. She wanted to push him away but she couldn't. Her desire for him was too strong; the sexual tension between them was always there, simmering away beneath the surface. It drove her crazy. She knew he was bad, but it only seemed to make her want him more. He was pulling at her clothes, her hands roaming all over his body. From somewhere deep within she found the strength and conviction not to give into the passion. She pushed him away with all the force she could muster. He stepped back, wiping his mouth with the back of his hand.

"You know you want me sugar, you always do."

Amber used the veranda to prop herself up, her chest pounding as she tried to regulate her breathing.

"Marcus, I mean it this time. I don't want you."

"Baby, you are so wrong, you can't get enough of me."

"Listen, I am not a victim, you think I'm gonna settle for you then your wrong."

"No decent guy would want you, you're damaged goods, spoiled, barren, infertile, and you're worthless," he spat the words out with such venom.

"I am not worthless."

She bit back tears at the harshness of his words. She would not let him see her cry. "You can go to hell." She lunged at him and grabbed at his face with her fingernails.

He shoved her back, hard, towards the veranda, she almost toppled over it, but Marcus grabbed her by her hair.

"You will never get rid of me, unless I wanna get rid of you. This is over when I say it is sugar," he spoke through clenched teeth. He let go of her and watched her fall over the edge on the snow below. He leaned against the rail as she heaved herself up. Fortunately the drop wasn't huge and as she looked back up at him she was only inches away from his face.

"The only way you'll get rid of me is when I'm six feet under sugar," he grinned and then turned to walk away.

"I'll be the one who puts you there and when I do I'll dance on your grave," she yelled after him.

As he disappeared out of sight he shouted back. "See you in hell sugar."

How she hated him.

Amber didn't like to think about the past, her way of dealing with things was to bury them so deep into her mind that they rarely saw the light of day, but now she'd opened the box the whole freakin' lot were tumbling out. She stared at herself in the mirror. She could remember that day out on the veranda as if it were yesterday. It wasn't unusual, it was typical Amber and Marcus, one minute the flames of passion would be burning intensely, the next they would be physically be fighting. Marcus never cared how much he hurt her, she would always be threatening to leave him, then they would have amazing sex and then it would all happen again. He'd been right about one thing;

she couldn't get enough of him. He was an addiction she found hard to give up, The main difference about that day was he had pushed her over the edge, literally, when he called her worthless and brought up the subject of her infertility. Marcus was the only person who knew she couldn't have kids, he'd found out by accident after he'd had a nightmare and shouted out in her sleep and in a moment of weakness she'd opened up to Marcus. Big Mistake.

Amber had and abortion at fifteen, although she never told Marcus exactly how old she was. She had been too scared to go to her doctor, he was a golfing friend of her dad's and she couldn't tell Summer she was too ashamed. So that left her only one option, some back street clinic. She got rid of her baby and was left infertile after the procedure. Amber had no future; she would never get married, have kids and live happily ever after. That was the reason that she went from one dead end relationship to another, she couldn't risk falling in love and getting hurt. Marcus didn't know the whole truth, the reason she neglected to tell him how old she was so that he wouldn't put two and two together and realise it was his baby she'd aborted. Years before they got together, they'd had a one night stand which resulted in her pregnancy. She should have left well alone and steered clear of Marcus, he'd already wrecked her life once before, but the chemistry between them was mind blowing and that was the only thing out of life she could enjoy. The damage had been done; he couldn't do any worse than he'd already done. That day when he called her barren had knocked the wind out of her sails, it had really hurt her and she knew then that she couldn't stay with him for the sex, he had ruined her life, scarred her forever and she could never forgive him. Three days later he was dead.

CHAPTER SEVEN

Claudia banged on the door of CJ's apartment. After a few moments Jackson answered.

"Hey Claudia."

She took no notice of him as she barged past him and shouted CJ's name. He emerged from the bedroom.

"I'm ready to finish our conversation from yesterday now." She stood in front of him, her arms folded across her chest. CJ looked from Claudia to Jackson then back to Claudia. Jackson slipped quietly out of the room.

CJ took a deep breath. "I know I've hurt you and you don't know how sorry I am. I shoulda been truthful from the start, I thought I was doing the right thing, I guess I didn't know how much you cared."

"I don't believe you're gay, you're kidding yourself, you slept with me for God Sake," she yelled.

"I told you last night, I was confused. As much as I hate to say it, sleeping with a woman confirmed any doubts I had. I just wish to God it wasn't you."

"That night was so special to me; I felt so close to you. I can't believe you could treat me like that. Not after what I went through with Marcus. How could you CJ? You of all people knew how messed up I was."

All the anger that had been building up inside her just exploded, she burst into tears, her legs felt like jelly. God she needed a drink. She flopped down on the sofa, sobbing uncontrollably. "Where did I go wrong?" She held her head in her hands as she cried.

CJ sat next to her. "God Claudia, you didn't go wrong, it was me that messed up. I would love to be the guy that was with you, but I can't and if I'd pretended then I would be cheating both of us. I know how much Marcus hurt you and believe me I'm glad he's dead. I could've killed him myself for what he did to you. I'm just sorry that you're hurting again and it's all my fault."

"I feel such an idiot, I threw myself at you and you weren't remotely interested."

They sat in silence, neither of them sure where their friendship was headed.

Matt sat at his father's desk in his father's study.. He glanced around the room; all his dad's personal possessions were still there as were the boxes that had been sent over from his Washington office that neither he or Summer had been through yet. His parent's bedroom was exactly as they had left it, the cream coloured room with its king size bed, walk in closet, private balcony and en-suite bathroom. It was a mirror image of Summer's room. The door to his parents' room remained shut. He felt like he was going back in time whenever he went in and the guilt always came back. Could he have prevented his parent's death? What if he had never gotten in the car with Marcus in the first place? What if Marcus had crashed the car killing himself, leaving his parent's still alive, meaning Summer wouldn't be tearing herself apart trying to find out who killed him coz' the jerk would have killed himself. Meaning, Summer would never have met Jez that night on Brooklyn Bridge. Jesus he was going stir crazy, he better than anyone had learnt to accept what life throws at you and not to spend hours dissecting the what if's and the if onlys.

Matt had a strange sense of foreboding that it was all about to come to a head and everything would change again forever. His cell phoned beeped, distracting him from his thoughts. It was from Amber, telling him she was working late. He almost laughed to himself, it wasn't like her to be so considerate, maybe she had a guilty conscience.

Amber, now there was the other problem in his life. Not only did he have Summer's obsession with Marcus to contend with but there was also Amber. What was he supposed to do about their relationship or lack of? Deep down he did have some affection for her, but was it enough? He didn't feel like he was in the right frame of mind to make any sort of decision about their future at the moment, but he knew something would have to be done soon. They seemed to have totally lost the art of communication, only speaking to argue or piss each other off and the sex issue, well he was just fed up of it. It wasn't that he didn't find her attractive, he'd have to be blind not too, but she was just so sexually demanding and dominant. That really turned him off. Like the time when he'd woken up handcuffed to the bed with her on top of him. He knew some guys would love that, but she just didn't do it for him. Amber was so detached, it was just sex to her, which would be fine if it was just a one night stand but they were supposed to be in a relationship.

There was that other time when Amber came to his office, he watched as the other guys' jaws hit the floor as she sashayed in wearing a long black coat, her hair pile don top of her head and glasses on. He knew something was going on the minute he saw the glasses, she always wore contacts, far to vain for glasses. She perched on the edge of the desk, letting the coat slip away from her leg so that only he could see what was underneath, nothing. She asked him to escort her to the lobby. The minute they were in the elevator the glasses were flung off, the hair was pulled out as she did an over dramatic hair flick and she un did the belt of her coat to reveal that she was totally naked underneath. It should have driven him crazy, but all he could think about was the security cameras and hoping to God they were turned off.

Matt had a feeling that their relationship had run it's natural course.

Over the other side of the City Amber was working away, her business was really taking off. She'd had calls from some Hollywood agents asking when she could redesign their A list clients' homes. Her waiting list was getting pretty long with some prestigious names on it. People didn't seem to mind waiting as her reputation preceded her, they knew she was the best. Which was why she'd ended up in her office on a Saturday night. A meeting with her accountant – who was exactly like Matt- boring beyond belief, advised her that by the end of the year she would be on her way to becoming very wealthy and she would need to invest wisely. She'd had to stop herself from yawning, yep it was just like speaking to Matt. If anyone ever asked her what her boyfriend did for a living she would never say accountant; just that he worked in the City.

Amber often wished that Matt had a more manly job, like Jez. You couldn't get a more masculine, testosterone filled job, all those rippling muscles, sexy uniforms. No wonder Summer had fallen for him when she saw him in his uniform. Her friend was totally lucky having a guy like Jez, but then he was lucky to have someone like Summer. They were sickeningly made for each other. Amber was happy for her, but she sometimes got a tinge of sadness when she saw them together, she would never have that type of love, that happy ever after. She sighed as she put her pencil down, she couldn't concentrate on the designs she was sketching.

Yep, Marcus had put paid to that, not that she could just blame Marcus, she'd been stupid too. What she'd give to turn the clock back, her life would be so different. She got up and went over to the coffee pot, maybe a caffeine injection would give her a boost and get her mind focused again. She didn't hear the door open behind her and almost dropped the mug when she turned round and saw Jackson leaning against the door frame.

"Jackson! You scared the crap outta me."

"Sorry babes."

"What are you doing here? I told you, no more secret meetings."

"I know, I know. I'm not here for that, although… your desk does look very tempting," he grinned.

She sat back down at her desk, he sat opposite her and put his feet up on her desk, resting his hands behind his head.

"So, what are you here for?"

"Well Claudia and CJ are having a bit of a heart to heart, so I've left them to it and I guess I got a bit of a conscience about you and me and I had no where better to spend my Saturday night, so I thought to myself where does the hippest girl in the City go on a Saturday night? So here I am," he shrugged his shoulders.

"You get a conscience?" Amber laughed. "You are a total bastard, in fact you are a bigger bastard than…" She hesitated. Jackson dropped his feet to the floor and sprang forward in the chair.

"Don't you dare say it, don't you dare Amber Gordon."

She had the good sense to look embarrassed.

"I'm sorry, I didn't mean it."

"We were just having fun, no one is any the wiser, nobody got hurt, we're both consenting adults we knew what we were doing."

She nodded her head. She was losing the plot where the hell did that come from? Why had she nearly accused Jackson of being like Marcus, he was right. They'd only been messing around.

Jackson leaned forward across the desk and took her hand.

"I know he hurt you."

"What are you talking about?"

"Marcus."

"Jesus, Jackson. Do we have to talk about him?"

"You need to."

"You're getting as bad as Summer now. Marcus is dead, he's in the past why can't everyone just get a grip and leave him where he is," she shouted. A lump formed in her throat, what was happening to her? She took a sip of coffee; she needed to regain her composure. Amber Gordon did not lose control.

Amber honey, I know what he did to you."
You don't know shit," she replied calmly.
"You talk in your sleep." he replied, seeing the shock register in her eyes.
"Shit."
"I know all about it Amber, I know about the abortion, I know it was Marcus' baby..."
"People dream," she muttered.
"Not the same freakin' dream every night."
"I didn't spend every night with you," she protested."
"Ok, every night we were together then."
She was quiet for a few moments.

"Why didn't you wake me?" Amber asked quietly.
"Believe me honey, I wanted too desperately, but I figured you would open up when you were ready."
"So why now? Why tell me you knew?"
"I didn't come here to talk about that, but you were about to say I was like him and I'm not Amber."
"I know." She could feel tears of relief running down her face. Jackson stood up, went around the desk and pulled her into his arms.
"You could've told any of us you know, we would have understood."
"I thought I'd learnt to cope with it and after Marcus died, well I knew I could never tell anyone."
"Why?"
""My abortion, it left me infertile... I can never have kids... So

there's a motive if ever there was one," she tried to smile.

"God Amber, can't believe you've been dealing with this on your own."

They fell silent again.

"Any how, I reckon we've all got motive honey, y'all not on your own there."

This time she managed half a smile, then her eyes clouded over again.

"Shit!"

"What?"

"Matt. If you heard me, then maybe he has too?"

"I think if he knew he'd say something, he wouldn't let you suffer on your own. Besides he could sleep through world war three."

"Jackson, I don't suffer, I'm not a victim."

He smiled. "Sorry, forgot who I was talking to there. It explains a helluva lot though, now I know why you end up in relationships that don't go anywhere."

"What's the point in investing all my time in a guy who is gonna run the minute it gets serious and finds out I can give him a child."

"How can you be so sure, not every guy wants kids. I don't."

"Will you marry me?" she joked.

"That's better." He stroked her face. "I'd marry you in a heartbeat, but I'm not good enough," he laughed.

"Also, you're gay, bi sexual – what the hell are you?"

"Just having fun darling. Listen, I really think you should speak to Matt. Neither of you seem very happy at the moment, you need to get this out in the open."

"I'm not ready yet."

"That's ok, just remember, you've got me to talk to now. You're not on your own any more. I know it's not in your nature to let people in, but just try. You might be surprised."

"You're a good guy Jackson."

"Thanks, I know."

"You know what else, you're great in bed too."

"I know that as well – right back at ya babe." He looked from her to the desk and back again. "What d'ya reckon ? For old times sake?"

She burst out laughing. "You never let up do you?"

"You can't blame a guy for trying." She leaned over and kissed him, a deep, passionate kiss. "That's all your getting," She spoke as she pulled away. "We'll keep this on a friendship only basis from now on. Come on take me home." She picked up her bag and ushered him out of the door.

"Can't we be friends who sleep together?"

"C'mon. Home!" she ordered.

"Ok, what about once a month?"

She glared mockingly at him, he spun round to face her, walking backwards.

"Christmas? Birthdays? Thanksgiving?"

"You're pushing your luck now D'arby. Friends, period." She tried to sound serious but she couldn't help laughing.

"Ok, friends it is." He held out his hand to shake hers. "Please to be your acquaintance."

"You jerk."

He flung his arm round her shoulders. "C'mon friend, I will escort you home."

Summer was lying on her bed, propped up at the elbows reading Cosmo. She'd just got out of the shower and started to dress, but as she put her on her underwear, she realised it wouldn't be long until Jez was home. It really wasn't worth getting dressed! So, there she was waiting for him in a lacy black lingerie set. They were a bit restricted living with Matt and Amber, unless they had the penthouse to themselves they had to keep their love life in the bed room. She didn't really mind, their sex life was great.

The bedroom door swung open and Jez walked in, he grinned when he saw her on the bed.

"Jeez Summer are you a sight for sore eyes," he smiled that sexy smile of his which instantly sent a wave of desire through her body.

She got up off the bed and walked towards him, never breaking eye contact, she was still looking deep into his eyes as she began to slowly undress him. She tilted her head and leaned forward to kiss his lips, just as he started to kiss her, she moved her mouth away, still not breaking eye contact. She licked her lips then kissed him again. He took her face in his hands, pulling her as close to him as possible, not wanting to let her go. She moaned into his open mouth. He moved his mouth to kiss her cheek, her neck, her shoulders as he trailed his fingers across her soft skin and down to the clasp on her bra, expertly unhooking it and letting it fall away. He took in every detail of her as he let his eyes wander all over her body. She pressed up against him.

"God Summer, you don't know what you do to me," he murmured into her hair, taking in the freshly washed smell of coconuts as he ran his fingers through it. He gently tipped her head to face him, the love and sensual look in her eyes made his heart contract. He lowered his lips to hers, this time she didn't tease him and pull away, she surrendered totally to his kiss, he felt her body literally sink against his. He ran his fingers down her back in the way he knew she loved and then moved his hands round to the front of her body, gently caressing her breasts, she let out another moan. He bent his head and began to flick her nipple with his tongue. She reached down, inside his boxers. The sensation of feeling her erect nipple and the feel of her touch was sending him crazy. He scooped her up on his arms and laid her on the bed. She wriggled out of her knickers breathlessly, he lay down next to her, she positioned herself on top of him and eased him inside her. As he moved beneath her he let one hand roam across her body and moved the other one to between her legs. He could tell she was close to orgasm, as she came he moved his hands round to her butt and gave one final thrust as he exploded inside her.

"That was…" he breathed.
"I know…" she replied as she flopped down on top of him. He tenderly stroked her hot skin and sighed."
"That was a big sigh."
"It was a happy sigh."
He put his arms around her and flipped her onto her back so he could look at her as he spoke. "Baby, I've got everything I ever wanted or needed right here in my arms. As long as I have you I'll never need anything else."
"Jez, you've got me. All I want is you too."
"You make me complete, I never thought I'd ever have this…"
"I know. You don't need to worry."
"I would do anything for you Summer. Anything, I just want to make you happy."
She cuddled in closer to him. "You make me happier than I've ever been. I know it doesn't seem like it at the moment, but I will get over this Marcus thing. I won't let it ruin what we've got, you're too important to me. I want to start concentrating on our future. I just need a bit of time to get my head sorted, that's all."
"I will get you through this Summer, I swear." He kissed her lightly on the lips and tightened his grip around her.
"Just promise you'll never let me go, I feel so safe in your arms and I need you now more than I've done."
He could hear the waiver in her voice. "I'm not going anywhere babe."
She gazed up at his face, seeing the concern in his deep blue eyes, but still flashing that amazing smile at her. She reached up and ran a finger over his lips. She could never get tired of looking

at him, he was so sexy, so gorgeous and she loved him with all her heart.

Claudia hadn't left Jackson and CJ's apartment. She was still angry and confused and generally feeling let down. Not a word had passed between them for the last twenty minutes, both lost in their own mixed up heads. Claudia broke the silence and was actually surprised to hear her own voice.

"For once, please be truthful with me…"
He nodded his head slowly.
"That night in the log cabin, what made you and Jackson argue? What made you choose then and me to decide who you are?"
CJ was quiet, she could almost see the thoughts whirling round his head. He took a deep breath and sighed.
"We argued because of Marcus."
"Jesus Christ, does everything have to be because of him?"
"Jackson and I had been for a walk, wandering through the woods close to the cabin. We hadn't been seeing each other for long and we hadn't told anyone else about us. It wasn't our intention to keep it a secret for so long. Anyway as we got to the edge of the wood, in sight of the cabin, we held back a bit. Dusk was falling and we thought we wouldn't be seen…so we had a kiss."
Claudia shifted uncomfortably on the sofa. He moved on quickly.

"When I went into the cabin, I walked straight into Marcus. He'd been looking out of the window. My heart sank, I knew he'd seen us. He just grinned at me. He didn't come right and say it, just said something along the lines of, isn't it amazing what you see from a window when people don't know you're watching. I didn't know what to do. I wasn't ready to come out and I knew it wouldn't be long before Marcus outed me. I told Jackson what had happened, thinking he'd be sympathetic, but I was wrong.

He couldn't understand what the problem was and we should tell you guys about us. I told him I wasn't ready. Jackson started to question me, suggesting I might not be gay and maybe I didn't really know what I wanted. We had a huge row about it. I went to see you, my best friend, hoping I could maybe try and tell you what was on my mind, but then you started telling me about this guy you liked an it dawned on me that you were talking about me. Before I knew it we were kissing. I was so wrong to mislead you but..." he paused

"So, what you're trying to say is that I came on to you is that it? That it was my fault?"
"No, no of course not. It was me that messed up and I don't know what to do to sort it out."
The silence was back again.

"So, Marcus would've outed you?"
CJ nodded.
"You didn't want that?"
"What d'you think?"
"I think that's a motive for murder."
"Jeez Claudia, I'm not the only one with a motive."
He held her gaze as she got up off the sofa.
"I don't think we've got anything left to say to each other."
He jumped up and followed her as she stalked across the apartment.
"I'm sorry, I went too far."
"On which occasion are we talking about now?" She walked straight out of the door without looking back.
He ran his hand through his blonde hair. He couldn't lose Claudia's friendship, but who could blame her for the way she was reacting, he'd been a total jerk. It was easy to blame Marcus, he stirred everything up, but in the end CJ was responsible for his own actions.

CHAPTER EIGHT

The next morning Summer woke up early, well 9.15am was too early for a Sunday morning. She was still basking in the after glow of all that sex last night. Jez was an amazing lover; he knew how to turn her on without even looking at her. Out of no where a black cloud appeared in her thoughts and darkened her mood. She had this horrible feeling, she couldn't explain it, but she knew something bad was about to happen. It made her feel like staying in bed and hiding under the duvet to escape whatever it was. She felt her skin prickle and goose bumps appeared on the surface of her skin. Jez lay next to her, breathing slowly. She stroked his arm gently as she watched him sleep. She knew she was lucky to have found someone like Jez and she felt guilty for feeling so down when she had this guy who loved her and wanted to spend the rest of his life with her. Her depression had worsened since CJ's revelation. For a few hours on that Friday night, she thought she would finally be able to put the past behind her. Now she was back at square one, except things felt worse than before.

Summer was falling deeper into despair, her head felt like it was going to explode, and she was going crazy. It bothered her that everybody else seemed to be able to get on with their everyday lives without giving Marcus a second thought whilst she struggled to get through the day thinking about anything else but him. She found it increasingly difficult to look at her friends in the same light, when it came down to it, one of them was a killer. Simple as that. Why didn't any one else seem to care? Why was she they only one who wanted to find out the truth? She was so grateful that she had Jez, she loved him so much. He was always there when she needed him. He'd hold her in his arms and she knew that was her safe haven. They connected on every level, they were soul mates. She gazed at him again, he had such strong features. She supposed that reflected his personality, he was the strong one. He was the one that held her together. She sighed deeply, as much as she wanted to stay in bed with him; she needed to get away from her dark thoughts. She'd feel better after a shower.

Jez woke up alone, Summer's side of the bed was empty. He glanced at the clock. 9. 30 am. He couldn't believe she was up at this time on a Sunday. They normally woke up late and had a long lie in together. He reached out and pulled her pillow close, he could smell the faint smell of coconuts, the fragrance of her, so fresh and pure. He couldn't even begin to explain how protective he felt of her, he just wanted to keep her safe from everything. She had already been through so much and if he could shield her from anymore pain he would. She was so precious to him, she loved him unconditionally and that made him feel like the luckiest guy on the planet. No other woman could hold a candle to her. He couldn't imagine what his life would've been like without her; he didn't even want to think about it. His main concern now was getting her over this Marcus thing. He knew she was feeling pretty bad, but he didn't know what to do. A thought struck him.

Jez reached across the bed to the bedside cabinet and opened the draw. He felt around till he found what he was looking for, he pulled a lilac book out.
Her journal.
He knew it was invading her innermost thoughts and in normal circumstances he would never even think about reading it, but he was getting desperate. He watched her sometimes, with a faraway look in her eyes and he felt like she was a million miles away; he couldn't reach out to her. He needed to know that things weren't as bad as he thought. If he read through her

thoughts he'd be in a better position to help her, he reasoned to himself as he tried to justify his actions. He began to flick through the pages. He smiled when he read the entry when he'd proposed;

"I feel like the luckiest person in the world, I can't wait till we are married."

He smiled to himself, the feeling was mutual. The smile disappeared as he scanned some of the more recent entries. He flicked to yesterday;

Feb 3

I feel like I'm going crazy, crazy like I need a shrink. I think about Marcus all the time, when I'm not thinking, I'm dreaming. Dreaming that I killed him. I look at my friends when they're sitting there laughing and talking and go through their motives. Some I know, some I make up. Some days Amber is the killer, other days it's CJ, Claudia, or Jackson and in my darkest moments, Matt or Jez. They are the hardest ones to think about so I try not too. I need someone to blame and in the absence of truth, I blame myself and in effect it is my fault. I suggested the vacation. So if it wasn't for me, there would be no hot tub and no dead body in it and nobody would be a murder suspect. Of course there is the other possibility that I'm the killer. Everybody else seems to have coped just fine and got on with their lives, except me! Just because I don't remember doing it, doesn't mean I didn't. I could have regressive hypnosis and find out if I did it. But I'm too scared. I am slowly going insane. I don't know how anyone could live with themselves for all this time with the knowledge that they killed someone and not get any conscience...but if I'm the killer, it explains it all.

I'm so glad I have Jez, the nightmare of Colorado will haunt me forever, but without Jez I wouldn't have anything and then there really wouldn't be any point....

Jez put the journal back and lay down on the bed, his hands behind his head. He felt like he'd been kicked in the stomach. He couldn't believe she blamed herself, did she honestly think she was capable of killing someone? She was tearing herself up over something she couldn't possibly have done and what was all that shit about having nothing without him. What was she trying to say? Did she feel suicidal? It was the other way round, he was nothing without her. He knew Marcus had been on her mind, but not to this extent. As from now he would do all he could to stop her pain even if it meant hurting other people. He couldn't bear to think of her having nightmares night after night and being consumed by guilt for something she didn't do.

Summer was in the kitchen making coffee when Amber came in.
"Hey Amber, you ok?"
"Fine."
Once she'd made the coffee Summer sat down next to Amber at the breakfast bar. Something was up. Amber had listened to her

go on and on about Marcus, it was time she started acting like a friend too.

"What's wrong?"

"I'm sexually frustrated."

"What?"

"Will you please explain to your brother what sex is?"

"Err, I'd rather not." Summer felt a bit awkward, she and Amber had always talked about their sex lives but since she'd been seeing Matt, it kinda felt a bit weird talking to her best friend about her brother's performance in bed.

"He hasn't touched me for months. I'm fed up trying to get him in the mood." Amber carried on regardless of Summer's protest. "He doesn't even bother to kiss me let alone have sex with me."

"Why don't you talk to him about this?" Summer suggested, regretting asking Amber what the problem was and wishing Claudia was here instead.

"I have, he says he's too tired, what kinda pathetic excuse is that? I've got a line of guys waiting for me. If he doesn't sort himself out soon, it's over. I have needs Summer, I have a high sex drive."

"I really think it's him you need to speak to. Find out what his problem is."

"I know what his problem is, I'm too independent. I'm my own woman and he doesn't like that. He likes to be in control, he's the same in bed. I wont let him be like that with me, it's me who's in charge and he hates it. It makes him feel less of a man. He'd have it in the missionary position every time if he could. Matt needs someone sweet and submissive, someone like you."

"Amber! That's gross, he's my brother. Anyway, I'm not submissive."

"I said someone like you – not you. You are so compliant. Jez is your big hero, he protects you, you let him and you love it."

"My relationship with Jez has got nothing to do with you. We are perfectly happy how we are and if you want my opinion, I think it's you with the problem. You are obsessed with sex."

"I can think of worse things to be obsessed with."

"Oh yeah, like what?"

"Marcus for starters."

Before Summer could answer Jez ran out of the bedroom.

"Honey, I've been paged. I gotta go to work. I'll be back soon. Love you." He kissed her on the cheek and disappeared out of the door before she had chance to tell him she loved him too. She turned her attention back to Amber.

"I am not obsessed with Marcus."

"You know as well as I do that you have a major problem dealing with it."

"Well someone has to care, nobody else seems to and maybe when this whole 'Marcus thing' is sorted we can get on with our lives."

"Honey, everyone else is getting on with it; you're the only one living in the past."

"Don't you even care that he's dead?"

"If he wasn't dead, if he'd moved to the other side of the country you wouldn't even miss him."

"That's not the point, he's not living happily in California, he is DEAD!" Summer stood up, slamming the coffee cup down on the table.

"Oh for God sake Summer, will you just snap out of it and change the God damn record while your at it!"

"Thanks for your support; it's nice to have friends you can rely on."

"Summer, the first rule in life is you can't rely on anyone except yourself, it certainly didn't help Marcus did it?"

"Well maybe that's why I'm happy and you'll never be, I let people into my life, I'm not some cold hearted bitch."

That comment really stung, but Amber tried not to let it show. "Look who's calling who a bitch."

"First you ask my advice, then you start insulting me and you expect me to let you. Y'know what Amber, you've got me all wrong. I'm not some doormat and I wont take anymore of your shit. I hope you and Matt do split up, you obviously aren't right for each other. At least Jez and I don't have any problems with our sex life."

With that she turned on her heel and walked out.

Claudia had lazed around her apartment in her pj's all morning feeling sorry for herself. "This is stupid."

She got up off the sofa and went into the bedroom, she picked up the photo of CJ and dropped it in the trash can. She picked up her laptop and logged onto her emails, she scrolled down until she found what she was looking for – Leyton Carter's cell phone number. She punched the number into her phone quickly, and then just as quickly snapped the phone shut. She took a deep breath.

"C'mon Michael's don't be a wuss."

This time she pressed the numbers in slowly. As she heard the ringing tone her stomach was doing flip flops.

"Leyton Carter." She heard the cool crisp voice at the end of the line. Two minutes later she had a date for that night, her first date in two years, he may not be the love of her life but it was a step in the right direction. The girls would be so proud when she told them. She ran a hand through her hair, God it felt awful. When was the last time she washed it? First step to recovery, the shower. As she got up off the bed she spotted a half empty bottle of wine. She picked it up and took it with her. She headed straight for the kitchen and poured the remainder down the sink, now that was the real first step to recovery. She'd wallowed in self pity and alcohol for long enough. She wasn't gonna fall apart over some guy. She smiled to herself as she headed off to the shower.

Jez sat on a bench in Central Park, the same bench he'd sat on all those years before when he'd left foster care. Hell, this bench was almost family. He watched a young family, the dad was trying to teach his daughter how to rollerblade, the mom was laughing as she watched. He sighed, some people had big ambitions, like Matt, he wanted to be a big cheese on Wall Street or Amber who would be a self made millionaire with her design business, but not Jez All he wanted out of life was to marry the girl he loved, and boy did he love her. He needed Summer physically, not just the sex, but when he wasn't with her, he didn't feel complete. Kinda like now. She meant everything to him. He had been so cynical growing up, didn't believe in love until the day Summer came into his life. Everything changed for the better then. She was his future. As the product of an affair, resulting in him spending his childhood in a kid's home, he decided very early on that if he ever had kids, and that was a very big if, they would have a stable and happy upbringing. He had that stability with Summer. He ran a hand through his hair. Except, things didn't feel that stable at the moment. What he'd read that morning disturbed him. If he wasn't careful, Marcus' evil streak could reach out from beyond the grave and destroy him and Summer. The question was... what did he do about it?

Summer was really messed up and it broke his heart to think of what she was putting herself through. The only way to stop it would be for the truth to come out. She'd stop blaming herself then. He knew the truth, he knew who killed Marcus, he'd known all along. He hoped it might all blow over, kinda stupid when he thought about it, this was murder they were dealing with here. So, now it was time. He could not and would not let

Summer carry on torturing herself, he was about to blow the whole thing wide open. He dared not let himself think of the consequences. He got up off the bench and slowly walked away, dodging the girl on the rollerblades.

CHAPTER NINE

Feeling at a bit of a loss after Jez's call into work Summer headed over to Claudia's apartment. She hadn't really had chance to speak to her since CJ's revelation. In normal circumstances she would've spoken to Claudia straight away, but at the moment she was slightly pre occupied with other matters. Or as far as Amber was concerned, obsessed. She hadn't even had the chance to probe Claudia about how she was feeling, she was far too mad at Amber and her accusations.

"....Then she had the audacity to tell me that Matt needed someone submissive, like me!"

"Y'know Amber, tells it like it is. Although I wouldn't say you were submissive, you're just not the most independent person I know."

"Whadd'ya mean?"

"Well, you're used to people looking out for you. You like the idea of being protected by some strong, masterful guy. The original princess looking for her prince charming and yours rode up on a fire rig and rescued you."

"Claudia, I wouldn't put it quite like that."

"Yeah. I know, but you're quite happy to let Jez stride into your life and take control of it."

"Jez doesn't control me. We work together in our relationship, we're a team," Summer protested.

"You do it subconsciously. Little things like wearing the clothes he likes, letting him choose the restaurant or what movie you see."

"He doesn't tell me to do those things; it's not him controlling me. I just like to please him."

Claudia shrugged. "Like there's a difference?"

"So I'm not some feisty ball breaker like Amber or a strong

feminist like you, I'm just easy going. Jeez, there are enough arguments between Amber and Matt in the apartment. I prefer things to be different between Jez and me. It works for us, we're happy and so what if we're passionate and affectionate with each other. I sure wouldn't want it any other way."

"You are such a hopeless romantic."

"You're just as bad; you lived in a fantasy world as far as CJ was concerned."

Claudia's face fell at the mention of his name.

"I'm sorry; I shouldn't have said that, I'm still worked up over my row with Amber. I know how much you wanted to be with him," Summer apologised.

"I just wish he'd told me from the start that I didn't stand a chance."

"Well the hopeless romantic in me believes that everyone has a soul mate out there and hopefully yours is just around the block!"

"The strong feminist in me has actually already asked a guy out on a date."

"You go girl!"

"Well he may not be the love of my life, but I've got to start somewhere. He's a lawyer I know through work. He's asked me out a few times and I've always said no, because of, well CJ and all that. So I thought I'd ring him up and see if his offer of a date is still on."

"What's his name? What does he look like?"

"His name is Leyton Carter and to be perfectly honest I've only ever spoken to him on the phone, he's got a very sexy phone voice though," she laughed.

"When's the big date then?"

Claudia glanced at her watch. "In about four hours."

"Oh my God! You've got to get in the bath, wash and style your hair, decide what you're wearing. Paint your toenails. What the

hell are you doing sitting here? Go and get ready!" Summer ordered as she stood up and pulled her coat on. "I want full details tomorrow." She headed off towards the door. "You never know he could be your soul mate."
"Get outta here Stevens."

Jez walked into the lobby of their building. He felt sick to his stomach. He'd needed some space today to try and clear his head and to think. He knew he had to stay strong for Summer. He knew the bombshell he was about to drop over the next day or so would change their lives all over again. He hadn't really worked out a plan of action; he assumed he'd have to wait till everyone was all together. He'd just have to hang on until the opportunity presented itself. Whatever happened, there wasn't going to be an easy way to say what he had to say. He stepped into the elevator and pressed the button for the Penthouse. He leaned back against the hand rail. Was he doing the right thing? He really didn't see any alternative. He couldn't let Summer spiral any further into depression. He hadn't let himself think too much about what might happen once the truth was out, he couldn't. If he did it might stop him doing what he hoped was the right thing. The elevator doors opened and he stepped out onto the penthouse floor. He hoped Summer was still up. It was kinda late; he'd spent most of the day wandering around on his own. He wasn't very good with his own company and right now he needed Summer more than he'd ever needed her before.

He opened the apartment door. He needed her, he wanted her, to feel her in his arms, to look at her beautiful face, lose himself in her striking green eyes, kiss her soft lips, run his fingers through her silky hair and stroke her smooth skin. He wanted to be totally consumed by her. His breath quickened as he strode across the suite to their room, undoing his shirt as he walked. He wanted to explore every part of her body, to feel her moving rhythmically against him. He felt like his whole body was screaming out her name. He reached the bedroom door and gently pushed it open. The room was in darkness, but the light from the hallway illuminated the bed. Summer was asleep; the duvet had slid down her body to reveal her bare back, just stopping, teasingly at the base of her spine. He smiled to himself, even in her sleep that girl was sexy, and that girl was all his. He pulled off his jeans and the remainder of his clothes and slid into bed next to her. He began to kiss her back, starting with kisses on her shoulders and then trailing them right down her back. She moaned his name sleepily. He worked his way back up her body, as he reached her shoulder he gently turned her over onto her back. She was still asleep. He stopped and just looked at her, struck yet again by how beautiful she was. He bent down and kissed her throat then moved his lips to hers. He felt her stir and pulled away slightly as she opened her eyes.

"Hey gorgeous," he whispered.

"Hey you, where have you been? I was getting worried."

"Doesn't matter babe, I'm here now, right where I belong," he kissed her again. "Sorry for waking you, But I want you, right this second. D'you mind if I carry on what I was doing before you rudely interrupted me?"

"Be my guest," she smiled as she lay back, enjoying the feeling of his tongue flickering all over her body.

Claudia was having a surprisingly good time on her date with Leyton. She certainly hadn't expected to enjoy herself as much as she had. It was purely an exercise in helping her get over CJ. In fact she'd almost told the cab driver a million times to take her back to her apartment. She didn't really know Leyton that well, what if he was an axe murderer or a complete psycho? She knew she was being irrational, not all guys were like Marcus. If she was ever going to get over her issues with men she needed to get back out there. Despite Summer's insistence that she spend four hours getting ready she actually only spent an hour and a half. She wore her auburn hair loose so it framed her face and brought out the colour in her hazel eyes. It was so long since she'd been on a date that she didn't have a clue what to wear. She didn't want to seem too overdressed; neither did she want to look like she hadn't made an effort. She decided on black trousers and a pale pink top.

She walked into the restaurant, nervously looking around for a guy that looked like she imagined Leyton to look. She spotted a guy leaning against the bar. His hair was sandy coloured and his tall frame making him look suave and sophisticated in the suit he had on. However she could imagine him to look just as sexy in Levi's and a T-shirt. Before she could even hope that the guy was Leyton he smiled at her and wandered over to her.

As they sat down and ordered their meal there was none of the awkwardness she'd been expecting on a first date. The conversation flowed freely. They shared a lot of the same beliefs regarding the judicial system. It was gratifying and a nice change that she could talk to a fellow colleague without being belittled and he actually admired the work she was trying to do in women's law. They were coming to the end of the meal. He reached over to fill her glass up, she was drinking water. She hadn't forgotten the promise she made to herself to get her life back on track.

"So, can I ask a question I've been dying to ask all night?"
"Go on."
"What changed your mind?"
"About you?"
"I've been asking you out for months and you kept knocking me back and then all of a sudden you call me up and ask for a date."
"You know I'm a feminist, you were doing it all wrong," she laughed.

"Ah, so I shoulda waited for you all along." He raised an eyebrow at her as he took a sip of his drink.

"Well, not quite. What is it they say? If you fall off a bike you gotta get back on."

"So, you've just come out of a relationship?"

"It was more of a one sided relationship. We're friends and we kinda had a thing once and I hoped it would turn into something more, but it never did."

"He must've been crazy or gay to turn you down."

She took a deep breath. "Gay, actually."

Jeez, what was she doing? This was not a first date topic of conversation. Any second now Leyton would be making a sharp exit out of the nearest door. To his credit Leyton hid his reaction well, he didn't burst out laughing nor did he seem shocked. He just nodded his head slowly, prompting her to go on. As he was still sitting at the table he obviously wasn't about to run out on her. Maybe she wasn't the failure she thought she was. She may as well carry on with the whole sorry tale; if the date didn't work out at least he'd have something to laugh about in the office tomorrow.

"Well, I was kinda an experiment. He didn't know if he was gay or straight and apparently sleeping with me solved the problem for him, he is now officially out of the closet."

"Nice guy huh, and he's supposed to be a friend?"

"He didn't deliberately set out to hurt me, he was just confused." As she defended CJ she knew their friendship would be ok, she wouldn't let any one say anything bad about him.

"Well I can assure you I am 110% heterosexual," he laughed.

"That's what you think; I have the power to turn men gay. Wish I coulda picked a better super power, but there you go." She was now laughing with him. He drank some more wine and as he lifted the glass to his mouth he didn't take his eyes off her.

Claudia couldn't stop looking at him either; he had such kind, warm chocolaty eyes full of laughter. She felt so at ease with him, she normally felt a bit threatened in social situations like these. Not tonight though, the misgivings she'd had earlier in the evening felt like a million years ago. She'd been so open with him; she certainly hadn't expected to tell him the whole CJ debacle. As Leyton put his glass down on the table he reached out to hold her hand. She didn't want the evening to end. They carried on talking until they were the last ones in the restaurant.

It felt completely normal to go back to his apartment for coffee. It felt totally normal to spend the night with him and it was definitely ok to call her office the next morning as she lazed in bed with Leyton and tell them she was working from home.

Jez woke early the next morning, although he couldn't be sure if he'd even been asleep. He had a gnawing feeling running through his body; he just knew that today was gonna be the day of reckoning. Could he really go through with it? He was about to blow the bottom out of everybody's world, it seemed too important just to let it go. He turned to face Summer who was still sleeping peacefully. He reached out and gently pushed her hair away from her face. She was so perfect and he loved her more than anything. He wanted to take her nightmares away. He wanted to protect her, but could he save her from this? He thought he'd done the right thing in Colorado, holding back what he knew. The memory of Summer's reaction when she found Marcus' body was something he'd never forgotten. He could've stopped her from going through that, but how was he to know where she was headed that morning? He would never forgive himself for that error. He knew he'd been wrong in keeping the secret he had hidden for so long, Summer needed to know the truth, it was the only way forward. He moved over and kissed the tip of her nose, every time he looked at her he fell in love all over again. His whole life was about her and nothing else.

He wasn't a believer in God, but he sent up a silent prayer that they would get passed this. They were about to go to hell and back and he was damned sure he was going to get them back in one piece.

"I love you Summer. I love you so God damn much."

After Claudia's day at *work* she called in on Summer, who was desperate to hear the details of her date. The two girls' were sitting in the kitchen with Amber. Summer and Amber's argument long since forgotten in the excitement of Claudia's date.

"Guys, it was amazing! We had so much fun and I felt like we kinda connected. Does that sound crazy?"

"Oh my God Claudia! You've found him, didn't I tell you how amazing it feels to find your soul mate," Summer gushed.

Amber rolled her eyes. "Oh for God sake, she's been on one date with the guy."

"Ok, maybe it's too early to decide if he is Mr. Right, but she's definitely on the right track."

"I have never felt so good; no one has ever made me feel like this before. It doesn't seem normal; shouldn't it take ages to fall for someone?"

"When Cupid aims that arrow, he doesn't take any prisoner's, you've got it bad girl and I'm glad to tell you that there aint no cure for it."

"Oh God Summer, I hope you're right."

"Claudia, do not encourage little miss romantic over there, it's bad enough she's all loved up, don't you go over to the dark side as well," Amber protested.

"The view from my side is just fine, you should try it sometime."

"No danger of that honey. I've got my head screwed on, no guy is gonna turn me into jello."

"D'you know what Amber? If it feels this good then I'm happy to take a walk on the wild side for a change, let myself go. I don't wanna be the uptight ice maiden anymore."

Summer shrieked with delight. "I love, love!"

Jez walked into the kitchen, Summer jumped out of her chair to kiss him.

"Hey what did I do to deserve that kinda welcome home?" he laughed.

"Nothing, I just love you. That's all."

"She's a bit hyper at the moment, it seems Claudia had gone and gotten herself her very own love bubble," Amber explained in a bored voice. "Escape while you can, the guys are in the other room watching the game. I'll be joining them soon; all this love an stuff is making me wanna puke."

"You never know Amber; cupid could be after you too."

"No way, that arrow aint never gonna get me."

Jez laughed. "I'll leave you guys to dissect, sorry discuss Claudia's date." He gave Summer a lingering kiss and then headed off into the other room.

"Seriously Claudia, all that loved up stuff isn't for me, but you seemed to have found a decent guy. I hope it works out, you deserve to be happy," Amber smiled.

"AND…. He was right under your nose all the time." Summer was beyond excited.

"D'you know what I can't believe though?" Amber sighed.

"What?"

"That Claudia Michaels, of all people took a sickie."

Jez sat on the sofa, a beer in hand watching the game. He was a huge Nicks fan, but even they couldn't take his mind off other things. The other guys were shouting at the TV willing the Nicks on. Unlike the giggling coming from the kitchen, there wasn't much conversation going on amongst the guys, the game was taking all their attention.

Although everyone was here, technically they weren't all together. Also it wouldn't be fair to interrupt the game. Summer had seemed so much like her normal self tonight, laughing and joking. Maybe the answer was just to distract her. They could go on vacation, have a whole change of scenery maybe that was all she needed. Except, when they came home the problem would still be here, Marcus was never going to go away. His ghost needed to be laid to rest. The girls came into the room, Summer sat down next to him. As they continued to watch the game he noticed that far away look come back into her eyes. Nope, enough was enough. Until the truth came out Marcus would always have some kinda hold on them. He'd made his decision, he had to stick with it and he wasn't about to chicken out now. The sooner he got this over and done with the better.

"Listen guys, there's something we need to talk about." He sounded braver than he felt. He felt Summer stiffen.
"Oh c'mon man, there's only ten minutes of the game left," Jackson moaned.
"It can't wait. It's been too long as it is."
"Then it can wait ten more minutes."
"Nope, sorry guys. I gotta tell you now."
In the space of a few seconds tension filled the room.
"This is getting a bit of a habit isn't it, all these big announcements." Claudia tried to lighten the mood. CJ smiled at her relieved that she seemed to be coming to terms with his deception.
"Jez is coming out of the closet my dears," Jackson laughed, taking Claudia's lead.

"Poor Summer," Amber continued.

"Stop, all of you just stop." Jez stood up. The room fell silent. Summer didn't know what the hell was going on, what was happening to Jez? He hardly ever raised his voice. He looked straight at her and for the first time ever she couldn't read him. She was scared, whatever he was about to say, she didn't want to hear it. Jez moved over to the TV to turn it off, it gave him time to gather his thoughts. He turned to face them again; vaguely aware of the glares he was getting from Matt and the confused looks from the others. More than anything he was conscious of the look on Summer's face.

"Please God; tell me I'm doing the right thing," he whispered, he couldn't back out now.

"I know who killed Marcus."
Summer felt the bile rise in her throat.

CHAPTER TEN

Everyone sat in a stunned silence, unable to speak. Summer could barely breathe, never mind utter a single word. Jez watched the group closely; he damn well had their attention now. He didn't even know how to begin relaying the sordid tale to them so he just took a deep breath, prayed to God that he was doing the right thing and hoped the words would somehow find themselves.

"We'd been stuck indoors most of the day; the storm had been real bad. Too bad for us to ski. So we spent the day in the log cabin."
He paused for a second; of course they knew the storm had prevented them from going out – they were there.
"You must all remember that being stuck with Marcus all day was taking its toll on all of us. He was being a bigger ass than usual. He'd totally pissed Amber off over the ski bimbo, he'd stirred things up between Matt and I and he'd also tried to beat the crap out of Summer."

Jez fell silent again. Summer glanced around the room, looking for the guilt on someone's face, but as it was their expressions were unreadable. She looked back at Jez who was now leaning against the wall, arms folded across his chest and staring at the floor. He looked up and began to speak again.

"Summer was upstairs in our bedroom and I have no idea where everyone else was. It was getting late, but I thought I'd just have a quick jump in the hot tub. Being stuck in all day was sendin' me crazy, I needed to get some air in my lungs. Marcus had beaten me too it, beer in one hand and a cigarette in the other. I didn't even speak to him; I just turned and walked away," he paused trying to gather his thoughts.

"He called out my name. I should've ignored him, carried on walking, but I didn't. I turned back round. He laughed at me, told me that I thought I was too good to speak to the likes of him. I said I didn't waste my breath on guys who beat up on women. He laughed again. I was still mad at him for what he did to Summer and he was pushin' me too far, thinking it was all funny. I turned to leave again."

"He called out to me again, this time telling me there was something I needed to know, something important. This time I didn't stop walking I just shouted behind me that I didn't wanna hear anything he had to say. He laughed again, God I wanted to shut him up. He had me so riled up, common sense told me to ignore him, but curiosity got the better of me. I turned back round and stood at the edge of the hot tub, me looking down on him, him grinning up at me, those horrible eyes of his taunting me."

"I knew whatever he planned to tell me, I didn't wanna know. He took a swig of his beer. Then a drag of his cigarette, enjoying making me wait. He said I'd really pissed him off, made him look stupid when I rescued Summer like some kinda super hero. This time I laughed. He was sick, pathetic. He said it was time to let me in on a little secret, so he could get his revenge."

Jez stopped again; he could see he had a captive audience. No one was even moving let alone speaking. It was almost like he was talking to a bunch of statues. God, if only he was.

"Marcus jumped out of the tub and grabbed his wallet from his jeans. He pulled out a load of newspaper cuttings. Before he handed them to me he said he'd had this information for a while, but was just biding his time. Apparently by knocking the crap outta him, the time had arrived. He passed me the papers."

"The newspaper story didn't make much sense to me; I didn't know why he was showing it to me – until he explained. What he told me would blow my whole world apart, the love, security and happiness I'd finally found with Summer would all be gone. My stomach turned, I was totally stunned. He had that stupid grin on his face and said he was looking forward to letting Summer in on the secret and that he bet I wished I had a gun to blow his brains out."

"He laughed again, I couldn't listen to his God damn laughing anymore, and not when in the space of five minutes he'd ruined my life. I didn't need a gun. I grabbed the belt of one of the gowns hanging up. I couldn't let him destroy what I had with Summer, no way."

Jez was looking at the floor again; he couldn't look at them, especially not Summer. He couldn't bear to think what must be running through her mind right now. He carried on.

"I totally lost it, all I could hear was the laughing ringing in my ears. Before I had time to think about it, I'd wrapped the belt around his neck. I only wanted to stop his laughing and when it did, I let go of him, he fell back into the tub. He'd destroyed my life; I did the same to his. I honestly don't know if I meant to kill him or not, he just pushed me over the edge. I don't know how long I stood there, looking at him. I heard a door close back in the cabin, I realised I had to get outta there. Perhaps if I'd shut the door we wouldn't be in this situation now, you'd have all though it was just some random killing. By leaving the door open I implicated all of us."

"I jumped in the shower and stayed there for ages, petrified that you'd all find him and know it was me. Eventually I went to bed, knowing that I'd killed a man and left him to die. I am totally and truly ashamed of myself, I'm trained to save lives not take them away. But more than that…"

He looked up and for the first time met Summer's gaze, tears filling his eyes as he saw the distress on her face.

"…I'm sorry I caused you so much pain, I never meant this to happen. All I wanted to do was to love you and protect you."
The tears were now streaming down his face, he couldn't tear his eyes away from her, no matter how much it was ripping him up inside.

Summer shook her head slowly and her mouth formed the word, no, but no sound came out. She couldn't believe what she'd just heard, she was having another nightmare, she must be. Jez, her Jez had killed Marcus, it just couldn't be true.

Amber broke the stunned silence. "What was in the newspaper article? What did Marcus say to provoke you?"
Jez was taken aback by her directness, but he knew he couldn't tell half a story and this would be the hardest part to tell, even harder than telling the woman he loved that he was a murderer. Boy, would it all hit the fan now.
He turned to face Summer.

"Baby, please understand I did this for us, because I love you. God I love you, I'm nothing without you. Just please understand….please," he pleaded with her, although he doubted it would do any good by the time she heard everything.

"My whole life was a mistake; you all know I grew up in a kid's home. My mom didn't want me, so she dumped my on my dad, who didn't want me either. I reminded his wife of the affair he'd had with my mom, which resulted in me. Up until the night of Marcus' death, that was all I knew. I never really wanted to know anymore, I guess I thought I knew enough. I mean how many times d'you need to hear that your parent's don't give a shit? I was never interested in finding my family, they didn't care about me, I didn't care about them. I'd made my mind up, in this life the only person you could count one was yourself, everyone else just let you down. At least that's what I thought until I met Summer."

"When she was in the car crash, there was nothing more important to me than getting her out. My emotions had totally taken over, this girl was special. It didn't take me long to realise I'd met the girl I was gonna marry. By the time we went to Colorado I was totally loved up, big time. I'd have done anything for her and I never wanted to be without her."
As he spoke, trying to justify his actions he didn't look at anyone, just stared into the middle distance as he told his story.

"When Marcus showed me the newspaper clips, he could see they meant nothing to me. He asked me if it clicked yet. I just shrugged, I wasn't really taking him seriously. You couldn't trust the guy as far as you could throw him. Besides, I couldn't concentrate on anything except that stupid laugh. He said it was about a politician having an affair. There was nothing unusual about that, I'd figured that out for myself. I read the story again. A mistress had sold her story, he'd gotten her pregnant and left her on her own. Alarm bells started ringing."

"The politician's name seemed familiar, and then it hit me. Marcus must've seen the realisation on my face cos he said, meet your dad. George Stevens, Summer's dad. My mom was the mistress. I was Summer's half brother. That's when I lost the plot; he was a lying sick bastard. All he did was laugh in my face and said I was the sick bastard. He had taken everything good in my life and turned it upside down."

"Summer, I am so sorry for what I've put you through, I did it for us. I couldn't let him ruin what we have. I couldn't let it happen. If he hadn't told me, we'd be none the wiser; it wouldn't have made any difference. We're soul mates Summer, you and I, me and you. Nothing will ever change that, please forgive me babe, please," he pleaded, his cheeks wet with tears.

The silence was deafening, nobody could take it in, least of all Summer. She couldn't move, frozen to the spot. It had to be a nightmare, this couldn't be real. Why of all the people in the world did it have to be Jez? Why? She felt too numb to even cry.

"Summer, say something."
"I… I… don't know…." she finally mumbled her voice barely audible.
"Summer, I know we can work this out, we love each other." He knelt down and reached for her, she recoiled from his touch. Matt grabbed Jez and pulled him up by his collar, shoving him against the wall.
"Don't you dare go near her again you asshole, you're sick. I wanna kill you." Matt shouted as he began to punch Jez.
Jez brushed him off easily, but Matt came back for more, catching Jez, by a pure fluke square on the nose. Jackson and CJ pulled him back. Jez instinctively reached up to his nose to stem the blood.

"Matt, calm down, you'll kill him."
Matt shrugged Jackson and CJ off him. "That was the idea."
Jez looked Matt directly in the eye. Matt looked like he was

gonna hit out again. Sensing this, Jackson pulled him away.
"C'mon man, chill."

Jez looked over to Summer; she was slouched on the sofa, her face in her hands. Her whole body shaking as she cried. Amber and Claudia, either side of her comforting her.
"Look what you've done to her," Matt growled.
Jez stared at her. God, what had he done? He wanted to hold her in his arms, tell her it was gonna be ok. Why did he have to open his big mouth?
"Summer, I'm sorry."
He didn't know what else to say.

She found enough strength to lift her head up and meet his gaze. He had humiliated her, why had he done it like this? Confessed in front of everyone, they were all watching her fall apart. She was so angry. No secrets, they'd said. He'd lied all along She had a strange sensation that she couldn't explain. Jez was her half brother, so why, when she looked at him couldn't she stop herself from loving him. One part of her felt concerned that he was hurt and made her want to reach out and touch him, whereas another part wanted to finish what Matt had started. She could see his eyes searching hers, those dazzling blue eyes that she'd looked into a million and one times before, trying to work out what was going on in her head.

He was the same Jez he'd been half an hour ago when he was her fiancé, but now when he'd become her half brother how was she supposed to turn her feelings off like that? How was she supposed to stop loving the man she thought she would be spending the rest of her life with? Realisation hit her and nausea welled up in her stomach at the thought – she would've married her half brother. That thought over took every other emotion she was feeling, she knew she was about to throw up. She stood up and ran to the nearest bathroom, just about making it. She felt dazed and disorientated. She could hear raised voices coming from the other room; she passed out on the bathroom floor.

Summer woke up in her bed; she could just make someone out at the end of her bed. As her eyes adjusted to the darkness of the room she realised who it was.

"Amber, is that you?"

"Sure is honey, how are you feeling?" Amber reached out to stroke Summer's hand.

"My head hurts, I had the worst nightmare. It was about Jez and…."

"Honey, it wasn't a dream."

"WHAT?" Summer sat bolt upright.

"Summer, lie down. You need to rest."

"Where's Jez?"

"He's at Jackson and CJ's. Matt's outside waiting to see you."

"I don't want to see him; I don't want to see anyone."

"Listen, just try and get a good night's sleep. Matt and I are only next door."

After Amber had gone Summer wished she'd asked her to stay, she felt very lonely all of a sudden. Lying there all alone, the bed felt a million times bigger. She lay on her side and buried her face in Jez's pillow. She could smell his aftershave and felt comforted by it. That worried her. She wanted to feel his strong arms around her, which worried her too. Her head and her heart felt like it was gonna explode. She reached across to her cabinet and took three sleeping pills. All she wanted to do was sleep, she felt exhausted. She didn't want to think or dream. Just sleep.

CHAPTER ELEVEN

Jez sat at the breakfast bar in Jackson and CJ's apartment. He rubbed his hand over his tired face, the stubble itchy against his hand and his eyes stinging from lack of sleep. All he could think about was Summer. He'd missed her like crazy last night, lying there in an empty bed, now he knew how she felt when he was on a night shift. He lifted his cup of coffee to his mouth and winced at the bitterness. He wished he'd never opened his big mouth. There must have been another way to help her with her obsession without telling her what really happened, there must've been. He should've thought it through properly. Now he'd ruined everything. Would she take him back? Would she ever forgive him?

"How ya doin buddy?" Jackson sat down opposite him.
"Like your average murderer and liar."
"Jez, you had a moment of insanity, he pushed you to the limit. Let's face it, all of us had motive to kill him."
"Yeah, but it wasn't anyone else, it was me. I thought I was protecting Summer, all I've done is hurt her."
"It is kinda gross sleeping with your sister."
Jez slammed the coffee cup down. "She's NOT my sister, she's my half sister."
"Tomato, Tomata. Same diff."
"A sister, half sister, whatever is someone you grow up with. Not someone you meet one random night on Brooklyn Bridge, fall in love with, have all these plans together and then find out you share the same fuckin' dad. I was supposed to marry her for God sake. I couldn't give up on the only good thing that's ever happened to me. The love I have for her is the real deal, so strong on every level. I can't live without her Jackson, I just can't," Jez's voice began to waiver.

Jackson took a deep breath. "Are you positive Marcus was telling the truth?"

Jez ran a hand through his hair as he contemplated Jackson's question. "I know he was a sick bastard, but I don't think even he would do something like that as a joke. I saw those articles, I saw the proof. Why go to the trouble of setting something like that up for a joke?" Who could even imagine that kinda stunt up?"

Marcus. Jackson kept this thought to himself, now wasn't the time. He didn't want to give his friend a glimmer of hope. He had a gut feeling that something wasn't right about this, but Jez wasn't the person to discuss it with. The poor guy was an emotional wreck. Instead he leaned over and put a hand on Jez's shoulder.

"Just give it time; you never know what'll happen."

Amber and Matt were sitting on the balcony of the penthouse. They were feeling stifled in the suite, but didn't want to leave Summer. Fortunately it was coming to the end of spring and it was quite a balmy evening, reminding New Yorker's that the winter had passed and the intense heat of a Manhattan summer's day was not far off.

"I was right about Jez wasn't I? I knew he was up to something and I was right."

Maybe," Amber replied absent mindedly as she took a sip of white wine.

"Whaddya mean. Maybe?"

She set her glass down and turned to face him. "How would Marcus know all this when you didn't? It just doesn't add up. You've been through your parents' documents after they died. Your dad was a decent guy. If he knew he had another child out there he would've left them well provided for in the event of his death. It seems far too much of a coincidence that of all the guys out there, Summer should fall in love with her half brother. I don't buy it."

"This is too sick even for Marcus. You will come up with anything just so you don't have to agree with me, wont you? All I know is my little sister is locked up in her a room, a complete mess and it's all that jerks fault. I hate him for what he's done to her, when I think of all the times he told me he loved her he was talking through his ass."

"No he wasn't, he does love her, that's obvious. It must've been a shock to find out he was Summer's half brother. How would you feel if you really loved someone and they turned out to be your long lost sister?"
"Stop defending him!" he stood up as he shouted then sighed. "I would do the decent thing and break up with you of course."

"No. Not me. Someone you really loved." Her reply hung in the air and for some inexplicable reason he felt stung by it. Now was so not the time for this.
"We're not talking about us," he started quietly. "I just can't believe you would take Jez's side."

"Oh Matt, don't be so childish, I'm not taking sides. Besides, if I'm on anyone's *team*, then it's Summer's. All I'm saying is keep your mind open to other possibilities. I don't think this is a cut and dried as you think and don't forget I knew Marcus better than any of you. I've played his mind games before. He played to win and even now he could still win this game if we're not careful."
"Now who's being childish, taking about games?"
"Look, let's not argue, as much as I'd love too, we need to conserve our energy for Summer."
He nodded silently. She stood up from the chair and went back

into the suite, she couldn't be bothered speaking to him.

Despite the sleeping pills Summer tossed and turned all night, by the time it got to morning she was exhausted. She didn't think she had enough tears left to shed. This time yesterday her life was all planned out, she was going to marry Jez, they were going to start a family and everything was going to be perfect. Now, less than twenty four hours later her life was in tatters. She didn't know where to go from here. It wasn't just the whole Marcus thing, she'd found out a whole bunch of stuff. Her dad, who she idolised, had cheated on her mom. Was this a one off? Or was it a regular occurrence?

Obviously the biggest shock had been finding out about Jez. How could he have known all this time and not say a word? He knew more than anyone how much she'd tormented herself over Marcus' death, how she blamed herself and now this situation really was her fault. If she'd just let it go like the other's had said then everything would've been ok. Jez would not have had to tell her what happened that night.

What was she thinking? She buried her head in her pillow. Of course she needed to know the truth. A marriage cannot be built on lies. What would've happened if they'd had kids? God what a nightmare that would've been. All those conversations about what they would call their kids, how much they'd love them. Surely he must've known there could never be any children.

She turned on her side, hugging his pillow close to her. It felt so weird lying their without him. Questions whizzed through her mind.

What was he doing now?

Was he thinking about her?

Was he missing her?

She knew she still loved him, how could she just stop like that?

Life was so unfair. She loved Jez so much and now they could never be together. Her dad always said there was a fine line between love and hate, she'd never understood that. She did now, loved him like she always had done, hated him for what he'd put her through and it was the worst feeling in the world.

"That's so not the answer dude." Jackson grabbed the almost empty bottle of JD off the breakfast bar. Jez had only moved from that spot once all day, to get the liquor.

"Got any better ideas?" he slurred.

Depressed Jez was bad, drunken Jez was even worse.

"You gotta talk to her man. You can't spend every day going through a bottle of JD."

Jez laughed. "Like Matt's gonna let me anywhere near her."

"You aint tellin me that you'd let Matt stop you?"

Jez shook his head.

"Anyways, I'll speak to Amber; Matt doesn't even need to know."

"It's not Matt I'm scared of, it's Summer." Jez seemed to sober up in an instant as reality hit him. "I know in my heart we can't be together. I always knew, if it ever came out, that'd be it. But, I can't be without her, from the moment we first met she blew me away. She was so brave in that car, she looked at me with those big green eyes of hers and I felt like I could see her soul. Know what I mean?"

Jackson just shrugged, obviously the liquor was bringing out Jez's emotional side.

Jez carried on. "I knew that I was gonna marry her. I love her so freakin much." Tears stated to fall down Jez's cheeks. "I know when I see her, she'll confirm my worst fears and I'll never be able to hold her in my arms again and the thought of that hurts so much."

Jackson cursed CJ for being out, he was the good one in a crisis. Where as he was the one who made all the jokes, except there was nothing funny about this at all. He was managing to support Jez in his hour of need and he was proud of himself for doing so, this wasn't the kind of situation he was comfortable with, listening to someone pour their heart out. Whatever Jez had done it didn't matter to him, he was his friend and he wouldn't turn his back on him.

"Like I said, you gotta talk, the longer you put it off the worse it's gonna get. She'll need to talk to you too. Just remember – if you really are her half brother, then it's already over."
Jez looked up and slowly nodded his head. "I'll talk to her, but if it's over then I'm over."
"No way man – I won't let that happen."

Claudia was busy reading through some case notes when her secretary's voice came over the intercom.
"I have a Chad Jensen here for you Miss Michaels. He says he has an appointment, but there isn't one in the diary."
Claudia smiled at the annoyance in her receptionists' voice. No one got past Gloria without an appointment; it was a brave person who tried. CJ must've been putting up quite a fight to even get her to buzz through.
"It's ok, I know what it's regarding. It was my fault Gloria. I forgot to tell you I'd scheduled a meeting."
She hoped that would appease her.

CJ strode across her office.
"What was so important that you didn't have time to make an appointment? You will have put Gloria in a bad mood all day," she said sternly as CJ sat on the chair on the opposite side of her desk.
"She's vicious," he looked past her, through the huge window behind her. "Great view." he made himself comfortable.
"So, what are you here for?"

"I wanted to check that we're ok, y'know after our heart to heart the other night."

"You really hurt me CJ. You abused my trust in you."

"I know," he looked down. "Believe me, I feel real shitty about it."

"I'm trying to turn the experience around positively. Amber said if you fall off the bike, you gotta get right back on. So that's what I'm trying to do, you might've just given me the push I needed to sort my sad little life out."

"Amber told me you'd been on a date."

"Just a date, nothing serious. Just a bit of fun, we're going out for a drink tonight actually. To be honest, it's good to have a break from everything that's going on with Summer and Jez. I know it sounds awful, but I can't bear to see her hurting anymore."

CJ nodded. "Know what ya mean. It's a bit tense at our place, Jez is a mess."

"I can imagine. Poor guy."

The intercom buzzed again.

"Sorry to interrupt Miss Michaels, I have Leyton Carter on line two."

"Thanks Gloria, put him through." Claudia knew she was blushing. CJ raised an eyebrow.

"Hey Leyton, what can I do for you?"

She nodded in response to Leyton's question. "Yeah, eight is fine...no, no, yeah cool. Looking forward to it." She smiled into the receiver and then giggled at something. "I'll see you later then." She was still smiling as she put the phone down.

"Was that lover boy then?"

"He's a friend," she replied defensively.

"Hey, I'm happy for you, go out there and have some fun. There are a million guys out there who won't treat you as badly as I did. Don't put barriers in the way of relationships just 'coz I was a jerk and I let you down. I'm a shit, but I'm only human."

"I know you're a shit, but, we're gonna be fine. I value your friendship too much to lose you. I'll get over you. You're still my best friend and I'm grateful for that."

CJ stood up and moved towards her, he pulled her close and hugged her tight. "No, I'm the one that's grateful and I do love you... just not the way you wanted."

Over on the other side of the City Summer was still in her bedroom and wouldn't come out. Matt had been pleading with her to let him in. She couldn't face anyone yet. What would she say? Was there a way forward from here? She sure as hell couldn't see one. No one could possibly understand what she was going through. There wasn't a single person she knew who'd managed to fall in love with their half brother, who also happened to kill someone. If it wasn't so tragic it'd be funny. How could Jez do this to her?

They loved each other so much, she'd never even dared imagine what life would be without him and now she found herself in that situation it was worse than she could've possibly thought. He was everything to her. Even sitting here in the safe sanctuary of their room didn't feel right. He was everywhere, all his clothes, his CD's, photos his whole aura was here. This room was their private world. How many times had they made love in this bed? How many times had they been out on the balcony planning their future? How many times had he lain down on the bed watching her put her make up on? How many times had he told her he loved her and would never hurt her...?

She felt a bubble of anger well up in the pit of her stomach. He had broken so many promises, hurt her so much. For the first time in days she felt energized, the anger was like a rush or adrenalin. She looked round the room, all she saw was Jez, she couldn't take it much more. She jumped of the bed and went over to the dressing table; in one quick movement she knocked all the photos to the floor. The glass smashing, just like her dreams. She pulled all of his clothes out of the wardrobe, each item felt like she was ripping her own heart out. She grabbed the scissors and slashed the clothes, heart wrenching sobs leaving her body as she got more and more angry.

After she had ruined all of the clothes the venom still hadn't subsided, it only fuelled her even more. She grabbed a box that contained all the cards and letters he'd ever sent her. She ripped them up one by one, scattering the paper like it was confetti across the room. It was only after she'd destroyed the last card up and surveyed the damage that she slumped to the floor, the energy drained from her body. She clasped the one item of clothing that had escaped her wrath, one of his FD t-shirts and held it close to her. Clutching it like it was a life raft. She felt betrayed by the one person she loved more than life itself, she knew she was nothing without him, without Jez...she couldn't go on.

Amber's ringing cell flashed up Jackson's name.
"Jeez, just what I need," she flipped her phone open. "'Sup Jackson?"
"Baby, I need a favour."
"Don't baby me. I hope this favour isn't what I think it is, just friends remember."
"Sorry to disappoint, but it's not your gorgeous body I'm after."
"That can't be right, you're obsessed with sex."
"Ha. That, coming from you!"
"Oh c'mon. just get on with it, I haven't got all day."
"Now, that is a first, never heard you say that before."
"Like I said – you're obsessed."
"Ok, so I'll cut to the chase. I need you to get Summer to speak

to Jez. He's goin crazy and by the sounds of it, she's not doing much better. They need to talk, if Jez really is her half brother, things need to be sorted."

"What d'you mean, if?"

"I wouldn't put anything past Marcus; it could all be some sick stunt."

"Exactly, I've said as much to Matt."

Jackson laughed. "Bet that went down well."

"I thought he was gonna burst a blood vessel."

She could hear Jackson's laughter down the phone; it was nice to hear someone laughing. The atmosphere at home was getting near breaking point. She could always rely on Jackson to make her laugh even when the whole world felt like it had gone crazy.

"Listen, get Jez to come round later. I agree with you they need to talk. We need to have a chat too. We can't ignore these gut feelings, we both can't be insane can we?"

"You may be darling, but I'm totally sane."

"Whatever."

She flipped her phone shut and smiled, she loved to get the last word.

Jez couldn't explain the mixture of emotions as he stood at the door of the penthouse suite, he felt like an intruder. The thought of seeing Summer again was making him break out in a cold sweat, how would she react to him? Jackson squeezed his shoulder.

"C'mon man, let's do it." Jackson pushed open the front door; Jez followed him down the hall and into the living room. It was strange to think that up until a week ago this had been home.

He was met by a glaring Matt, he went to stand up, Amber put a hand on his shoulder to signal to him to sit down. As he did he made a growling noise, never taking his eyes off Jez. However uncomfortable he felt, he would not let Matt intimidate him. All he cared about was Summer, not Matt. Who was he anyway? Just some jumped up City guy who happened to be his half brother.

Amber broke the awkward silence. "She hasn't come out of her room since all this happened."
"D'you think she'll talk to me?" Jez asked.
"Well she hasn't even wanted to talk to me, so I doubt she'll speak to you. Besides which, she's locked herself in," Matt said, still glaring.
"That's my day job, breaking down doors." He strode across the apartment towards the bedroom.
Matt stood up. "I'm not letting you see her."
Jez pushed him back down on the sofa as if he was as light as a feather and didn't give him a second glance as he carried on walking. When he reached the bedroom door he tried the handle, the door wouldn't open.
"Summer, honey, it's me…Jez. I need to speak to you."
There was no answer. "Honey, if you're near the door, move away." He dropped his right shoulder and with one easy push the door was open.

He stood rooted to the spot as he took in the scene that met him. He didn't see the carpet, it was blanketed in strew pieces of paper, clothes, photos and in the middle of the mess was Summer, just sitting there holding one of his work T-shirts. he heard the others gasp behind him. He spun round to face Matt.
"Why the hell didn't you break the door down sooner? Look at the state of her. Look!" He grabbed Matt by the collar and pushed him to one side as he turned his attention back to Summer.

He went over to her; he gently picked her up and sat her on the bed. He couldn't believe how much her appearance had changed in the space of a week. He thought he was close to breaking point; it looked like she was already there. She looked so pale and gaunt, not like the girl he knew so well.

"Summer, we need to talk," he whispered softly. She nodded her head slowly.

Amber pulled Matt away from the door and closed it over. Matt protested but Jackson pointed out that the last thing they needed was an audience.

Summer spoke first. "What happened Jez?"

"Summer, I wish to God I'd never said anything. I want everything back to normal. I miss you, I want to be back here where I belong...with you."

"It can never be the same again, you've changed everything."

"We can just go back to before all this happened, please."

"Jez, you killed a man...I don't know what's real anymore, my parents who I thought were devoted to each other, weren't. The last person I suspected of killing Marcus did. I have a half brother and guess who it is? You! And you think we can carry on as normal?"

"I never meant to hurt you," he whispered.

"You haven't just hurt me, you lied to me, humiliated me, ruined my life and smashed my heart to pieces," her voice was wavering as she spoke but she was determined to get the words out.

He could hear the anger in her voice rising as she spoke and the tears that he put in those emerald eyes mirrored his own. Just as she snapped earlier on, the anger was her driving force again. "You were supposed to love me!" With strength that took Jez by surprise she pushed him off the bed, crying as she lashed out at him, punching and kicking out. He let her, she needed to get the anger out. Eventually she wore herself out and flopped backwards onto the bed, her head in her hands as she continued to cry. He knelt down beside her.

"I would do anything to protect you, that's why I killed Marcus. What we've got is too special. I couldn't let him ruin it and I thought I was doing the right thing not telling you what happened that night. I thought we'd just carry on."
She still had her head buried in her hands as he spoke. He carried on.
"When we met, that was it, I'd fallen for you. I know you know that but I never get sick of telling you. I went through all the normal emotions when you first meet someone, but this time was different. Like something I'd never experienced before. My feelings were so intense; I couldn't get enough of you. When I wasn't with you, part of me was missing. I love you with all my heart and I have done from the moment you first said my name. The night of the car accident, I couldn't sleep; you filled my thoughts and I wanted you in my life. Then when I found out that you were my half sister, I knew I couldn't let you walk away, 'coz that's what would've happened if you found out. Then after Marcus was gone, I tried to forget about it, I went into denial. You were Summer, my fiancée; no way could I imagine that you were my sister, no way. You were my girl, always have been, always will be."

She lifted her face up to meet his, he was so handsome, with his strong jaw line and rugged good looks. Although she wasn't used to seeing him with stubble. And those eyes, so blue, how she hated to see so much pain in them.

He was gazing at her, his Summer, her radiant smile just a distant memory, the sparkle in her eyes replaced by the anguish he'd put there. He hated himself for what he'd done to her. He professed to love her, how could he cause so much pain to someone he loved with all his heart and more?

"I'm so confused. I'm sitting here, looking at you, into those eyes I know so well. I know the truth, I know what you've done, who you are and yet it would feel like the most natural thing to fall into your arms, but I know I can't."

"You can, we can forget it all happened, start again. Go some place new and begin again," he pleaded.

"You might be able to live like that, but I can't. We wouldn't be able to have kids; we couldn't make all those dreams come true that we used to talk about. You were living in a dream world Jez. We've got no future together. I-can't look at you in the same way, but I can't switch my feelings off like that. I love you, I always will. I felt it too that night on the bridge, just as much as you did. But now it's all wrong. I can't be with you."

"We're soul mates, we're perfect together, you're perfect. I can't live without you Summer."

Tears ran down her face, he reached out to wipe them away. Their eyes locked, he pulled her close and held her tight.

"If it had been any other reason why you killed Marcus, we probably would've got through it, I could've forgiven you. I know it sounds crazy, but I would've stood by you. But I can't forgive you for this."

"Please don't say that babe, please don't leave me," he sobbed into her hair.

It took all her strength to push him away again, although this time it was her emotional strength she needed.

"You can't hold me anymore, we can't see each other. It hurts too much. I am trying so hard to be strong, but I can't do it," she was worn out from crying. "Please just go, before I give into you."

"I can't leave you like this. There must be some way we can sort this out."

"Jez, you're my half brother, that says it all," she sounded stronger than she felt. It was unnerving her seeing Jez so distressed. He was normally the strong one, he held her together. It was killing her telling him to go. He stood up and leaned over to kiss her softly on the cheek, she turned her face slightly towards his and they stayed like that for a few seconds.

"I love you Summer, don't ever forget that. I'm not gonna let you go. I'll find some way for us to be together, sweet dreams babe, you'll be in mine – tonight and every night."

"Maybe that's the only way we can be together, in our dreams," she whispered softly.

She watched him leave. "I love you," she mouthed as he shut the door. She buried her head in her pillow and cried herself to sleep.

CHAPTER TWELVE

A few days later Amber and Jackson were in her office attempting to shed some light on Marcus' story. Jackson was logged onto the internet doing a search on Jez's name and George Stevens.

"Tell you what darling, I prefer the other stuff we used to get up too in this office."

"You may feel comfortable cheating on CJ but I certainly don't."

"CJ knows I'm not totally faithful to him. He asks me no questions, I tell him no lies. It's his bed I'm in every night," Jackson shrugged.

"Touching, wish I could say the same thing about Matt." Amber was sitting at her desk also on the net, she was trying to trace the foster home where Jez was left.

"Have you spoken to him yet about you two?"

"Nope, we're far too busy trying to keep Summer together, I kinda think that once this is all over, we'll just fizzle out."

"Onto the next pointless relationship."

"You don't know what you're talking about."

"Don't I? The way I see it is, despite what you think, you and Matt could be really good for each other if you just gave yourself a chance."

Amber took a sip of her skinny latte. "Enough already, we've got work to do," she dismissed the conversation. "D'you think we're heading down a dead end here?"

"I don't know, but it's worth a try. We both know Marcus was more than capable of something like this. It's worth a shot."

"The little shit, this has his name written all over it, you could never trust a single word that fell out of his mouth."

"Don't forget, we've got all those boxes to go through in the study. I know Matt hasn't gone through those."

"He hasn't?" She asked surprised.

"Not as cold hearted as you think hey? He makes excuses, says he's too busy but I know he thinks he can't handle it. See you're both vulnerable. Just open up to each other."

"Quit with the psych lesson Jackson."

"For now I will. We've got a mystery to solve."

Summer had yet another restless night, in fact she couldn't remember the last time she'd slept properly. She was exhausted, all she wanted was a good nights sleep and to feel like she was getting back to normal. Seeing Jez again had really freaked her out and made her more confused than ever. She couldn't deny that she still loved him, despite how wrong that was, but she also knew it was over. She'd always been a hopeless romantic, believed that love would conquer all. In this case love didn't stand a chance, it wasn't as simple as just following her heart.

She wished she could just switch her emotions off, but it wasn't that easy. She missed him like crazy. The first few seconds of the day were the best, for a few moments everything was ok. The she'd turn to cuddle into Jez and he wasn't there, then the pain would start all over again and it totally consumed her. Her heart felt heavy, she felt sick, her head hurt and her body ached for him. It had seemed so right to fall into his arms the other night, how easy it would've been. Her heart was all for it, her head kept telling her no. No wonder she was so confused. She had to keep her distance from him, it was the only way. Last night he'd said she was perfect. If she wasn't perfect he wouldn't want her anymore. She pulled herself out of bed and went into the en-suite. She studied her reflection, she hardly recognised herself. Her eyes were all puffy and swollen, her face pale and hollow. She pulled her long dark hair back from her face. If the sight of her like this hadn't put her off Jez then maybe this would, she reached into the cabinet and took out the scissors. She systematically began cutting huge chunks of hair off.

Claudia was on her way round to Leyton's apartment after a fairly stressful day. Not only was she dealing with her normal workload, but Amber and Jackson kept calling over this idea that Jez wasn't really Summer's half brother and to ask her advice on various scenarios they'd concocted. Those two were insane, it would probably do more harm than good. She was under strict instructions not to tell Matt or Jez about it. As if they hadn't had enough of secrets to last a lifetime, but apparently not.

By the time she'd reached Leyton's apartment she was ready to forget her day and just enjoy being with him. They'd been seeing a lot of each other. She was trying not to take it too seriously, she didn't want to get hurt again. They were having fun but she didn't want to get her hopes up. She was staying in control this time and the best thing was, she wasn't feeling the need to drink so much. She pressed the buzzer.

"Hey you, come on up."

The door to the apartment was slightly ajar, she pushed it open and gasped. The room was lit by fairy lights and candles were dotted around the place. As she walked further in she noticed the dining table set up for a romantic meal for two. Leyton was leaning against the doorframe, still in his suit, but his tie loosened. She thought there was something sexy about a guy in a suit and there was definitely something sexy about Leyton. She must've been out of her mind to turn him down all those times. What had she been thinking?

"Hey you," he smiled seductively at her, his chocolate coloured eyes twinkling with mischief. "Thought we could eat in tonight, ok with you?"

She could only nod. She felt like all her senses were heightened, her body was tingling all over and she knew the moment he touched her she'd just melt. She thought she was in control? No way! He sauntered over to her, pulling her close to him as he reached her. He kissed her with a passion she'd never known. Thank God he had hold of her, her legs didn't feel strong enough to hold her up. She responded to his kisses with the same amount of urgency. He pulled away.

"Come into the bedroom, I want to show you something."
She giggled. "Is that the best chat up line you can do?"
He held her hand and led her into the bedroom, there was a bucket containing champagne and a huge bowl of strawberries.
"I thought we could start with dessert first."
"God Leyton, you really know how to sweep a girl off her feet."
"I pursued you for long enough, just making up for lost time."
"Believe me, you're making up for it," she whispered.
"This is just the beginning," he replied as he pulled her back into his arms and fell back onto the bed. Claudia thought she'd died and gone to heaven.

Amber and Jackson were back in his apartment going over with CJ what they'd found so far.
"Well, we have a copy of Jez's birth certificate," Amber started clearly quite pleased with herself. "It lists a Mary Louise Stanford as his mom, father unknown. Obviously this doesn't prove or disprove Marcus' story."
"It also looks like we found the exact same article that he showed Jez. The lady in question who sites George Stevens as the father of her unborn child is called Louise. Is this Mary-Louise or a totally different lady and it's just a coincidence?" Jackson finished, he'd been pacing the room as he spoke, looking or trying to look like a TV detective.
CJ burst out laughing. "Sorry guys, I know you're taking it seriously but when Jackson gets all theatrical like that I forget what I'm supposed to concentrating on."
Amber nodded her head in agreement. "All he needs is the dirty

mac and he's Coloumbo."

Jackson pulled a face.

"I have to say guys, I think it looks like Marcus was telling the truth. Unless George was having a string of affairs, it's probable that this Mary-Louise and Louise are one in the same person," CJ sighed.

"I disagree. I have a gut feeling that I can't ignore. We just need to keep looking. We'll find the answer wont we darling?"

Amber nodded. "I'm with Jackson. I'm not ready to give up yet."

"I hope for Summer and Jez's sake you find what you're looking for."

"I hope so too."

"Although there is one way we could find out for sure...DNA."

"Yeah, great idea but I don't think we can do that," Jackson said.

"You can't, I can. I have access to equipment at work, I'm sure I could do it."

Amber got excited. "You could do that?"

"I am a scientist. All I need is something off them both..."

"We need to be discreet, we don't want either of them knowing. Where is Jez anyway?"

"He's gone back to work," CJ replied.

"Work? You're joking?"

Jackson shrugged. "He said it'll help him get his head together.

"How's Summer doing?" CJ asked.

Getting worse, she's trashed her room, we can't leave her alone. She looks awful. The only person she's spoken to is Jez, I haven't got a clue what she's thinking."

"Maybe she needs professional help."

"She won't need it once we find out the truth. We'll go through George's study tomorrow," Jackson said.

Amber's cell rang. "It's Matt," she checked the name flashing on her phone.

"Yeah?" she was quiet for a few moments as she listened. "I'm on my way."

She was halfway to the door. "Sorry guys, gotta go. Summer's lost the plot. Catch ya later."

"Wait!" CJ shouted after her. "We're coming with you."

CHAPTER THIRTEEN

When Amber and the guys arrived back at the Penthouse they found Matt sitting on the sofa with Summer. Amber did a double take when she saw her.

"Jesus," she heard Jackson whisper behind her. She ran up to Summer and sat down next to her. She reached up and touched her friends' hair which appeared to have been hacked to pieces. Summer just sat there, oblivious to what was going on around her.

"Oh my God Summer, what happened?"

"I found her in her bathroom cutting her hair," Matt began, "I can't get any sense out of her. I don't know what to do."

"Honey, why did you do this?" Amber asked gently.

"Jez says I'm perfect, not perfect now," she mumbled still staring into space.

Amber put an arm around her. "Oh honey."

"We're all here for you darling. We want to help," Jackson said.

CJ sat down on the coffee table opposite her so he could face her. He took her hands in his. "We're gonna get you through this, but I think we need to get you some professional help. I have a friend who you could talk to in confidence."

"She doesn't need a shrink. I can look after her," Matt interjected.

"Matt, I know you promised your mom and dad you'd look after her, but everyone needs help sometimes. You won't have failed," Amber said.

"It's got nothing to do with that. I can cope."

"She's only one step away from self harm. We've got to do something," CJ advised.

"Yeah I agree with CJ, it sounds like a good idea."

Matt sighed. "Look, we'll see how she is after the weekend. If she gets any worse...then I'll think about a shrink."

Amber reached up to touch Summer's hair. "Let's get your hair sorted out. Why don't we get you down to the salon?"
Summer seemed to snap out of her day dream; she jumped up off the sofa. "No! I'm not going anywhere. You're all talking 'bout me like I'm not here or like I'm some kinda object. I have feelings, feelings that are broken and shattered. No one can put me back together, no one. I can't go out, I won't go out," she ranted.
"Its ok honey, we'll stay here." Amber jumped up and put her arms around a sobbing Summer who buried her head in her shoulder. Amber gently stroked her back and chopped up hair. "Ssh, it's ok. Let it all out."
Once the floodgates opened Summer couldn't stop crying.
"It will never be ok," she cried. "Stay with me tonight, don't let me be on my own."
The total desperation in her voice made Amber's heart ache. "Course I will sweetie," Amber replied only just managing to control her own voice.

The following morning Claudia woke to the feeling of finger tips running up and down her back.
"Mmm," she smiled happily. She turned on her back and felt the finger tips on her stomach; they lingered on a sensitive part just below her belly button. She opened her eyes slowly and saw Leyton gazing down at her.

"Good morning sleepy head, did you sleep well?"
"Mmm, this bed is so comfy," she nodded her head.
"D'you have any plans for today?"
"Nope, none at all." She had taken a few days off work.
"Well, how 'bout I make us breakfast in bed, then we could

spend the day chillin out in bed or we could go out somewhere if you want."

"Staying in bed sounds pretty good to me," she smiled as she slid further down the satin sheets.

"Don't move I'll be back in five minutes with your breakfast."

"A girl could get used to this," she replied as she sat up in bed, the sheet just covering her. She watched him get out of bed. Noticing what a cute butt he had. As he stood up his sandy coloured hair fell perfectly into place. Leyton looked just as good out of a suit as he did in it she decided as she watched him walk naked across the room. She remembered back to last night and the feel of his body against hers. He grabbed a towel and tied it loosely around his waist.

He grinned. "Five minutes."

"Make it four," she smiled back.

She leaned back against the headboard; she had honestly never felt this happy before. Her cell phone rang. She felt down the side of her bed for her bag and pulled out her cell.

"Amber, this is so not a good time," she grinned into the phone.

"I'm sorry hon, but I really need your help with Summer," she quickly explained the situation.

"I'll be right over," she was already out of bed pulling on her clothes.

Leyton was just putting the finishing touches to the breakfast tray as he laid a rose down next to the toast. He'd liked Claudia for ages and couldn't believe it when she called to arrange a date. He'd almost given up hope. He knew she'd been hurt before and although she seemed at ease with him, he could tell she was holding back and that she couldn't put her trust in him yet. He would have to prove himself to her and he was prepared to do whatever it took. He would show her how good it felt to be in a loving relationship. Just as he picked up the tray Claudia ran out of the bedroom, fully clothed. His heart sank, he'd scared her off. But as she came closer, he could see she was smiling, albeit apologetically.

"Leyton, I'm sorry, I have to run. I just gotta call and one of my friends really needs my help. She's having a really bad time at the moment and well, I need to be there for her. I'll be back as soon as I can, keep the bed warm for me," she leaned over and kissed him.

"Hey it's ok; I know your friends are important to you."

"You're important to me too."

As the words came out she took a step back. She hadn't meant to say that, she'd let her guard down for a second. She could see in Leyton's eyes, he'd seen it to. He moved closer minimising the space between them.

"Go and see your friend. I'll still be here when you get back and someone to lean on if you need it," he bent down and lightly brushed her lips with her own.

As he watched her leave the apartment he couldn't help but smile, he'd break down those walls she'd built around herself.

Claudia got a shock when she arrived at Summer's apartment and saw her sitting at the breakfast bar, pale, drawn and her hair…God only knew what had gone on there. She stood opened mouthed in the door way. Amber had warned her how bad their friend was looking, but it was still a shock to see her in the flesh. Amber stood behind her with a pair of scissors trying to make the best of Summer's hair. She could hear CJ and Matt arguing in the other room.

"Summer," Claudia finally managed to find her voice.
There was no response.
"Claudia's gonna do your hair for you honey, you'll feel better

once your hair is sorted," Amber said.

"Pity it's not so easy to sort my head out," Summer replied sarcastically.

Claudia and Amber exchanged a look.

"Let's see if I can remember my training from that Saturday job at the salon," Claudia joked, trying to lighten the mood. She took the scissors from Amber and got to work.

"What was all this about?" Claudia asked gently.

"What d'you think? My whole life has fallen apart."

"You'll get through this, you're a strong person."

"You don't understand, I was supposed to be with him forever. My life has no future, no purpose."

"Summer, don't say that," Amber pleaded.

They heard the front door slam, footsteps down the hall and more raised voices. Despite Matt's protests Jackson had called Jez, he felt he needed to know what was going on with Summer and the others agreed.

"Where is she?" Jez demanded.

Matt ignored him. In a reversal of roles it was CJ who was getting irate and shouting at Matt. "She needs professional help, I've already told you that."

"You don't know shit," Matt shouted back.

"Where is she?" Jez asked again.

Jackson was sitting in the corner of the room, wishing he was a million miles away. "Kitchen," he mumbled.

"If we don't do something soon, she'll get worse."

"D'you think I don't care CJ? She's my sister. I know what's best for her and she'll be a whole lot better without you around," he turned to Jez, venting his anger out on him. "I think you should leave."

"No way man, I ain't going nowhere," Jez plonked himself down on the sofa, putting his feet up on the coffee table and folded his arms across his chest.

"I think CJ's right," Claudia came in from the kitchen. "Her personality has totally changed, her behaviour is completely erratic. I don't think any of us can predict what she'll do next. I know you want to help her Matt, we all do, but you can't take her battle on for her on your own. It's too much."

"I agree," Amber added as she appeared behind Claudia.

"Me too," Jackson moved from the corner of the room.

"So… you're all ganging up on me? Well, while we're all here, can I just point out that Jez is actually a cold blooded killer and since we found out that he killed Marcus not one of you has reported him to the police. He has committed a crime."

"In case you'd forgotten, we're all an accomplice to that crime, dumb ass," Jackson reminded him.

"Irrelevant. The guy still messed up my sister's life and you're all sitting here with him like nothing's happened. Jez, maybe if I called the cops it might encourage you to GET THE HELL OUTTA HERE."

"No one gets the cops involved. If anyone does, I'll tell them I did it."

Jez spun round at the sound of Summer's voice, she'd spoken quietly but with conviction. Yet again he was shocked by her appearance, she looked tiny standing in the door frame. She'd lost even more weight since the last time he saw her and what the hell had happened to her hair? It shook him to the core to know this was all down to him, he'd caused all her pain and the worse thing was she was still sticking up for him against Matt, he didn't deserve that. She owed him nothing, nothing at all.

"Summer, I…" he began.

"Jez, I can't do this anymore. I want it over."
He wanted to go over to her and hold her, he missed her like crazy. She looked so vulnerable. He stood up and slowly walked towards her. She didn't take her eyes off him. He put his hands on her shoulders, the bones poked thorough. God he hated himself for this.

"Baby, I need you," he whispered.
"I don't need this."
"We can get through this, just have faith in us...I have. We are so good together."
"Jez, please don't. I'm not strong enough to cope with this. I have to tell myself over and over again that we're over, 'coz if I don't...I know I'll give into you and that can't happen. I can't be with you, no matter how much I still, I still love you. It really is over, it hurts like hell, but there is no other choice. Maybe once you can accept that, then I can get my head together."
"I can never accept we're over. I love you Summer, why can't that be enough?" He ran his hand through her hair, resting his hand on her cheek, gently stroking it with his thumb.
"Don't...don't make this harder for me, please."
He dropped his arms to his sides, hung his head and walked away. Summer stared after him, desperately wanting to run after him, but knowing she couldn't.

Later that afternoon Matt was out on the balcony of the Penthouse, watching the moving City below but not really paying any attention. Maybe the others were right, perhaps Summer did need professional help. He couldn't reach out to her, that's for sure. He'd always looked out for his little sister, now he just felt like a failure. Amber was driving him crazy with her half baked ideas of a conspiracy theory, he was sure she was up to something. He had to admit though that since Claudia had fixed Summer's hair into a neat bob she looked much better and she'd seemed to be in control when she spoke to Jez. In fact it looked like Jez was going to pieces then, not Summer. He had walked out of the apartment like a broken man, not that Matt cared. Perhaps she had turned a corner. He'd keep an eye on her over the next few days and then decide what to do. That seemed like the best idea. Since his parent's death, he didn't just feel like Summer's brother, he almost felt like he had a parental role as well. As for Amber, he'd address their relationship when this mess was all over…if it ever was.

Jez folded the paper and put it in the envelope, together with a CD. He wrote Summer's name neatly on the front. Her parting words, that she'd be ok if he wasn't around, were stuck in his mind. It tore him to pieces to see what he'd done to her, he'd never forgive himself, but he couldn't accept that it was over. He couldn't picture himself in ten years time without her by his side. He knew technically they were related, but he could never get his head round that. Matt and Summer as brother and sister, yeah, but whenever he thought about himself and Summer all he knew was that he'd found his soul mate. He didn't know what he would do without her, he didn't see any point in carrying on. His life would be over anyway. So what were his choices? Stay here and see the woman he loved fall apart or move away and start again without her? If he went away he knew exactly what his life would be like.

He would never love again, he couldn't, there was only room in his heart for Summer. He'd go back to how it was before they met, meaningless relationships, one night stand after another. No emotional attachments, then every night when he went to bed, he'd think about her; hoping that she'd moved on, that she was happy and had found someone who loved her as much as he did – if that was possible. If he went away would she forget him? Would she miss him? If it meant that she could get her life back together then he would have to sacrifice never seeing her again which would break his heart, but she had always meant more to him than he'd ever meant to himself. He got up off his bed and went to find Jackson, he was in the other room watching T.V.

"Hey man, can I ask you a favour?"

"Sure, go ahead."

"I'm thinkin' 'bout taking off. I can't bear to watch Summer in so much pain and knowing it's down to me."

"Listen, man. Y'all gotta stay."

"I wish more than anything that I could stay and be with Summer, but that's never gonna happen."

"If you go, Marcus has won."

"If I stay he wins, if I go he wins too. There aint nothing I can do," Jez sighed.

"Listen, just don't go yet. Leave it a few weeks. You never know what might happen."

"What are you talking 'bout?"

How could he tell him that right now CJ was doing a DNA test on Summer's hair and some of his hair that they got from his pillow? "I can't tell you, just please trust me. I am your friend, I promised you I was gonna be there for you and I will. I just need you to trust me on this one. Hopefully I can tell you soon and things might look better."

Jez gave a half smile. "I appreciate your help, you've been a great friend, but this is it. I've got to the end of the road and I need to make a decision."

He handed Jackson the envelope. "If I go, you'll just wake up one morning and I'll be gone. Can't handle goodbyes. I wont leave a forwarding address. Please give this to Summer for me. I hope it'll help her move on. I just want her to be happy."

"What if she wants you to stay? What if she wants you back?"

"Jackson, we both know that will never happen, she's made it perfectly clear. Its enough, no, its not enough, but it eases the pain slightly to know that she still loves me, even if she can't act on that love."

"Just hang around a bit longer."

"A few days and then I'm gone."

CHAPTER FOURTEEN

For the first time ever, Matt reluctantly left for work on Monday morning. Amber was working from home that day so he knew Summer wouldn't be on her own, it didn't stop him from worrying though. As soon as Matt left, Amber rang Jackson; they were going to resume their investigation.

Jez pulled on one of his FDNY T-shirts and grabbed his jeans. Jackson thought he was crazy going back but he didn't want to let the guys down. Working as a team was doubly important when you were a fire fighter. Even if just one member of the team were missing it could have a huge impact when responding to an emergency. Besides which he was going stir crazy just sitting here in the apartment, getting on with his job might give his life some kind of purpose.

He felt like an emotional wreck, he knew he would never stop thinking about Summer. He felt so desolate and empty without her, but it was his own stupid fault. He knew that, but he couldn't let go. He was so worried about her, seeing her last night looking so fragile broke his heart. Was it the right thing to just up and leave? He didn't know right from wrong anymore. In the middle of the long lonely nights since they'd been apart, he imagined that he'd never told her the truth. Instead he helped her come to terms with Marcus' death, she bounced back to her normal self and she'd walked down the aisle to him, making him complete, not the broken man he was now. During the day he tormented himself as to whether this could actually happen. He really didn't know how to get through this. If he decided to go he could try and get on with his life, hoping that she was doing the same. But he would always be haunted by what he'd done to her. Had he hurt her so much that she would never be able to trust anyone again and let them into her life? He hoped not. He also knew that if she did find another guy, he couldn't sit around and watch it happen.

To see her in some other guy's arms would finish him off. Eventually that day would come, he was sure of it. He couldn't handle it, but if Summer was happy, he'd find a way to cope. Stay or go? He didn't know what to do for the best. He didn't think he was ready to make that decision yet, maybe it would take longer than the few days he promised Jackson he'd stick around for. He pulled on his boots and lastly put on the watch Summer bought him for their six month anniversary, it gave him little comfort.

Jackson and Amber were busy going through all the unopened boxes in George Stevens' study.
They had been going through them for over two hours and still they hadn't found anything that they were looking for. Still it might help if they knew exactly what they were hoping to find.

"D'ya think we're wasting our time? Maybe we've made something out of nothing," Amber sighed.
"Never fear my dear, we'll find the final piece of the puzzle."
"I didn't know we'd found the first bits, wish I could be as positive as you."
"Look, we can't give up now. Hopefully we'll find the evidence to prove that bastard Marcus wrong, then he really can rot in hell and more importantly Summer and Jez will be back where they belong, together."
"My God, you almost sound like you care."
"I'm not the callous bastard you think I am, well not all the time anyway. Besides, we'll have an answer one way or another today, CJ is excepting the results of the DNA test, he's been working on it all weekend."

"God, I didn't think it'd be that quick."

"He's moved heaven and earth to get the results."

Amber sighed. "It still doesn't change the fact that he did kill Marcus. What if we find out he was lying after all but Summer doesn't take him back?"

"That's a chance worth taking. If I know Summer I think she'll go running as fast as her legs can carry her into Jez's arms. True love and all that."

"Yeah, you're right; she did tell him the other night that she still loved him. She'd forgive him for Marcus; the only thing keeping them apart is this damn brother/sister palaver."

"C'mon then, less talkin' more lookin'."

"After all this is over we should go into partnership, fight crime or something," Amber laughed.

"We could be Cagney and Lacey – except I don't fancy being a woman," Jackson replied as he lifted another box up. "This looks promising, it's already open."

He tipped the contents out onto the floor. There were lots of personal letters inside and newspaper articles. The letters were from different women over a period of ten years. All of them had a similar theme, expressing undying love to George Stevens and promising to wait for him to leave his wife. Evidently they were still waiting as he never left his wife, probably had no intention on leaving his glamorous and powerful wife, Eleanor Stevens.

They searched for a letter from Jez's mom, Mary-Louise, but so far they hadn't found one. They did find one from the mysterious Louise, who they read about in the article the other day. It threatened to expose George as an adulterer. The article they had previously read about her showed a very pregnant Louise telling her story of how she'd fallen in love with senator George Stevens, how he'd swept her off her feet, promised her the earth, gotten her pregnant and then dumped her.

"I never knew George was like that, he always seemed kinda cool," Amber said.

"That's guys for you. As much as I hate to admit it, it looks like Marcus was right. This article is dated four weeks before Jez was born, that woman looks like she could pop at any moment. All the evidence points to Jez being Summer's half brother. The Mary- Louise on the birth certificate must be the Louise in these letters. Without Louise's surname we can't prove Marcus was wrong. She's only referred to as Louise in these articles," Jackson sighed. "Looks like we were wrong."

"Not quite," Amber jumped up excitedly, waving a piece of paper in her hand. "Listen to this."

Dear George,

Not that it's really any of your business, but I thought you might like to know you are the 'proud' father of a baby girl. If you have any interest at all in your daughter, we will be returning home from hospital tomorrow. If I do not hear from you by the end of the week, you will have no contact with your child.

Yours Sincerely,

Louise Madison

Jackson smiled. "Jez's mom was called Mary-Louise Stanford so she obviously isn't the same woman as this Louise Madison."

"This is dated two weeks before Jez was born."

"So Jez obviously isn't the child referred to in these articles."

"Yeah, and the fact Louise gave birth to a girl you dope."

"So, let's get this straight, unless George managed to get two women pregnant at the same time, which we haven't seen any evidence of here, then there's no way Jez is George's illegitimate son. There is no mention of Mary-Louise Stanford in any of this stuff," Jackson said.

"So, I think we can be ninety percent certain that our hunch was right."

"We just need CJ to get back to us with…" Jackson was interrupted by his cell ringing. "Shit, it's CJ. God this is fate, I can't answer it." He flung the phone at Amber.

"Hey CJ, it's Amber…" she paused to let CJ speak, she nodded her head a few times. "Ok, we'll meet you there in ten."

"So…?"

"Make that 100% certain Jackson baby, we were right. Summer and Jez aren't related."

"Holy cow, jeez Marcus was one sick guy."

"Believe me honey, Jez did us all a favour I could've quite happily killed myself."

"Well my dear, that's case closed," Jackson concluded. "Let's go and tell Summer."

"Wait, CJ wants to meet at the firehouse, give Jez the news, I think she needs it to come from him."

"Yeah, you're right, quick grab what we found, can't hurt to back up the DNA result…although I'm sure they wont question that."

Summer was beyond tired, she needed sleep. She'd run a hot bath and had lit candles in the bedroom to try and relax her, it hadn't worked. It just reminded her of the romantic nights she used to have with Jez. She was sitting on the sofa, waiting for the coffee machine to do it's job. She was all alone, she heard Amber go out earlier.

She closed her eyes for a second, they felt so heavy, and her whole body ached with tiredness. Her eyes stung as she shut them, sore from the lack of sleep and all the crying. She kept them closed a bit longer; she knew opening them would sting even more. Within seconds she was asleep. She didn't hear the coffee machine beep and she was oblivious to the smoke coming from under her bedroom door where one of the candles had toppled over.

Jackson and Amber made their way to the fire house as quickly as possible; they pulled up right along CJ. Jez was on the forecourt washing down one of the rigs. He panicked when he saw them.

"Summer?"

"She's fine Jez, everything's fine," Amber grinned. "We've got some great news."

"You guys are freakin me out, what the hell's goin on?"

"You are not Summer's half brother."

"What?"

"We've got proof. Marcus made it up, he lied," Jackson explained.

"His sick idea of a joke," Amber added.

"A joke! He ruined my life for a joke?" he took a breath. "I killed him for nothing…"

"It's not ruined. Don't you see? You and Summer can be together. This is what I couldn't tell you about the other day, we had to be sure. It would've been cruel to get your hopes up," Jackson said.

"Oh my God, this is great, but…what if she doesn't believe me?"

"Oh yes she will," Jackson waved some papers at him. "If she doesn't believe what she reads here…"

"…I'm sure she'll believe the DNA test I've just completed on you both," CJ smiled.

"Oh my God, Oh my God," Jez began shouting. It was over. It was all over, everything was going to be ok. They'd be back together; he already knew she still loved him.

"I need to see her." He began to run off then ran back towards them. He picked Amber up and swung her round hugging her, he did the same to Jackson and CJ. "Thank you, thank you for caring. I owe you guy's big time."
"Just go and get her," Jackson ordered.

Just as he was about to ran back into the fire house the emergency bell rang. His colleagues immediately ran out to the rig.
"Fire, East 9th Street. Penthouse."
The four of them froze on the spot.

Amber and Jackson followed the fire rig as it raced through the City, sirens blaring. CJ was behind them in his car. Jackson was trying to keep as close to the rig as possible, speeding through red lights and honking his horn in order to keep up. Amber was trying to reach Matt at the office, apparently he couldn't be disturbed. That was until Amber informed the secretary that his sister was trapped in a fire and he had to get his backside home. Amber clicked the cell shut; she didn't wait for the secretary's response. It seemed to take forever to cut through the traffic. Jackson kept glancing in his mirror to check CJ was still there. Amber could only imagine what must be going through Jez's mind and Summer…she couldn't think about what might be happening to her right now.

"Jackson, she can't die," her voice cracked with emotion.
"Jez wont let that happen."

They didn't speak for the rest of the journey, too scared to voice their concerns. The rig screeched to a halt outside the apartment block. They saw Jez jump out as they pulled up behind it. Amber could see the smoke billowing out of the penthouse windows. Jackson and Amber were out of the car, running towards the rig; Jez was already running to the building.

"Walsh! Get back here and get your breathing gear on," the fire chief yelled at him.
Jez ignored him and carried on running.
"WALSH!"
Jez turned round, running backwards he shouted back. "Chief, my fiancée is in there; I gotta go and get her."
With that he disappeared into the building.
"Dante, Kowalski, get your gear on and get after that son of a…" the chief ordered.

Summer thought she was dreaming she felt disorientated. The room was hazy and there was a strange smell. She closed her eyes again, sleep was calling her. She opened then as quickly as she shut them. She must keep them open. Something inside her told her she was in danger. She knew she was on the floor. She tried to get up, but her head was too heavy to lift. The air around her was starting to suffocate her. She got as close to the floor as possible where the air was more breathable, but it was still choking her.

She tried to pull herself along the floor, but her limbs felt like lead. She didn't even know if she was moving in the right direction. A thick dark acrid smoke covered her like a blanket. After what seemed like forever, she gave up, she couldn't move anymore. She lay down and closed her eyes. She felt like she was falling in a deep sleep, a strange sensation came over her. She thought she was never going to open her eyes again. As she lost consciousness images of Jez flashed through her mind. How she'd loved him. She could feel him now, close by, she could almost hear him…

Jez kicked down the door of the apartment, the smoke billowed out into the hallway, he ducked underneath it.

"Summer!" he shouted as he entered the burning suite. He pulled his jacket over his mouth and noise and shielded the rest of his face with his other arm. He got down closer to the floor; the smoke was already stinging his eyes. It was so thick with smoke, he could hardly see. All he knew was that he had to find her. The heat was intense and he began coughing, but he would not give up.

He began to crawl along the floor to maximise the dwindling oxygen. As he moved her stretched out as far as he could, feeling for her. He tried to call out again but the smoke filled his mouth before he could get the words out. His throat and lungs were starting to burn. He crawled into the living room, she was there, she'd managed to crawl to the door way. He grabbed her and pulled her along the floor, her body was limp. He knew he had to keep going; he had to get her to safety.

I will not let you die; I will not let you die. Listen to me Summer. He willed her to hear his thoughts. As he got back out into the corridor he picked her up in his arms, he was going to run for it. A flashlight dazzled him momentarily. He knew it was one of his colleagues. He leaned against a door frame to support his weight; he passed Summer over to the guys. One of them gave him his breathing mask. He slumped against the door frame as he quickly put the mask on and tried to regulate his breathing. Within seconds he had air again. He watched his friend get Summer to safety.

Please God, don't let her die.

Now he could breath properly he was about to head off after them, he didn't need to wait for the guys to come back for him.

He heard a cracking noise, he looked around him. He couldn't see what it was and then, too late he realised the noise was from above. He had no time to move as the door frame gave way, taking the ceiling with it and pinning him to the floor. His last thought before everything went black was that Summer was safe.

CHAPTER FIFTEEN

The engine of Matt's car was still running as he ran toward the gurney being pushed into the ambulance rig. He could see Summer lying there with an oxygen mask over her face. She was lifted into the ambulance, he jumped straight in. He heard Jackson's voice as the doors were closing.

"We'll follow."

Amber grabbed Jackson and they ran towards the cars.

"Wait!"

They turned back round to CJ. "Jez," Amber whispered.

"Where the hell is he?" Jackson ran over to one of the fire fighters.

"Where's Jez? Why isn't he out yet?"

"There was a problem, they just radioed down. He's on his way now."

"Is he ok?" Jackson asked.

"Sorry guys, I know as much as you," the fire fighter apologised.

Amber ran over to the gurney as soon as she saw it come out of the door. She was shocked by what she saw. Jez's body was charcoal coloured, his hair was singed and he was covered in blood. His eyes were flickering.

"Jez," she cried.

"Tell her...tell her..."

She was pushed out of the way as the ambulance crew raced to put him in the rig. She found herself in Jackson's arms, burying her head in his chest.

"He was bleeding," she sobbed.

"They'll be ok baby, they'll be ok," he said with conviction he didn't feel.

Matt was in the corner of the ER waiting room, looking uncomfortable on the plastic orange chairs when the others found him.

"What's happening?" Amber asked as she sat down next to him.

He shrugged his shoulders. "They took her straight through and told me to wait here. They said they'd keep me informed but I haven't heard anything yet."

Amber could hear the deep concern in his voice, he had paled in colour. She placed a hand on his knee.

"What about Jez?" CJ asked.

"I saw him rushed in, but I don't know anything. I didn't realise it was him who got her out."

Jackson tried to laugh. "You know Jez, a regular hero."

"This is such a mess. Just when we thought we'd got it all sorted out," Amber sighed.

"What d'you mean?"

"Oh My God Matt, it was all a sick joke. Marcus lied. Jez isn't related to you and Summer. We found Jez's birth certificate and did some research on your dad."

"You did what?" Matt whispered loudly.

"Amber and I both thought something wasn't right, so we did some investigating. We found some news articles and we looked through your dad's stuff. Some of Marcus' story was right. Your dad did have an affair, well quite a few in fact..." Amber elbowed Jackson in the ribs, too much information.

"He did get one of his mistresses pregnant, but she had a girl, this was around the time Jez was born. So by omitting certain information it would be easy to trick Jez into thinking he was the product of that affair. Especially as he'd known all along that Jez's mom had an affair with a married man, he just played devil's advocate."

Matt looked shell shocked. "Are you, are you sure?"

CJ nodded. "I did a DNA test, there's no way they are related."

"Jeez, I can't take this in. I knew Marcus was warped, but this is crazy. What did he think he'd achieve? Son of a Bitch, if he wasn't already dead I'd kill the bastard myself. The state Summer got herself in over him and now she's in hospital fighting for her life all because of him. If anything happens to her...she's all the family I've got." Matt broke down in tears and put his face in his hands, Amber had her arms around him.

"Mr Stevens?" They all looked up to see a doctor standing in front of them.
"Mr Stevens, I'm Doctor Jordan. I have some news concerning Ms Stevens and Mr Walsh."
The doctor showed Matt into the relative's room. He gestured for Matt to sit down. He sat opposite him and cleared his throat.

"We're having trouble trying to locate Mr Walsh's relatives. Do you have any contact details for them?"
Matt shook his head. "Jez doesn't know who his parent's are, Summer is his family."
The Doctor nodded his head slowly. "So, Ms Stevens is his next of kin?"
"Yeah, I suppose so. Look, what's happened to them? When can I see my sister?"
"I'll take you through in a moment. There are a few things I need to discuss with you first. When Mr Walsh arrived in the ER he was badly burnt, his lungs were filled with smoke and he'd suffered massive internal bleeding."
"Bleeding? In a fire?" Matt was confused.

"It seems he got your sister out just in time. He became trapped after getting your sister out. The fire crew got him out as quickly as they could...but his injuries were too extent," the doctor paused. "I'm sorry."

"But, but Jez is a fire fighter, he does this every day. He knew what he was doing...you're wrong."

"He ran into that building with no protective gear on, no one is invincible I'm afraid."

"Oh God, how am I gonna tell Summer? She's alive isn't she?" he asked worriedly.

"Thanks to Mr Walsh, she will be just fine. She's had a lot of smoke inhalation so were helping her to breathe at the moment and clear her lungs out. Her wounds are superficial. However, we've taken the decision to keep her sedated for the time being," Doctor Jordan explained.

"Sedated? Why?"

"As well as the previous conditions I have just mentioned, it seems your sister was ten weeks pregnant, unfortunately she has miscarried."

Matt could only shake his head in disbelief, how bad could things get? "Please tell me this is all a bad dream," he pleaded with the doctor.

"I wish I could Mr Stevens. We felt that your sister needed to gain some strength before we told her about her fiancé and baby. Did she know she was pregnant?"

Matt shook his head. "I don't think so, she err, hasn't been too well, she probably wouldn't have realised."

"I can take you to see her now."

"I better speak to my friends first, they're worried. Thank you Doctor," Matt replied numbly.

Matt stood up at the same time as the Doctor, who reached across and opened the door to let him out.

"I'm sorry to be the bearer of bad news. When you're ready to see your sister, give one of the nurses a call. They'll take you through," the Doctor advised him kindly.

Matt nodded his head and gave a faint smile. The Doctor watched the deflated young man walk down the corridor to inform his friends of the news. He ran his hand through his hair and leant against the door frame. Sometimes he hated his job.

Jackson saw Matt first and also the look on his face. "Oh God. No," he whispered.
"What?" Amber looked up and straight into Matt's eyes. "No," she mumbled.
It seemed to take forever for Matt to reach them, by which time Amber felt her heart plummet through to her feet.
"What's happened?" Amber had only felt this scared once before in her life.

"It's Jez," Matt replied slowly, not sure which part of this nightmare to tell them first. It was then he noticed two fire fighters on the other side of the waiting room. He went over to them, aware that Amber, Jackson and CJ were right behind him. It somehow seemed easier to tell these guys than see the pain on his friends faces.

"Are you from Jez's firehouse?"
The two men nodded slowly. "He didn't make it, did he?"
Matt shook his head. "I'm sorry guys," he heard Amber whimper behind him.
"It's a bitch losing one of your own. He was a good guy."
"The doctor mentioned internal bleeding, what happened in there?"
"We gave Jez a breathing mask to help him while we got his fiancée out. The building looked secure and she was unconscious. Our first concern was to get her out. We left her with the team outside and went back for him. The door frame collapsed, bringing the roof down too. We freed him as quickly as we could, but looks like the damage was done. He saved your

sister's life. Another ten seconds, she'd have been trapped too. Matt nodded slowly, realisation sinking in.

The other guy began to speak. "I can't believe it. He was always so aware of keeping himself and the crew safe. He never took risks, said he had too much to live for..."

"How is his fiancée? He talked so much about her, his face used to light up whenever he spoke 'bout her. Never knew a guy so much in love, we called him Romeo back at the firehouse."

"She's gonna be ok, thanks to Jez," Matt replied suddenly hit by the injustice of it all.

"We better get going, tell the guys the bad news."

Matt watched the guys walk away, their heads hung low; they'd seen death over and over again, never made it any easier.

He spun round to face the others. Amber was in the middle of Jackson and CJ, both with their arms around her, looking like they were keeping her upright.

"You're wrong, he can't die," Amber shook her head.

"What about Summer?" CJ asked.

Matt sat down, those chairs not getting any more comfortable and sighed.

"She's gonna be ok, but it's complicated. They want to keep her sedated at the moment, she's pretty weak and they don't think she's strong enough yet to cope with Jez's death or the fact she's suffered a...a...miscarriage."

"Miscarriage!" Amber practically fell down onto a chair.

"Summer was pregnant, in the early stages. She's been so spaced out she probably didn't know, but that wont make it any easier when she finds out," Matt sighed.

"Poor Summer. Jesus, she still doesn't know that Marcus lied and then to find out Jez is dead and their baby...How much more shit is life gonna give this girl? It's all down to Marcus. A perfectly happy couple has been torn apart, resulting in Jez's death and the loss of their unborn child. I hope he's burning in the fires of hell," Jackson spat. He rarely lost his temper, but the realisation that his friend was dead and Summer had more heartache to come made him angry. He needed someone to blame and that blame lay quite clearly with Marcus. As far as he was concerned, Marcus killed Jez. He slumped down onto the chairs.

"For someone who despised Jez, I owe him so much now. I have great respect for him, he ran in to get her out, without a second thought for himself. This should never have happened. God, what I'd give for him to be alive so I could apologise for being a jerk."

"You should go and see Summer," Amber said.

"We need to go and find Claudia, she's got no idea about this," CJ sighed.

"You guys feel free to use our apartment for as long as you need," Jackson said.

"God, I forgot we haven't got a home," he turned to Amber "I don't wanna put the guys out, go and book us into a hotel. I'll see you there, just leave a message at the nurses station, let me know where you are." He pulled her close and kissed the top of her head.

He watched the three of them walk down the corridor, never feeling more alone in his life.

The nurse showed him into Summer's room. She lay there with tubes coming out of her mouth, she looked deathly pale. Tears stung his eyes. He pulled a chair over and sat next to her. He gently took her hand in his.

"Summer, I am so, so sorry. I don't know what to do to make it right. I'm sorry I gave Jez such a hard time, you were right, I was wrong. He was a great guy; I never should've doubted how much he loved you. I was jealous. I thought you didn't need me anymore. I didn't make a very good job of the promise I made to mom and dad to look after you did I? I should've realised you'd never push me away. You don't deserve all this hurt and pain. Just please say strong, I promise everything will be ok, I promise," he wiped the tears away with his other hand. He rested his head on the bed and cried.

CHAPTER SIXTEEN

Claudia lazed on the sofa in her apartment, drinking champagne. She was sticking to one glass; she knew she didn't need alcohol to make her happy. Leyton gave her much more of a buzz than a few glasses of wine ever could. She was watching him over by the CD player, choosing some music; he flicked through her music library with a smile on his face.

"Bon Jovi?" he raised an eyebrow. "Not really the romantic music I was looking for.
"It's sexy as hell; you gotta listen to the words."
"Ok, I'll take your word for it," he popped the disc in and joined her on the sofa.

He'd never felt so at ease with someone, they'd spent all afternoon chatting about their tastes in music, to films, politics, childhood, the legal system. Here he was sitting here in this gorgeous woman's apartment, after taking the afternoon off work, drinking champagne and listening to Bon Jovi, feeling like he was on top of the world. He looked over to her and grinned.

"What are you smiling at?"
"You."
"Why?"
"I just never had you down as a rock chick, that's all."
"Why not?"
"Cos you're a no nonsense lawyer."
"And there's a contract we have to sign to say we can only listen to boring jazz is there?" she giggled, taking a dig at his taste in music.
"No, it's just don't you have loads of tattoo's or piercing' to listen to this stuff?"

"Like I said, listen to the lyrics."

She shifted on the sofa to sit upright. "Ok, I'm gonna get deep now, but this music is the soundtrack to my life. I grew up with it. Each track has a million memories for me, from my school days to unrequited love," she half smiled.

"I like it when you get deep, I know you feel comfortable with me and I'm working through those barriers."

"I'm not used to the feelings I've got, of trusting someone, of being myself. Of feeling…" she paused, unable to look into his eyes.

"Loved?" he finished for her.

She nodded.

"Is that what you meant?" he asked.

"Is that what you meant?" she returned the question. She looked up, meeting his gaze.

He knew this was the most open she'd ever been in a relationship; he knew he had to be open with her too. Even if it meant scaring her off a bit.

"If I told you I was falling in love with you, would it scare you away?"

"It's all happened so fast. I wasn't looking for a relationship. I thought we'd go on a few dates, I'd get CJ out of my system and I'd feel better about myself, but it didn't quite turn out like that."

He moved closer to her, taking the champagne glass out of her hand and held both of her hands with his. He stared intently into her eyes.

"So, would now be an appropriate time to tell you I love you?" he whispered softly, leaning in and kissing her. She could barely breathe, let alone speak, so she carried on kissing him instead. He wrapped his arms around her, pushing her back down on the sofa.

They we're interrupted by the intercom.

"I'll get rid of them," Claudia said as she reluctantly pulled away from his kisses. She moved over to the door and pressed the buzzer.

"Claudia, its CJ."

She glanced nervously at Leyton; he just smiled and shrugged his shoulders.

"Sorry for interrupting," CJ apologised as he walked into the apartment.

"It's ok, we weren't doing anything, I mean, we were, I mean, oh I don't know."

She felt uncomfortable having both CJ and Leyton in the same room; both men had politely smiled at each other. She was about to make introductions when she noticed the troubled look on CJ's face.

"What's wrong?"

"I've got bad news."

"Summer?"

"Err, can I sit down?"

"Of course, you've never had to ask before." She sat down next to him; he instinctively reached out for her hand. She noticed Leyton flinch slightly.

"There's been a fire, at the penthouse."

"Oh my God. Was it bad? Is anyone hurt?"

CJ looked down to the floor, then back up at her worried face.

"There's no easy way to say this... Claudia, Jez was killed."

"NO! No, he can't be, he's a fire fighter, no, no," she shook her head.

"He was killed rescuing Summer, she's in hospital, she'll be ok."

Claudia couldn't speak; all she could do was shake her head as the tears spilled down her cheeks.

"That's not all...Summer was pregnant, she's lost the baby."

"Jesus, I can't take this in."

"The theory Amber and Jackson had was right," CJ was aware of Leyton watching him, he didn't want to reveal too much in front of him. "Marcus was lying. Amber and Jackson were on their way to tell Jez the truth when they heard about the fire. He never got the chance to tell her," he finished sadly.

This was too much for Claudia, she broke down in floods of tears into CJ's arms and they both just cried.

Leyton didn't know whether to get up and go or stay, he felt like he was intruding. He wanted to comfort Claudia, seeing her in CJ's arms made him feel uncomfortable. He knew he was being irrational. She was just sharing her grief, but it still felt weird.

After a very long and horrible day Matt was in the elevator up to the suite at The Plaza, nothing but the best for the son of a senator. He felt like he was asleep on his feet, although he doubted he'd get much sleep tonight. He'd stayed with Summer all day; she was still in an induced sleep. He'd left reluctantly; Doctor Jordan told him he'd be no use to Summer when she woke up if he hadn't had enough sleep. He desperately wanted her to come round, but he was dreading telling her all the horrible things that had come to light. He swiped the card to open the door, the room was in darkness. He thought Amber was in bed until her saw her silhouette in the window, a glass of wine in hand. She hadn't seemed to hear him come in.

"Amber?" She didn't reply, so he went over and put his hand on her shoulder. She looked startled.

"You ok?"

She shook her head.

"Stupid question." He went over to the mini bar and poured himself a large JD.

He sat down next to her, neither of them spoke. Matt stared out of the window, lost in thought. He just wanted this nightmare to be over, things were going from bad to worse. He was distracted by a strange noise, he looked round and realised that the noise was Amber crying. He'd never seen her cry before; she always kept her emotions so well hidden. He was a bit taken aback and unsure how to react.

"Hey, it's ok to cry. It's been a shock."
"How's she gonna cope. Jez is gone and so is her baby."
"We'll be there for her, that's how," Matt replied.
"She's lucky?"
"Lucky? How'd ya figure that one out?"
"Lucky to have people around her, people who love her and know what's happened. I had no one."
"I don't understand...You never had anyone for what?"
"I had an abortion," she downed her wine.
"What? When? Not our..." he started.

She shook her head quickly. "No you didn't get me pregnant. I was fifteen. Usual story, too much to drink at a party, went off with some guy, didn't use protection and I end up pregnant. Sluttish or what hey? I couldn't tell anyone, not even Summer. I had a bit of a reputation and I was scared she'd think badly of me. There was also the problem of the baby's father...it was Marcus," she waited for him to say something; he didn't so she carried on.

"I know she would've helped me but I was too scared. I couldn't go to my Doctor; he was a member of my dad's country club. I definitely couldn't tell Marcus. I got the money together for an abortion and I went to a clinic, if that's what you could call it. It was dirty and smelly; they hadn't even bothered cleaning up the previous patients sick and blood. They didn't take my name or address, I could've died on that table and they wouldn't have a clue who I was.

The nurse was hardly sympathetic, she just shoved me into the so called operating theatre. The doctor was a horrible. Sleazy, dirty looking old man. I wish I'd run, but I didn't know what to do. At the time the thought of having a baby scared me more than thought of the operation and besides I knew loads of girls at school who'd had an abortion and were fine. He told me to lie down and take off my jeans. He gave me anaesthetic which is all I remember till I woke up in the middle of it all, screaming in agony. It was the worst pain I'd even known. He just carried on and didn't even blink at my screams. I was ill for ages but couldn't tell anyone, I had to pretend I had a bug. I had to deal with the fact that I'd killed my baby and I couldn't confide in anyone."

"Jesus, Amber...I never knew. You could've told me. It was a long time ago. I wouldn't have thought badly of you. You were just a kid and Marcus shoulda known better."

"He never knew, I never told him. You see, that's not the end of it. You may have noticed over the years how I go from one bad relationship to another, married guys, sleazy guys, commitment scared guys, guys who are workaholics..."she raised an eyebrow at him, he returned the gesture. "...I was in these pointless relationships because the abortion had made me infertile. I was never gonna be able to get married and have a family. So I knew there was no point in looking for my Mr. Right. He'd run a mile once he knew I was damaged goods." She stared straight ahead, hugging her knees to her as she told the story.

"Marcus knew I couldn't have kids, but he didn't know it was down to him and I wasn't gonna give him the satisfaction of knowing it was all down to him."

"You shoulda told me."

"Why? So you coulda done a runner instead of wasting your time with me? Let's face it; our relationship is hardly worth the bother."

"No, I would've understood you more. It all makes sense now,"
He reached across and took her hand. "Despite what you think, I care about you. You've gone through a helluva lot by yourself and I think that's pretty amazing."

"We've got no future. I'm just gonna keep going from one dead end relationship to another."

"Is ours really that bad? We could make it work."

"What's the point? We could put our heart and soul into this and then it's come to the point where you want kids and it'd be bye, bye Amber."

He stood up and pulled her close to him. "Come here."
He led her over to the sofa and sat down. "You never asked me what I wanted, I can't say I ever thought about kids."

"You will eventually."

He stared at her for a while.

"God, I'm sorry. This isn't the time. It's been a long and difficult day," she apologised.

"No. I'd say this conversation was long over due. We need to talk and we need to be honest with each other."

She nodded slowly.

He grabbed the bottle of JD and two glasses. "I don't think I woulda slept tonight anyway, so now's as good a time as any."

CHAPTER SEVENTEEN

Claudia sat on the window seat in her apartment, she refilled her wine glass

and put the half empty bottle beside her. She quickly gulped it down; old habits die hard after all. She arrived at the hospital earlier just after Matt had left, according to the nurse. She found her way to Summer's room and sat next to her almost lifeless body.

The nurse told her she should be able to hear everything that was said. As she took Summer's hand in her own, the tears slid down her face. Claudia didn't know what to say, what d'you say to someone who has just lost the love of their life and their baby, but doesn't yet know? So she just sat there, stroking her hand. She couldn't bear it for too long, she leant over and kissed Summer on the cheek and left.

She cried all the way home and was still crying now. She'd told Leyton she would go over to his apartment after the hospital, but she went home. She needed a drink. So, there she was, sat in her own apartment trying to drown the grief in alcohol. She couldn't believe Jez was dead, life was so cruel sometimes. Summer and Jez were made for each other and now it was all over. She moved over to the sofa and grabbed another bottle of wine. Summer and Jez had been so happy, they had their life all planned out and it had all gone horribly wrong. She lay back against the sofa and closed her eyes, the tears still leaking from her eyelids. Tears for Jez and tears for Summer.

Leyton was starting to get worried about Claudia. She'd raced off to the hospital as soon as CJ had left. She should've been back hours ago. He'd offered to drive her to the hospital, but she'd said she needed to be on her own. He paced the floor as he tried her cell again, it was gone ten o'clock, she should well be home by now. He only got her machine when he tried her apartment; he'd even tried her office.

Enough was enough; he grabbed his jacket and headed over to her apartment. Understandably she was upset, her friend had just died. He just needed to know that she was ok. He managed to talk the security guy at her apartment into letting him in and when he found her she was slumped on the sofa, a couple of empty wine bottles on the floor. He shook her gently to try and wake her. When she didn't respond he whispered her name. There was still no movement.

He said her name slightly louder. This time she mumbled incoherently and before he could move she'd vomited all over his shoes. He picked her up and carried her into the bathroom and cleaned her up. She remained slumped over him and kept mumbling. Once he'd sorted her out he carried her into the bedroom, laid her down on the bed and stayed with her till morning.

Amber woke up in a strange room, in Matt's arms, which was even stranger. She felt disorientated, and then she remembered. Remembered the terrible tragedy the previous day and also the fact that she had finally disclosed her deep dark secret. Despite his horrendous day Matt had listened to her well into the small hours and had been supportive, he'd even shown a sensitive side that she didn't even know existed. It was actually quite a nice feeling waking up close to him; the warmth of his body was comforting. Normally they woke up as far as possible from each other.

Last night he promised he'd be there for her…if she wanted him to be. She felt guilty at the thought of burdening him with her problems when he had enough to deal with. Hell, Summer didn't even know Jez was dead yet. She should've been a shoulder for him to lean on. God knew, when Summer did find out about Jez, he was going to need someone to turn to. She didn't know where their relationship was headed; they had talked long into the night. All she knew was she didn't feel as hostile toward him as she normally did.

The next few days passed in a blur for Matt. He spent most of his time at the hospital. The damage to the penthouse had been extensive. He'd arranged for work to start immediately on fixing it up. Once the structural work was done Amber was going to redesign the décor. He didn't know how long it would take, weeks? Months? He didn't care; at the fore-front of his mind was Summer. Therefore he would be staying at The Plaza for the foreseeable future. Jackson and CJ kept offering their apartment but he didn't want to impose, besides he and Amber had been having some pretty serious talks and were definitely benefiting from having some privacy.

He couldn't get his head round what she'd been through, no wonder she was emotionally scarred. It was easy to see why she'd behaved the way she did in relationships. He felt like they'd turned a corner. She had shown him a vulnerable side and let him know what was going on inside her head. He felt sure they could make this work, but that was dependent on whether she was willing to invest in their relationship or not.

He was sitting beside Summer's bedside, she had been drifting in and out of consciousness all day although she was very disorientated and groggy. Most of the time she wasn't sure who he was. She had however said Jez's name. It turned his stomach every time at the thought of what she would wake up to. Doctor Jordan advised not to tell her anything until she was properly awake. He had discussed with the Doctor what to tell her, he had kindly offered to pass on the news but Matt felt it would be better coming form him. The Doctor understood this but said he would be on hand if Summer had any medical questions that she wanted answering.

Thankfully the Fire Department were taking care of Jez's funeral; otherwise it would've been left to him to organize that too. There was only so much he could take. He hoped Summer would be well enough for the funeral, it would help with the grieving process. He was dreading having to tell her, he knew she would be heartbroken and he was seriously worried that it might tip her over the edge. He looked down at his sister; he wished things would stop going wrong for her. All he wanted was for her to be happy and come out the other side. He held her hand and began to talk to her while she slept.

Claudia had been so embarrassed when she'd woken up the morning after her drunken binge to discover that Leyton had found her passed out and then she proceeded to throw up over him. He'd been so nice about it and said he'd understood why she was in such a state. She thought she'd got her drinking under control, but the alcohol was the only thing that seemed to numb the grief. Now her heart just felt heavy, she couldn't get her head around the injustice of it all. Jez died saving the love of his life, doing something he did every day. She knew Summer would be distraught and even more so when she found out she'd been carrying Jez's child. She had loved him so much and Jez had felt exactly the same.

She sighed heavily, she was supposed to be working on her case, but her mind wasn't focused. She spun her chair round to face her huge floor to ceiling windows. As well as worrying about Summer and grieving for Jez she was also concerned about Leyton. Despite his understanding the other night she was petrified he was going to leave her. She had let him closer to her than anyone other guy, well with the exception of CJ. What if he thought she had too much emotional baggage and it was too much work? Before CJ called about the news of Jez's death Leyton had told her he loved her. He hadn't mentioned anything since. She knew how she felt for him; at least she thought she did. Now she was feeling insecure and didn't know what to do about it. She took her glasses off; the tears that were falling were splattering her lenses. She didn't hear her office door open; she was too lost in thought, when suddenly Leyton's voice snapped her out of her thoughts. She spun back round.

"What's wrong baby?" He perched on the end of her desk and took her hand as the tears rolled down her cheeks.
"God I can't stop crying."
"Understandable, you've just lost a friend."
"It's not just that...it's us."
"Us? What's wrong with us?"
"Nothing. I hope, she wiped the tears from her face. "I was just getting a bit stressed over what happened the other night."
"Look, I already told you, I didn't really like those shoes anyway," his chocolate coloured eyes twinkled as he spoke.
"I just thought I might've put you off, things had been going really well. You said some really special things to me and then I go and make an idiot out of myself."

He tilted his head to one side. "Special things? Like, I love you."
She dropped her gaze and nodded.
"I know you're having a rough time at the moment and I know it's gonna take you time to realise that I am not gonna hurt you. I just didn't wanna get all heavy when I know you're grieving right

now. I just wanna be a shoulder to cry on."

"You mean you don't love me anymore?" she asked slowly.

He pulled her up and put his arms around her waist. "Claudia I am crazy 'bout you, you've completely bowled me over and I do love you. I just know you feel insecure and need to learn to trust me."

"You don't think badly of me that I have issues? There are things I haven't told you about yet; I will tell you...I'm just not ready."

"Claudia, I think you're amazing, you're beautiful, intelligent and a million other nice things and I'm in this for the long run, no matter what we come up against, we'll deal with it together, ok?"

She nodded her head. Why had she nearly let this amazing guy slip through her fingers? He tipped her face towards him and gently kissed away her tears.

The following day Summer woke up properly from her induced sleep. Matt was by her side. She wasn't sure how she got to be in this cold, clinical room. She smiled slowly at Matt, why did it feel like ages since she'd seen him? There was another guy standing by Matt, he was tall. Attractive and he wore a white coat. It was then she realised she ached all over. Her chest felt sore and as she tried to speak her throat burned.

"What happened to me?" she croaked.

Matt cleared his throat. "There was a fire at home, you were trapped inside," he paused for a second. "Jez rescued you."

She smiled. "Jez?" her whole face lit up.

Jeez, this was gonna be harder than he thought.

"Where is he? Why isn't he here?" she licked her cracked lips, they felt so dry.

"Summer, d'you remember what was happening between you and Jez? What Marcus had said?" he asked quietly. He didn't want to reveal too much in front of Doctor Jordan.

She nodded her head slowly, it was coming back to her now, That's why Jez wasn't here…they weren't together anymore, but surely he'd want to know if she was ok?

"Well Marcus, wasn't telling the truth, it was supposed to be a joke."

"You mean everything's gonna be ok? Why isn't he here? You're not still pissed at him are you? Why won't you let him see me? I need him," she tried to sit upright but her arms were too weak. "How long have I been asleep?"

"A few days."

"A few days! Why was I asleep that long? Why isn't Jez here? He wouldn't leave me on my own." She was starting to get distressed.

"The Doctor's felt you needed time to recover."

"I'm fine. What's going on Matt? You're worrying me."

"Oh God Summer, I really don't know how to tell you this and I wish I didn't have to. Jez isn't here because, because he died saving your life."

"No, no, NO! I don't believe you; you just don't want us to be together. He's not dead, he'd never leave me."

"Summer, I wish I was wrong. He ran into the building with no breathing equipment, he was that desperate to get you out. He got you out but something collapsed on him and…" he turned to the Doctor who stepped closer.

"I'm Doctor Jordan, I treated your fiancé. We did all we could but his injuries were too severe; we couldn't stop the internal bleeding. I'm so very sorry Ms Stevens."

"No, you're lying."

Matt held her hand. "It's true."

"He doesn't know how much I love him, he doesn't know," she cried. Tears rolling down her cheeks.

"He does know, he's always known."

"How can you say that? You hated him."

"Not anymore Summer, he saved you're life. I will forever be grateful to him for that."

"So, he finally gets your approval, a bit late now," she spat.

"I'm sorry. I shoulda made more of an effort, but that's something I have to deal with now for the rest of my life."

"And I have to spend the rest of my life without Jez."

He hung his head. "I know."

"We were getting married. You don't know how much I hated Marcus for tearing us apart. I so wanted to be his wife, have his children."

Matt exchanged a worried look with Doctor Jordan; he quickly looked away, but not quick enough. Summer had seen the look that passed between the two men.

"What?" she asked numbly.

Matt looked at his sisters tear stained faced, the shattered look in her eyes and he just couldn't carry on. He couldn't tell her the rest. He turned to the Doctor once more.

"I'm sorry, I can't," he whispered, tears stinging his eyes.

Doctor Jordan nodded. His heart went out to this poor girl and her brother who was trying so hard to keep it together. He sensed something bad had already happened prior to the accident. What, he didn't know and it didn't concern him. He just hoped his patient was mentally strong enough. He sat down on the edge of the bed.

"Ms Stevens, I'm afraid there's more bad news," he didn't think she could get any paler than she actually was, but in that second she turned grey. He carried on. "It seems you were in the early stages of pregnancy. However, you had begun to lose blood; we were unable to stop the bleeding. You miscarried."

Summer couldn't speak, she was stunned. She hadn't even had a clue she was pregnant. Now she'd lost the baby, her baby, Jez's baby…now they were both gone Jez and their baby all in the same day. She began to sob, her whole body shaking. "Jez, Jez, I need you," she cried.

Matt hugged her. "I don't know what to say to make it better," he was also crying.

The Doctor stood up and slipped out of the room, leaving them to grieve together.

Matt stayed until Summer finally fell asleep. He gently let go of her hand and quietly left. Once the door closed behind him Summer opened her eyes, she'd pretended to be asleep so she could be alone, now she really was, no Jez and no baby.

She remembered the last time she'd seen him. She'd told him she couldn't be with him and it was all over between them. She recalled the look of pain in his eyes and it'd broken her heart.

"Damn you Marcus, damn you to hell," she whispered into the darkness.

She tried to picture his face, wishing he was still there. She would give anything to touch him again, kiss him, feel his arms around her. She loved him so deeply, he had been everything to her and now he was gone. She wished she was dead too, she had nothing to live for anymore. She thought how happy he would've been to have found out he was going to be a dad.

Her mind wandered back to her last conversation with him, had she told him she still loved him? She hoped to God she had, but did he know that she could never stop loving him? A memory flashed across her mind, of being trapped a dark blanket of smoke around her, she knew she was going to die. She was scared, so scared that'd she'd imagined Jez was calling out to her. She must've really heard him; he'd really been there when she needed him...just like he always promised he would.

He'd rescued her. "Jez, I love you so God damn much, I hope you know that."
She felt like she'd been crying for an eternity, her weary body craved rest, she needed to sleep. She knew she hadn't been asleep long when something made her wake up. Someone was sitting by her bedside; it took her eyes a few moments to adjust to the dark. They reached out for her hand, she'd know that touch anywhere.

"Jez..."
"Hey baby, sorry it took me so long, got her as soon as I could."
"I knew you'd come, I've been so scared without you."
"He smiled and kissed her gently. "Never ever feel scared, I'll always look out for you Summer, I'll be the one to show you the way, you know that babe."
She nodded her head.
"Don't ever forget how much I love you. Promise?"
"I promise Jez. I love you forever. Please don't leave me," she pleaded.
"I'll never be far away."
She gazed up into his handsome face, those blue eyes always full of laughter, that strong jaw line and kissable lips, like she'd done so many times before. She closed her eyes, trying to commit it to memory.

When she opened them again he was gone. She shouted his name into the darkness, but there was no reply. She leaned back against the pillow and tried to regulate her breathing. The memory of her dream whizzing around her head, but it wasn't a dream, it couldn't be. She could feel him all around her; still taste his kiss on her lips. He'd been here. She desperately wanted to go back to sleep to see him again. Another memory flooded her mind, the night he'd broken the door down to get to her, they'd talked. He told her he'd see her in his dreams, she'd replied that was the only way they could be together. How true that was now.

CHAPTER EIGHTEEN

Doctor Jordan was pleased with Summer's physical recovery but was worried about her emotional state and said as much to Matt. She was ready to be discharged but he was going to speak to her about psychiatric help, she'd a lot to cope with. He'd chatted to Matt about this, but he didn't seem to think she'd agree to it. The Doctor hoped that between them, they'd get her to see sense. She was only young and if she didn't get through this in one piece it could have serious repercussions on the rest of her life, he'd seen it happen too many times before.

He entered Summer's room; he was surprised to see her up and about. She was packing her belongings. She actually looked well, her hair and make up were immaculate, not the normal concerns of someone who had just been bereaved, and he knew he was right to be worried. She lifted her head and gave him a strained smile.

"Are you ready to let me out of here?"
"You have certainly recovered well physically, so I'd say you were fine to go home. I just wanted to see how you feel about getting help with your emotional injuries."
Summer laughed bitterly. "Emotional injuries? I've heard it all now. I'm perfectly fine, it's not my head that hurts, it's my soul and as far as I know there aint no medical cure for that."
"If you ever feel like it's getting too much, I've given Matt some numbers of people who'll be able to help you."
"I won't be needing them."
"Well then Summer, I hope every thing works out for you and I'm truly sorry about your loss."
She picked up her bag. "Don't take this the wrong way, but I hope I don't see you around."

"Me too," he said quietly as he watched her leave the room. That was one troubled lady.

Amber was rushing around the hotel suite. Matt had called to say he was on his way back with Summer. She was still feeling shaken up by events, especially as it had brought her own buried memories closer to the surface. Maybe her experience would help Summer.

"Amber, stop running around, the place is spotless," CJ sighed as he watched her behave totally out of character.
"Everyt'ing gonna be alright." Jackson slipped into his Caribbean lilt when he was feeling the pressure.
"Come and sit down for five minutes, it's gonna be hard enough to know what to say when she gets here. Just chill and get your head together."

Amber stood still for a second and ran her hand through her long blonde hair. She looked at the guys, the strain of the last few weeks showing on their faces. They were all here to support Summer; their own grief would have to wait.
"For the first time in my life I don't feel in control. I don't know what to say or do and that's not me. I don't know what to expect when I see her. She was fragile enough before, but now without Jez and the baby. I'm worried what it'll do to her," Amber sighed. Before anyone could answer the door to the suite opened.

Matt stood in the doorframe with a weird look on his face, Summer stepped out from behind him, looking like she'd never done before. Full make up (she was strictly a lip gloss girl), hair scrapped back off her face in a hair band and a vacant look in her eyes. Amber reached out for her and hugged her.
"Honey, I'm so sorry."
Tears welled up in Amber's eyes, since she'd told Matt about the

abortion, the floodgates refused to close. Summer untangled herself from her arms.

CJ stepped forward. "We're here for you Summer."
"Of course you are 'coz my life is straight out of some fuckin' soap opera, so freakin unbelievable, it's almost funny. Well I'm fine, I don't need anyone's sympathy and I don't need your pity. Despite what you all think, poor little Summer is not gonna fall apart. I can cope." She stalked across the room and went into one of the bedrooms.
Amber stared open mouthed, Summer was not the type of person who normally sounded so harsh and hard, in fact she sounded just like Amber.

"What the hell just happened?" Jackson asked.
Matt just shrugged. "She was like that in the car the whole way back. She doesn't need anyone apparently and especially not me."
"Why?"
"I'm the bad guy, I never gave Jez a chance and now he's dead. The thing is, she's right, I did hate him and I can't make amends. She says the last thing she needs is my false sympathy."
"That's a bit harsh," CJ said.
"She's hurting real bad, I'm the closest person to her. She needs to hit out and blame someone and I'm it. Doctor Jordan explained that it's all part of the grieving process. Until she's ready to move on to the next stage, I'm her punch bag."
The guys all looked at each other. "This is so not the way I expected her to react, it's gonna be harder than we thought," Amber sighed.

Amber poked her head around Summer's door. She was sitting on the bed staring into space.
"Summer, honey...I need to speak to you."

Summer glanced in her direction but didn't speak.

Amber sat down next to her on the bed.

"Look, I know you think you can do this on your own, and that's fine…you just need to remember that you don't have to do it this way."

"If you've come to lecture me, then don't bother. Jez is dead Amber, DEAD!"

Amber felt herself well up. "I, I didn't come in here to patronise you… Oh God Summer, I saw Jez when they brought him out of the building…"

Summer's head instantly snapped back towards Amber.

"He was barely conscious, but he knew I was there…he said, tell her."

"Tell her? Tell her what?…Me?"

"Of course you, tell her, that Marcus lied, tell her I love her, tell her she was the last thing on my mind…I don't know Summer, all I know is he was thinking about you when he…when he…" Amber couldn't finish the sentence, she could hardly speak through her tears.

Summer crumpled against her friend. "I want him back, why didn't he make it?" The tears wouldn't stop, and she didn't think the pain of losing him ever would either.

Summer had to get out of the hotel suite and away from the others, she knew they were just concerned about her and she was lucky to have them as friends but there was only one person who would make everything ok again. She found herself wandering around Central Park, she needed space. She'd made a deal with herself, to look like she was coping, she would only cry on her own or in the dead of night, when she was lying awake thinking about him. That's when she would let the grief take over. He'd left a huge void in her life, she felt empty without Jez.

Her pregnancy wasn't planned, but she knew that baby was

supposed to bring them back together because that's where they belonged. Now she had neither, all her dreams had fallen apart. She missed Jez so much, if she thought the separation before the accident was bad enough, then this was a billion times worse. She was never going to see him again, never feel his strong arms around her, feel his passionate kisses, see his smiling face, hear him call her name. She missed everything about him, without him she was nothing.

She sat down on a bench, her legs so tired and weary. She knew she'd let him down. He was always there for her...right till the end and the one time he needed her she hadn't done the same. When he said he'd killed Marcus she hadn't stood by him. Amber and Jackson knew Marcus was lying, why hadn't she suspected the same thing? She should've been there for him. She just wanted to curl up and die at least they'd be together then, how she was going to get through tomorrow, his funeral, she didn't know. Maybe that was the time to show him how strong she could be and not to let him down again.

Summer was in the car directly behind the procession of fire fighters, leading to the church. It was a gloriously sunny spring day, it should've been raining...forever. She never in her wildest dreams imagined being the grieving widow at the age of twenty three, having just lost the love of her life, her soul mate. It all felt so surreal. She thought when she saw the coffin it would hit her, that this was the final goodbye. It hadn't, it wasn't her Jez in there, it couldn't be. She expected to see him everywhere she turned, every morning when she opened her eyes he should've been there lying next to her.
The car pulled up behind the fire rig. She took a deep breath, this was it.

Matt held the door open for Summer and helped her out of the car. He glanced around, the sight of so many fire fighters in full uniform took him aback. Jez's coffin was draped in the American flag, his helmet placed on top. His throat closed over, he wished to God that Jez had made it, he wished he had the chance to thank him face to face for saving Summer's life instead of through his prayers. He admired Jez so much now and would never get the opportunity to apologise for his childish behaviour.

He felt a hand on his shoulder, it was Jackson, CJ was behind him. He spotted Claudia with a guy he didn't recognise, he assumed it must be her new boyfriend. He thought it was nice that he'd come to support Claudia today. By this time six fire fighters had moved Jez's coffin onto their shoulders and another began to play the Last Post on a bugle. It made the hairs on the back of his neck stand on end. He followed the coffin, with Summer at his side.

Summer stared straight ahead. She sat in the first pew, flanked by Amber and Matt. She couldn't bring herself to look at the coffin or listen to the words of comfort from the young fire fighter who was giving the eulogy. Instead, she gazed at the huge photo of Jez that had been placed at the alter. He was dressed in his uniform, smiling at them. He had loved his job and she'd been so proud of him. She always thought he looked amazing in his uniform, he used to laugh and say it was the uniform she fell for. She'd tell him that she would've fallen for him no matter what. Then he'd grin at her and tell her that he was the luckiest guy on the planet. That smile of his made her heart contract. His blue eyes always had that mischievous look in them, but only she noticed, it was one of those secret looks that only she knew about. All those private smiles, secret looks between them were all gone. Everything she loved about him, gone. She blinked back tears, she had to stay strong, she'd promised him she'd be strong. She couldn't break down now – later yes, but not now.

She didn't take her eyes off the photo, she stared deep into his eyes, he was giving her the strength she needed.

Claudia couldn't stop crying, she was struggling to keep the heart wrenching sobs inside. Leyton had tight hold of her hand and wasn't letting go. She didn't want to accept that it was Jez lying there in that box. She'd glanced over at Summer a few times, she seemed to be holding it together. God she just wanted this day over with.

CJ was next to Claudia, without even looking at her he could tell how distraught she was. Out of the corner of his eye he could see Leyton stroking her hand. He wanted to take hold of her other hand, but he felt that might have been inappropriate. He kept his eyes trained on Summer, amazed at how well she was coping, on the outside. Knowing Summer she would be falling apart inside, not that he could blame her. How on earth do you begin to get your life back together after something like this? It struck him how unfair life was, here were two people totally devoted to each other and by a cruel twist of fate were separated. Sometimes he wondered if there really was a God.

Jackson hated being in church, even for a wedding, so funerals were even worse. Especially the funeral of such a good friend. He and Jez had been close, but had become even closer over the past few weeks. Jez choosing to confide in him and his and Amber's determination to uncover Marcus' lies made him feel like he was really fighting Jez's corner. He shifted uneasily in his seat, it was bad enough having to look at a coffin, and knowing who it belonged to but he really couldn't handle seeing all the fire fighters. They looked so smart and proud, so fearless, but he could see as he looked at their faces, their tears. Tears for a lost colleague, a friend. He couldn't bear too look at them anymore. He couldn't bear to be in this Goddamn church any longer.

Amber was trying to be strong for Summer, but the tears kept welling up. She couldn't get her head round the injustice of it all. Jez had been so happy when they told him the news that Marcus had lied, less than an hour later he was dead. His and Summer's dreams shattered. If Jez had waited, like his Chief had told him too, he might not have gotten to her in time and Summer could've died. It seemed like fate was playing a cruel trick, in order for Summer to survive, Jez had to die. The weird thing was, she was 110% sure that if someone had told him this before he'd run in for her, he'd have carried on regardless, that was the depth of his love for her.

Summer kept her promise to herself; she kept her composure right through the service, to the committal of the body, through to the wake where she had thanked everyone for their kind words and sympathy. Like that would make a difference.

It was only when she got back to the hotel room that she kicked off her shoes, flung herself on the bed and cried her heart out for the man who had loved her and who she loved and would always love with all her heart. She would never love anyone like she loved Jez; she never even wanted to love again. There was no room in her heart for anyone but Jez, her soul was with him. She belonged to him.

She felt hemmed in, the hotel room closing in on her. She slipped her shoes back on and quietly left the hotel suite so as not to wake Amber or Matt. She headed for the nearest bar. There was no shortage of guys offering her drinks, she accepted, she just wanted to numb the pain. There was also no shortage of cheesy chat up lines either, not that she was interested. They guys all looked the same to her, had she been talking to the same guy all night? She didn't know and she didn't care.

The bar closed, she went back to this guy's apartment. She didn't know if the sex was good or bad, she was just going through the motions, trying to find a way to cope. The following morning when she woke up in a strange bed next to some middle aged guy she was too shocked to cry. What the hell had she done? She grabbed her clothes and as quietly as she could, left the apartment and made her way back to The Plaza. She didn't even know the guys name. Jez would be so disappointed in her, this wasn't her.

"Where are you Jez? I need you, I need you so much, I can't do this on my own," she whispered. She carried on walking, the air stinging her wet face.

She ignored the questions an irate Matt was throwing at her when she returned and went straight to bed. Despite hating herself for what she'd done, that night set a pattern for the nights to come …

CHAPTER NINETEEN

Four months to the day since Jez's funeral, the penthouse became habitable again. The irony of it wasn't lost on anyone, least of all Summer. She awoke that morning glad that it was the last time she'd wake up in that God awful hotel room, but wishing she didn't have to go back to the Penthouse. How could she go back there without Jez? Claudia had offered her the use of her spare room, but Claudia and Leyton were very much in love and she couldn't handle being around them all the time. As much as she was happy for Claudia it reminded her too much of what she'd lost.

Jackson and CJ had also said she could move in with them, but Matt had practically ordered her to come back to the penthouse. He wanted to be there if she needed him, more like he wanted to keep an eye on her. His favourite phrase of late had been, "Get her back on the straight and narrow." He talked about her like she wasn't there or like she was some kid. She knew she was acting out of character and they were all just concerned about her nocturnal activities, but until she found a better way to cope she was going to have to carry on like this.

Whenever they voiced their fears to her, what if she went off with some psycho? Or caught a disease? Or got pregnant? She always had the same reply. She only ever went off with nice guys, made sure they used a condom and if she was unlucky enough for it to burst, then past experience should show that she was useless at carrying a baby. That last comment normally shut them up. Truth was, she hated herself more and more everyday. Just like that very first morning, she had woken up to some God awful sights. Sometimes they didn't even make it back to their apartment, a quite corner in a club would do or a toilet cubicle in a bar. She preferred that, it felt safer than going home with a guy. She knew she was taking risks, but the sane rational part of her disappeared the day Jez died.

She often let her mind wander to what he would think of her. Nothing made sense anymore, sometimes she would get angry with him for leaving her. If he'd just got out of the fire with her, everything would've been alright. Other times she hoped he understood that she was dead inside. When she slept with these guys it wasn't for pleasure, she had nothing left to give. Her life was going from one night stand to another and she couldn't see when it'd be any different. The one thing she wanted, she couldn't have. Matt was totally freaking out, but Amber understood. Even so, she'd tried desperately hard to get her to break the cycle, she told her it would only lead to more pain. Summer couldn't see that being true, her heart couldn't ache anymore than it already had.

Before Jez, she'd only ever slept with one other guy, Brad. Now she'd lost count – where would it all end? She was so ashamed of herself, there were names for women like her. She pulled the covers back off the bed and padded over to the en-suite. She looked in the mirror and saw a scared, haunted and lonely face looking back at her. A face she didn't recognise. When would she feel her old self again? When would she recognise the person in the mirror again?

Matt was in the new kitchen at the Penthouse, giving it a final once over. He was really impressed with the way Amber had re-vamped the place. The living area was now white and cream and minimalist, it looked like something straight out of a magazine. He wasn't sure about the kitchen at first, it was a fifties style, all pale blues. Black and white check flooring but it was growing on him. The second living area was more chilled out, warm colours to enjoy their pizza and DVD nights. The only thing that hadn't changed was Summer's bedroom, she had told Amber she wanted it exactly the same, Whether that was a good idea or not remained to be seen.

Amber walked into the kitchen carrying a box of beer, she placed it down on the table.

"Jackson's bringing more beer over in a minute."

"D'you think it's a good idea having this party tonight?"

"I'm not sure, I suppose it seemed like a good idea when Jackson suggested it, he was trying to cheer Summer up...we'll see," Amber sighed.

"At least we can keep an eye on her tonight. I really don't know what to do to help her anymore. She just seems to have gone down a dead end road. I mean she hasn't even got her job anymore after they sacked her, I don't think it's even entered her head to look for another one," he paused and turned round, he leant against the sink and looked out of the window. "Mom and dad would be so disappointed in me, that I've let her turn out like this. How many times have we caught her sneaking in after being out all night? Too many."

"Hey, you're not to blame," she came up behind him and rubbed his back as she rested her chin on his shoulder. "We're not her parents, she's not our responsibility. She's having a bad time but she'll turn the corner at some point. Until then we have to wait. I know it's not easy."

He turned to face her, taking her in his arms as he did so. "You're my rock, d'you know that?"

"You've supported me too."

"I know and I'm glad you opened up to me, 'coz right now you're the only good thing in my life," he bent down to kiss her with a new found passion.

"Shall we go and christen our new bedroom?"

"Thought you'd never ask," she grinned.

Summer came out of her bedroom and locked the door behind her. With her back against the door she surveyed the room in front of her. Everyone looked like they were enjoying themselves. She didn't want anyone disappearing into her and Jez's room. She shoved the key into her jeans pocket. There seemed to be laughter everywhere, what short memories people had. She grabbed a bottle of Bud and headed out onto the balcony. She felt suffocated, she needed fresh air and she didn't want to talk to anyone. She slipped out onto the balcony un-noticed, or so she thought.

Leyton and Claudia were in the kitchen getting more drinks.
"Enjoying yourself?" he asked.
"Surprisingly, yes. I thought it'd be weird coming back here, but there's a really good atmosphere."
From what you've told me about Jez, he doesn't sound like the type of guy who'd want people to be miserable."
Claudia smiled sadly. "He wouldn't, if he was here now he'd be enjoying himself as much as anyone. I just hope Summer's ok, this must be hard or her. I hope she manages to have a good time."
He pulled her close to him. "You can show me a good time anytime you like."
She giggled. "Leyton, you're so naughty."
"You love it really."
She nodded her head and kissed him. She felt like she was floating on air whenever he was around her.

"Sorry guys, didn't mean to interrupt."
Claudia jumped away from Leyton and blushed slightly as she saw CJ, he grinned at her. He picked two bottles up. "Needed more drinks, you two look like you're having fun."
Claudia felt herself redden even more. Leyton swung an arm

around her shoulders, pulling her close but keeping his gaze on CJ who raised an eyebrow in return.

"The best," Leyton replied.

"Well, I'll leave you two lovebirds to it." He took his beers and headed out of the kitchen. Leyton watched him go with mixed emotions. Leading Claudia on was really low and he disliked him for that reason, but Claudia had forgiven him or did she still have feelings for him? Would she have blushed so much if Jackson had walked in then?

Summer leant against the wall of the balcony, beer in hand. She was enjoying the feeling of the wind in her hair, closing her eyes she could almost imagine it was Jez running his fingers through it. God she missed him so much. When she went into her bedroom before, Amber had done as she'd asked, the room was almost identical. It was just missing the obvious, Jez. It made her feel closer to him, she could feel him all around her.

She just wished this party would end. Jackson thought it'd cheer her up. Her fiancé had just been killed, she'd lost her baby, her job, her self respect what could possibly help her get over that? A party? Yeah right, she was instantly over her grief. Jez had died in this apartment and now these people were all drinking and laughing, they may as well be dancing on his grave. She thought back to how many times, day or night they'd stood here. They'd watched sunsets, the sun come up, seen the City twinkling like a Christmas tree. They'd made plans, talked about their dreams, their future. They'd even made love out here. This had always been one of their favourite places, it didn't seem right that she was here on her own.

He stood watching her for a while as she gazed out across the City, looking like she was in a world of her own. Without being introduced he knew immediately that this was the girl CJ had told him about. She looked so troubled, he watched as she ran a hand through her hair and take a drink. His heart went out to her.

Even now, four months after his death the pain still felt raw. She didn't think she'd ever feel ok again and get her life back together. She'd lost everything and she was falling into a deep hole with no one to pull her out. Not for the first time she looked over the wall and down to the ground far below, how easy it would be to jump. She wasn't strong enough on her own. All she wanted was Jez, she began to cry. "Help me Jez, I need you."
All she wanted was to feel his warm, strong, comforting arms around her.
She almost jumped out of skin when she felt someone take her in their arms and hold her.

He couldn't leave her, she looked so distraught. She obviously came out here to be alone, but he couldn't let her drown in her grief. Without giving it a second thought, he went over to her and put his arms around her. Unsurprisingly she seemed startled at first, but he whispered to her that it was ok. She turned into him, looked at him briefly then buried her head in his chest and sobbed, He didn't let go, he held her close, stroking her hair.

Summer didn't know whose arms she was in, but for the first time in ages she felt safe. A soft voice told her it was ok. She pulled away and looked into his kind, sympathetic eyes. She'd never seen this guy before, it didn't matter, he was there when she needed someone. He held her tight, like he was never going to let go and she cried her heart out, holding him just as tight, too scared to let go.

CHAPTER TWENTY

"Urgh." Summer rolled over in bed, her head pounding like the party was still going on inside it. She rubbed the sleep away from her eyes and looked around the room to let her eyes focus; the first thing her gaze fell on was the picture of her and Jez that was beside her bed. Was this pain in her heart ever going to stop? Now she had a sore head to contend with too, her mind was a bit hazy. She knew there had been a lot of drinking, she knew there had been a party and "Oh God," she groaned, there was that embarrassing moment.

She tried to recall the events of last night. She remembered being out on the balcony feeling so alone and missing Jez like hell. She contemplated how easy it would be to jump, then that guy appeared out of no where. He'd pulled her back from the brink; did he even know how much she needed someone right then? They had talked for a while and he'd persuaded to join the rest of the party.

They had drunk some more and found a quiet corner to talk. He told her he was a friend of CJ's. She assumed he was gay, but he set her straight on that score. He was visiting from LA. He and CJ had been college buddies ay UCLA. That was all she could remember about their conversation, she rubbed her eyes again, not wanting the next bit to pop back into her consciousness – but she knew it was coming.

He had been so sweet to her, he hadn't seemed fazed by her puffy red eyes and bedraggled hair. He just acted like that was what she normally looked like. She ran that thought through her head again, of course he thought that's what she looked like. That thought made her sad. At some point during the evening she'd dragged him off into one of the guest bedrooms, she started to try and kiss him, undoing the buttons on his shirt. He'd broken away and asked her what she was doing. She'd just laughed and said all guys wanted to get laid. He told her that he liked to go on a few dates with a girl before jumping into bed with them. She felt her cheeks redden at the thought of how she'd come onto him. She'd felt so humiliated, he'd turned her down. He must've thought she was so desperate. She had run out of the bedroom and locked herself in the sanctuary of her and Jez's room.

What had she become? Jez would hate her like this. The guy last night had been lovely to her, not like the sleazy guys she'd been sleeping with left, right and centre. He was just a good guy who was trying to cheer her up and she'd totally disgraced herself and the worst thing was she couldn't even remember his name. She reached over for the photo and hugged it close to her.

"Why did you have to leave me? Can't you see I can't do this without you?"

Amber propped herself up in bed against the pillows, Matt had just brought her a coffee. He kissed the top of her head as he passed it to her. If anyone had told her six months ago that Matt would become this attentive to her she'd have just laughed. The reality was, there relationship had definitely turned a corner. She wouldn't say she was loved up, that was not her style. She would never go weak at the knees for any man. However, it was fair to say that for the time being she was happy. Sharing her secret with Matt was definitely a weight off her shoulders; he'd been a tower of strength. She didn't know if their relationship had a future, the whole issue of kids still worried her even though Matt assured her that it wasn't at the top of his agenda. If it became an issue, then they'd talk it through together.

He seemed to thrive on the feeling that she needed him. Maybe that was part of the problem before; she had always been independent, successful and didn't need him. That must've made him feel pretty useless. She knew she could always cope on her own, but it did feel nice to have a guy to confide in. Maybe passion and excitement weren't everything; she'd had that with Marcus and look where that had gotten her. Trust, honesty and companionship was what Matt was offering her, the sex wasn't great, but she was a great teacher, she'd whip him into shape in no time and at least that'd be fun.

"How are you this morning?" he asked as he sat down on the edge of the bed.
"My head's a bit sore, I might've had one cocktail too many," she grimaced. He leaned over landed a kiss on her forehead.
"It was a good night wasn't it?"
"Yeah, I had fun and I drummed up loads of business. So many people commentated on what I'd done with the place."
"It might be a good idea to think about expanding the business, the economy's good. It's worth a thought."
"I was thinking that myself, I might even talk to Summer about it and see if she wants to help me. It would do her good to have something to channel her energy on and break this downward spiral."
"Yeah, I think she'd go for that. She spent a lot of time with CJ's friend last night...what was his name?"
"Scott, I think."
"Did she go off with him?"
"I'm not sure."
Matt sighed heavily. "Well, we'll find out this morning if he's still around."

Leyton and Claudia had stayed overnight at the penthouse in one of the guest bedrooms. They thought it only right and proper to christen the room, impolite not to really.

"Mmm, I love it when you wake me up like that," Claudia murmured.

"It's scientifically proven to be the best start of the day," he smiled as he planted soft kisses on her neck a shoulders.

"It's also scientifically proven that I need a black coffee after a night of drinking."

"As much as I hate leaving you for a second longer than I have to, I will be back with your coffee."

He grabbed the fluffy white dressing gown that was hanging on the back of the door; he blew her a kiss and headed out of the door. She hugged herself happily. She had finally confided about what happened with Marcus and it felt so good to get it out in the open with him.

Leyton walked along the hallway, through the lounge, by passing a sprawled out Jackson on the sofa and into the kitchen. He collided with CJ.

"Hey man," he muttered.

"Hey," CJ mumbled.

Leyton went to side step him, CJ blocked him.

"Listen, I just wanted to say, I'm glad you and Claudia are happy. She's had a lot of shit and deserves some happiness."

"Too much shit," Leyton replied, staring him straight in the face.

CJ shifted uncomfortably, he obviously knew what had happened between him and Claudia.

"Just do a better job than I did, don't hurt her."

"I've got no intention of hurting her and your damn right I'll treat her better than you did."

"Look, I know I was a shit, but all I'm trying to say is treat her right. I know we haven't got to a very good start but I'd like us to be friends. Claudia's special to me and I know she is to you, so there's at least one thing we have in common," CJ reasoned.

"You're right, you are a shit, but if Claudia has forgiven you then I don't see why I should hold a grudge," he held out his hand out. CJ shook it.

Summer found CJ clearing up in the lounge, Jackson was awake but whether he was in the land of the living was debateable. He was stretched out on the sofa, oblivious to anyone around him. "Bad ass hangover," was all he kept muttering.

"Haven't we all," Summer mumbled.
"You don't look too bad, I've seen you look worse than that," CJ said.
"Thanks."
"Sorry, there was a compliment in there somewhere."
"I er, I enjoyed chatting to your friend last night…" she let the sentence hang in the air.
"Scott?"
Scott – that was his name. "Yeah, Scott. He was really nice. I didn't think I'd be able to cope last night, being here without…without Jez." God it hurt just to say his name. CJ reached over and squeezed her shoulder.

"Scott's a good guy; he's a good listener too."
"I know he's not in town much longer and I wanted to thank him for last night." She hadn't worded that particularly well. She tried to read CJ's face, but whatever he was thinking didn't betray him. She made a mental note never to play poker with him.

"I have his number right here." He grabbed a pen and piece of paper and scrawled on it, he passed it to her. He'd jotted down his number and underneath he'd written Scott Morgan. She ran his name over in her mind, Scott Morgan. It stood to reason that he'd have a good strong name like that, uncomplicated, straight to the point and she was going slightly crazy. How the hell could

you tell by a name what someone was like?
She smiled up at CJ. "Thanks."

"You're welcome," he took her hands in his. "It will get better Summer, I know it doesn't seem like it, but it will. I promise."
"I wish I could believe you CJ, I really do."
"Talk to Scott, he has a knack of making things seem better"
"Nothing will bring Jez back, and that's the only thing that'll make me feel better."
CJ hugged her; Jackson stirred again from the sofa.
"Bad ass hangover."
CJ and Summer smiled at each other. "I'm gonna have my work cut out sorting him out today.

Summer was back in her bedroom, she had nowhere else to go. She sat looking over the few photos that she had how she regretted flipping out and ripping them up all. Was that only five months ago? It felt like a lifetime. If everything had gone the way it was supposed to she and Jez would be nearly parents. She placed her hand on her flat stomach, wishing she could feel a swollen pregnant tummy. Fate just seemed to be dealing her one cruel blow after another. She was down and almost out.

She picked up a photo that had been pinned to his locker. One of the fire guys had brought his stuff round in a box, on the lid in scrawly writing was Jez "Romeo" Walsh, she'd run her fingers across his name, smiling sadly at his nickname. The photo had been the first thing she'd seen when she opened the box, it had been taken last summer in Central Park.

There arms wrapped tightly around each other, laughing like they didn't have a care in the world, so happy together. Seconds after the photo was taken he'd wrestled her playfully to the ground, they giggled as they kissed each other – oblivious to the passers by. She stared hard at the picture, feeling the strength of their love, the love she would always feel for him. Jez gazed up her from the photo, his familiar blue eyes, and his sexy smile. He felt so close she could almost hear him laughing. She kissed the picture.

"I miss you."

Amber knocked on Summer's door.

"Honey, it's me. Can I come in?"

"Sure."

Amber pushed the door open; Summer was lying on her front on the bed, a picture in her hand.

"Whatcha doin?"

"Just looking at him, I'm scared I'll forget what he looks like. How I felt when I looked into his eyes, how it felt to be kissed by him."

"Summer, you'll never forget him. He was the love of your life. Your memories are locked in your heart and they'll always be there."

"I thought I'd feel better, being back here in our room, but I feel like I've taken five steps back. I miss him more than ever, it's not right that he isn't here."

"Listen, you're doing better than you think, I just wish you'd stop going off with all those guys."

Summer blushed. "It numbs the pain, you understand that."

"You're damn right I do, but I also know it stops the healing process. In the long run it'll only make things worse. If I hadn't opened up to Matt about the abortion, I'd probably be in another dead end relationship by now thinking I was in control. When in actual fact my situation was controlling me. There has to be a point where all this guy after guy stuff stops and you let someone see the real you."

"But you're so strong, I can't be like you."

"Don't you see you are being like me, the wrong me. I knew I'd never be able to have kids so I put myself in situations where I couldn't get hurt, I was rejecting them before they could do it to me. You, me and Claudia, we're the same. Claudia hid behind CJ, too scared to go out and find a real relationship, I hid behind all my in control bravado and you are hiding behind all these one night stands. I mean, what happened last night with CJ's hot friend? You went off with him didn't you?"

Summer hung her head in shame. "Yes." She didn't need to look up there know there would be a look of disappointment on Amber's face.

"It's not what you think. I came onto him and he, he...turned me down."

"What?"

"He basically said that he likes to get to know a girl before he jumps into bed with them."

Amber nodded her head. "A man with principles, I like him already."

"Amber don't, I feel so ashamed. I threw myself at him, offered myself on plate and he didn't even want me. These last few months I've behaved like a cheap hooker. I hate myself and what I've become, what's worse is knowing what Jez'd think. I was his all American princess –not anymore."

"Don't be too hard on yourself, you're grieving it makes people do strange things. The Summer I know and love is still in there, she's just taking her time coming to terms with her loss, but I know one thing, she'll be back. Jez won't think badly of you, he loved you too much. He's looking down on you, knowing how much you're hurting. He may be gone from this world, but I know he's still looking after you, he won't let you down. Have faith in the love you two have, it's strong enough to get you through this. Remember everything you two ever believed it, that's what'll make you strong again."

Summer felt more tears on her cheeks as she listened to Amber's words. "I feel him all around me, am I going mad?"
"No, you were soul mates, your love will never go away. You may not physically be together, but even in years to come part of you will always be with him."
"Why are you saying this? You don't believe in love."
"You're right I don't, but I always believed in you and Jez. That's kinda how I knew Marcus was wrong, it just didn't fit."

Summer was quiet for a few moments. "CJ gave me Scott's number. I thought I should ring and apologise for my behaviour last night. He's only in town for a few weeks. I don't want him to go back to LA thinking us New Yorkers are crazy. What d'you think?"
"If you think it's the right thing to do, do it. He sounds like a decent guy; it's worth making that call."

CHAPTER TWENTY ONE

"It was a nice surprise when you rang, I wasn't expecting it."

"Neither was I, I dialled your number a million times before I let it ring out."

Summer eyed Scott shyly as they sat in the lobby of his hotel, Park Central. He was sitting in the chair opposite.

"Y'know, you had nothing to apologise for."

"I just wanted you to know that I'm not normally like that, as you know, I've recently lost my fiancé and I'm having a hard time dealing with it. I guess I've been acting a bit strange."

"Who says grieving is easy? You have to do whatever it takes to get you through."

He smiled at her; she returned the smile, noticing those warm green eyes of his again. Her mind flashed back to when she first looked into them on the balcony as he held her so tight. Despite the turmoil she was going through, thinking back to how lovely Scott had been to her gave her the first good memory since Jez died.

"Are you ok Summer? You seem miles away."

"I'm sorry...I was just thinking about when we met."

"I didn't mean to startle you out there that night; you just looked like you needed a friend."

"More that you will ever know," she paused. "You must've thought I was some crazy lady, crying in the arms of some guy I'd never met before."

"You are not mad and for the record you didn't need to come all the way down here to say sorry, but I'm kinda glad you did."

"Why?"

"Coz, despite what you think, I really enjoyed your company."

"I enjoyed myself too, right up until the part where I made an idiot outta myself."

"Hey, that's forgotten."

"Well, I just wanted to say thanks for being there really..."

He smiled warmly at her. "I'm glad I was."

She stood up. "I better get back; I don't wanna take up anymore of your time."

"I'm not in a rush if you're not, besides which, I've just had an idea. I've finished all the research work I needed to do before I go back west, which means the rest of my stay here is my own. Only problem is...I've got no one to show me the sights. I know you've got some time on your hands, so how 'bout it?"

"I, well, er I don't know," she stammered.

"Come on Summer and then I can tell the guys back home that I had a real bona fide New Yorker, a gorgeous one at that, showing me around New York."

"Well, when you put it like that, how can I refuse?"

He had been so kind to her and whether he knew it or not that night on the balcony had been a catalyst in how she felt. She had leant against the wall, her thoughts leading her to think it would be easier to end her life and there'd be no more pain. But Scott had pulled her back from those thoughts. Jez had saved her life, running in to get her, not giving one iota for his own safety. He wanted her to live, even if it meant sacrificing his own life. If she'd done something stupid and taken her own life then Jez's death would've been in vain. She could see that now. So it was a small price to pay to show Scott New York City. Hell, she might even enjoy it.

Scott jumped up. "That's my girl; can we start with the Rockefeller Centre?"

"What? Now?"

"There's no time like the present."

A few nights later, everyone except Summer was at the Penthouse. Matt had just ordered pizza.

"Right guys, it'll be about twenty minutes, have we decided on which movie we're watching yet?"

"The girls wanna watch Titanic- again," Jackson groaned.

"Hey you know you wanna watch it too, you love Leo," Amber grinned.

"Oh purleese, I do have some taste."

Amber's cell beeped, she opened the message. "Summer says save enough pizza for her and Scott and can we watch something other than Titanic."

"She's been spending a lot of time with Scott hasn't she," Claudia noted.

"The more the better," CJ interjected.

"What d'you mean?" Matt asked.

"Did I forget to mention what Scott does for a living?" he asked innocently.

They looked at him expectantly.

"He's a shrink."

"You sly guy, did you set this up?" Matt asked, obviously pleased with the revelation.

"Well, not exactly. I mentioned to Scott that I had this friend who I thought was on the verge of a breakdown. He happened to bump into her at the party and realized this was who I'd been talking about. He wanted to help, but he didn't want to be too pushy. So I was really glad when Summer asked me for his number, I knew it would all take its natural course."

"She does seem happier," Amber acknowledged.

"Scott is great, if anyone can help her, he can. I think we're all too close to the situation, we need to grieve for Jez too," CJ said.

"You're not just a pretty face," Jackson winked at him.

"Does Summer know he's a shrink?" Claudia asked.

"I don't know, he wouldn't hide it from her, but he wouldn't make it an issue either. If it came up in conversation, he'd tell her. As far as he's concerned it's just a job."

"I just don't think she'd be very happy if she thought she was being tricked."

They heard the front door slam and foot steps down the hallway.

"Hey guys, we haven't missed the pizza have we?" Summer asked as she came into the living room.

"On its way," Jackson informed her.

"Hey Scott, great to meet you again," Matt grabbed his hand and shook it.

Amber shared a bemused look with CJ. Now that he knew what Scott did for a living he would probably go totally over the top. Scott just grinned at Matt.

"Did you meet Claudia and Leyton at the party?" Summer asked Scott.

"I don't really remember much about the party except bumping into you," he smiled fondly at Summer then turned to face everyone else. "However, Summer has told me so much about you guys, I feel like I know you already."

"Well you should know me, we shared a room in college dufus," CJ grinned.

Summer pulled Scott over to the sofa." C'mon let's get the movie on."

Claudia sat at her desk the following day, trying to answer one of Doug's emails. He wanted to know all about Leyton. She couldn't concentrate, her mind was miles away. She spun round in her chair, looking out of her window; she never tired of this breath taking view that was Manhattan, it never ceased to amaze her. She sighed; she hadn't slept very well last night. She hadn't been able to concentrate on the movie; she was too busy watching Summer. For the first time in ages she'd seen some of the old Summer, she seemed comfortable in Scott's presence. She hoped CJ was right and Scott would be able to help her, he seemed like a good guy. Claudia had felt guilty these last few months that she had found happiness whilst her friend was in the depths of despair. Leyton had made her so happy; she couldn't believe she'd gotten that lucky. He had got through her defences and she was enjoying this new found feeling of loving someone and being loved in return. Her direct line rang.

"Claudia Michaels."
"Leyton Carter."
"Hey you, I was just thinking about you."
"You must be telepathic, 'coz I was just doin the same."
"What did you want?"
"Just wanted to hear your voice babe, I was missing you. Breakfast seems like hours ago."
She smiled into the phone. This heady feeling her gave her was better than anything she'd ever known.
"How 'bout I treat you to lunch in the park at one?" he asked.
"Sounds like an offer I can't refuse."

Summer sat at her dressing table, blow drying her hair. She was meeting Scott in forty minutes. She couldn't remember the last time she bothered doing her hair properly. She actually woke up this morning looking forward to the day.
She planned on taking Scott on the Staten Island ferry, show him New York from the river. Then Jackson had promised them free entry to the Statue of Liberty. It was years since she'd been up there.

She touched the photo of herself and Jez that she'd stuck to the edge of her mirror.

"Jez, baby, am I doing the right thing? Is this ok?"
He just smiled back at her, she felt like she was betraying him. She should be grieving for him forever, everyday should be bleak. She felt guilty for enjoying the time she was spending with Scott.
"Is this what you'd want me to do?" She kissed her finger and placed it on the photo. "Love you, always."

"I bet you never get sick of this view." Scott said as he leant against the bars of the ferry, amazed by the New York skyline.
"This sounds terrible but I probably take it for granted, I've lived here all my life.
"I can't wait to get to the top of the Statue of Liberty; it was good of Jackson to get us free tickets."
"That's what comes of having friends in high places," she laughed as she turned her head to face him. He smiled, looking intently at her.
"What?"
"It's nice to hear you laugh. I know you haven't had a lot to smile about lately."

She turned her head back and looked out across the water. "Some days are better than others."
"It's hard. Your life was all mapped out. You knew where you were going, who you were going there with and now it's all changed."
"Jez was everything to me. He was the most amazing guy, sexy, romantic; loving...just everything I ever wanted. He was always there and now, and now he isn't."
"CJ said you and Jez were made for each other."
"We were," she smiled sadly.

"I know everyone keeps telling you it'll get easier, but it doesn't Why should you forget someone you loved so much?"

"The guys, they all think I should just get over it, but you're right. I don't want to forget him."

"You wont, you'll just learn to live without him, that's what gets easier, the missing him won't."

"So how do I do that?"

"Just keep doing what you're doing, take one day at a time. Build your life back."

"Y'know, when I woke up this morning I actually looked forward to the day, to being with you."

"See, I have my uses." He reached across taking her hand and giving it a reassuring squeeze.

"You're very easy to talk to; you seem to understand where I'm coming from. I feel like I've known you for ages, you don't seem to get fed up listening to me pouring out my problems."

He shrugged his shoulders. "I'm used to it, it's my job."

"What d'you mean?"

"I'm a psychiatrist to the rich and famous, plenty of them about in LA."

"You are joking?" she almost shouted.

"Nope, I'm a bona fide shrink, got letters after my name and everything."

"So, I'm a patient now am I? I thought we were friends." She was starting to get angry.

"Now you're joking, d'you know how much I charge an hour? I have two Porsche's at home and besides you have to wait at least six months to even get on my waiting list," he grinned.

"That good huh? Why two Porsche's?

"One to drive and the other 'coz its LA so what the hell!"

She couldn't stay mad at him; he was making her feel so much better. "The guys have been goin on for ages about me seeing a shrink and here I am seeing one without even knowing. How stupid am I?"

"Hey, stop it," he started, getting serious again. "Yeah, you've had a tough time, but you're doing really well. In fact, I think you're amazing and if I can use any of my expertise to help you then I will. I like hanging out with you, you're not the doom and gloom you think you are. You're fun and if I can help you with your grief then that's a bonus," he pulled her round to face him. "You are a great girl and I would like nothing more than to spend the rest of my time in New York with you, is that a deal?"

He put his hands on her shoulders and bent his head closer to hers.

"Deal," she whispered. He hugged her to him.

"We're friends, forever. Right?"

She nodded, she couldn't speak. Right now he felt like her lifeline.

Scott flung his hotel key down on the table in his hotel room and ran his hand through his hair, sighing deeply. What was he doing? What the hell was he doing? The golden rule was never ever get involved and what was he doing? He knew it wasn't strictly a doctor patient relationship, but he had to be honest, when CJ first told him about her his interest was purely professional. But now...now, Jeez, he knew he had feelings that he just shouldn't have. She had gotten under his skin the first night he met her. He looked into her eyes and that was it. Every time he held her he didn't want to let go.

Even through her grief and pain he could see the person underneath, the girl with the big heart and the ability to make you feel like the most important person on the planet without even realising she was doing it. They had been inseparable this past week. She was so kind, sweet, loving and sensitive and she was also vulnerable, which was why he couldn't tell her how he felt. His main priority had to be helping her get her head together, not confusing her even more. She had come on so much in the short time they'd spent together. He had a feeling of protectiveness towards her. According to CJ a lot of people felt like that towards her, Jez and Matt for starters. And then there was the other he couldn't tell her that she made him feel alive, Jez.

Whatever he felt for her, she would never reciprocate to him or any guy for that matter. She was in love with a ghost. No man could ever compete with that, he was her soul mate and she would never let anyone else into her heart. She was a beautiful person, inside and out, she didn't deserve to be on her own. Every time he looked into her face and saw the sparkle, hiding behind those bewitching green eyes, he wanted to wave a magic wand and put the sparkle right back where it belonged. He didn't want to push things, at the moment just being with her was enough and whatever happened, at least it was the start of a beautiful friendship.

Summer sat on the balcony, watching the sun go down over the City. It had been another intensely hot and humid August day, so she was enjoying the slight drop in temperature. She reflected on the day, it was surprising her how much she was enjoying spending time with Scott. She was glad she hadn't backed off and flipped out when he said he was a shrink, after all, it was just a job. She just couldn't shake this feeling of guilt, Scott made her laugh, what did she have to laugh about? Her soul mate was gone forever. What would Jez make of this? She thought about it for a moment, he wouldn't want her to be miserable. He'd like Scott and would be glad he was helping her and at least it was better that sleeping with random guys she met in bars, Scott was just a friend.

Amber was right though, Scott was hot, but not in the same

rugged way Jez was. It was obvious he spent a lot of time outdoors in LA, his skin had a healthy sun kissed glow and his brown hair had been streaked by the sun, he had lovely warm green eyes. She knew he enjoyed surfing which kept him fit, he wasn't as athletically built as Jez, but when he held her, his arms felt muscular which felt safe albeit a bit strange to be in. Personality wise he was kind and caring, with a great sense of humour. He made her feel totally at ease, he didn't expect anything of her, he just wanted to be her friend and God knew she needed one right now. When she weighed it up, he seemed like the perfect guy, just like Jez...except, he wasn't Jez. Still, she was sure he'd make the right woman very happy.

"Am I the right woman?" she whispered.
Shit! Where had that come form? She wasn't interested in Scott like that. Jez was the only guy for her, nobody would ever come close. He made her heart beat faster; her stomach flip and her skin get goose bumps. In fact that was the main difference between Jez and Scott, none of those things happened when she was with Scott. Yeah, he was a nice guy but she didn't really know why she was comparing him to Jez. The only guy she ever wanted or needed was Jez.
"But he's gone," she whispered out into the night.

The thoughts she'd been having about Jez and Scott were obviously fresh in her mind as she slept that night. She was walking along a beach, Jez was walking on ahead, she shouted his name. He turned and waved. She ran towards him, but the more she ran the further away he seemed. She thought he was calling her name to, but she realised the voice was coming from behind. She stopped and turned around. It was Scott; she looked back over her shoulder to Jez. He was gone.

The following day Amber and Matt met for lunch at a nearby

deli. They sat outside to enjoy the summer sunshine, even though it was really too hot to be outside for too long. Amber took a sip of her skinny latte. She had been laughing with Matt about how enthusiastic he'd been about Scott once he discovered his occupation.

"If he did any other type of job, you'd be straight in there doing that big brother thing you do."
"Maybe, maybe not. I hope I learned my lesson after Jez...Anyways, he's just a friend isn't he?"
"For the time being."
"You think there's more to it?"
"I hope there's more to it. That girl deserves a break and he's good for her."

They were silent for a few minutes, Matt thinking about his little sister and hoping to God she could get her life back together. He knew he would have to stop being so over protective. It still preyed on his mind how badly he treated Jez. He would only start worrying about it if it became an issue. He couldn't see anything happening between Summer and Scott, for starters he was only here on vacation, he'd be going back to LA soon. Amber cut into his thoughts.

"This is really nice; I can't remember the last time we met up for lunch."
"Probably when we first started going out."
"We didn't treat each other very well did we?"
"Nope, but look at us now. I'm spending less time at the office 'coz I want to get home to be with you..."
"And I'm a totally different person," she finished.
"No, you're still the same person, you've just laid all your ghosts to rest and I'm so proud of you. I love you Amber Gordon."
"I do feel happy and contented now. I never thought I'd be in a

normal relationship."

"Well, the normal is debatable," he grinned. He stood up and bent down to kiss her. "I gotta run; I'm in a meeting at two. I'm planning on finishing early. Can you get out too?"

She quickly ran her schedule through her head. "Yeah, I suppose I could."

"Right, meet you at four thirty – in bed," he grinned. With that he was gone. She watched him until he got lost in the crowd. Yeah, she was happy; she'd never envisaged that she might be in a position to be in a stable relationship.

On the other side of the City Summer and Scott were sitting on a bench in Strawberry Fields in Central Park.

"I love Central Park."

"You do, why?"

"I feel like it's a tiny piece of sanctuary in the middle of all these skyscrapers," she replied.

"I feel like that about my house on the beach."

"You've got a beach house as well as two Porsche's?"

"Yes I have Miss Penthouse in new York," he grinned.

"Touché."

"Anyway, I love my beach house. It's almost magical watching the sun set or sun rise over the Pacific; everyone thinks the sky is just blue, not in California. It's purple, red, orange, yellow – any colour you want."

"Sounds lovely."

"Y'know what, when I go back home, you can come visit. I'll show you my town and I'll show you the best sun set or sun rise you've ever seen."

"What's better, sunset or sunrise?"

"Sitting on a beach, a fire beside you watching the sun come up, makes you feel like the only person on the planet."

"Sounds nice, I'd like that."

He already had the image running through his mind, he promised himself he wouldn't tell her how he felt but that didn't mean he couldn't think about it.

"It would be good to visit you in LA; my pasty features could do with some Californian sunshine."

"What you talkin 'bout, you're gorgeous."

"And you're too sweet."

They sat in silence for a few moments.

"Jez and I were going to move to the suburbs once we were married. We wanted a garden for the kids; we even talked about a weekend house in Connecticut. We had so many plans..."

"That's the sad thing when you lose someone, you'll always have the memories, but you'll never have the dreams."

"That's so true. I don't want the house in the 'burbs anymore. If I ever did meet someone else, I could never do any of the things I planned with Jez. I'd feel like I was betraying him, does that make sense?"

"Perfect, but y'know, you'll make new dreams and plans when you're ready."

"So, using your amazing skills as a shrink – am I completely insane?"

"Totally, the men in white coats are behind that tree over there waiting for you."

"Quit making fun of me," she pretended to tell him off, but she couldn't keep the smile out of her voice.

"Honestly Summer, you're doing great, stop being so hard on yourself. You know I enjoy being with you and I just hope that the next three weeks go real slow 'coz I'm in no rush to get back to LA and back to work with the nutcases."

She laughed. "So you'd rather stay in New York with this nutcase?"

"I've already told you, you're not a nutcase."

"Y'know what, I don't want you to go either Scott. You have no idea how much you've helped me, you mean a lot to me. You understand me; you've made me laugh when I never thought I would again. Promise me we'll keep in touch when you go home. I've found such a good friend in you, I don't want to lose you, I've lost too much already." Her bottom lip began to quiver.

"Come here." He pulled her closer and put his arm around her, she rested her head on his chest.

"You are stuck with me for life Summer Stevens. D'you know how many flights there are between here and LA everyday? If you need me, I will be on the first flight to you. Likewise, you can jump on a plane and turn on my doorstep in the middle of the night if you need to. I will always be around for you."

"Thank you," she whispered.

To any onlookers that were passing they might have smiled at the young couple on the bench, looking so much in love. The young handsome man with his arm wrapped protectively around his beautiful girlfriend, what a perfect couple they looked, but appearances can be deceptive.

Summer was feeling a great sense of unrest. It was comforting having Scott's arms around her, but just as she felt she would be betraying Jez by buying a house in Connecticut she felt just as bad being in another mans arms. A man she knew she had feelings for, she tried to tell herself they were feelings she had for a friend, like CJ or Jackson, but deep down she knew she was kidding herself. It wasn't like those one night stands, she'd been detached from them. It was just a process to numb the pain. This new feeling frightened her, she was trying to hold onto Jez, but he was slipping away from her. She was so confused and didn't know which way to turn.

Scott, on the other hand couldn't believe his luck. Here he was on a beautiful day, in a beautiful setting, with the even more beautiful Summer in his arms. He couldn't explain how she made him feel. Hearing her laughter made the hairs on the back of his neck stand up. He wanted to look after her forever, she made him feel special. She had an aura about her that she didn't even know about; she turned guy's heads without even realising it. Just sitting here he'd had at least six envious looks from guys passing by because he was with her and she was oblivious. Maybe that was her attractiveness, she was stunning, but didn't realize it. Such a refreshing change from all those plastic bimbos back home. She was like a breath of fresh air. Sitting her like this, he could at least pretend for a few moments that they were really together. He knew it was just a fantasy; she obviously had Jez on a pedestal. Was the guy really so perfect or had she immortalised him into some kinda saint? All he knew was she wanted this moment to go on forever. God a shrink would have a field day with him.

CHAPTER TWENTY TWO

Scott lay awake in his uncomfortable bed in his dull hotel room. He normally didn't have any trouble sleeping, but Summer was on his mind. He was thinking back to when he was telling her about the views for his beach house and describing sitting by a fire watching the sunrise. There were bits he'd left out, what was really going through his mind was that she was there with him.

They'd be sitting on the beach, Summer sitting in between his legs, her back leaning into him. He'd have his arms wrapped tightly around her and they'd be cuddled under a blanket. The fire would be crackling away beside them, the light from the fire casting a warm glow over her face. Every now and then she'd tilt her face up to his and he would kiss her so gently and lovingly.

The thought of it made him need a cold shower, but then that would wake him up even more. He sighed heavily and put his hands behind his head. He so wanted to be with her, but he didn't think Summer would ever let herself love anyone ever again. She was so devoted to Jez, by all accounts they were the all American golden couple. He'd seen a photo of the two of them together; they made a very good looking couple. Jez reminded him of all the High School jocks he'd ever met, the kinda guys all the girls wanted to be with. It made him feel quite inadequate, whether it was Jez's good looks or just the fact that he knew in Summer's eyes he would never measure up to Jez. He knew he was just as capable of loving Summer as Jez was. The question was, would Summer ever give him the opportunity?

"I was hoping to spend some time with Scott while he's here, but he seems to be busy with Summer." CJ passed Jackson the toast that he'd just made.

"Jealous are we?" Jackson took a bite of the toast.

"No, actually I think it's great for Summer to be spending time with Scott, according to him they're having a ball. I'm not sure it's good for Scott though."

"Why?"

"I've known Scott a long time, I know he's falling for her."

"Are you sure? They looked pretty normal to me the other night."

"Yeah, but it was the little looks he kept giving her when she wasn't looking, trying to be discreet 'coz he know she wont be interested."

"She might be."

"She's hardly in a position to be ready for a relationship is she? Jez hasn't even been gone six months yet. She'll never get over him and no one will ever compare to him, not even a guy like Scott."

"Scott seems like he can look after himself. Besides, whose to say a new guy isn't what she needs right now? A decent guy not all those guys she's been sleeping with when she was drunk."

"Yes, but she'll never get over Jez."

"I know, I heard you the first time, you're right she never will, but why should she? Why should she forget someone who she loved so much? She needs to move forward instead and maybe Scott's just the guy to help her do that."

"Yeah, that makes sense, I just want to see Summer happy, that's all."

"We all do," Jackson reached over and squeezed CJ's hand.

Scott woke up to a knock on the door.

"Jeez," he muttered. He looked at his watch, seven thirty. He yanked back the covers and made his way to the door, running his hand through his hair in an attempt to smooth it down. He was more than surprised to see Summer standing at his door when he opened it.

"Hey you, this is a nice wake up call. Room service has definitely improved."

"I know it's early…" she began, she kept her eyes trained on his face, she was very aware that he was naked except for his boxer shorts. She really was trying not too look, but she couldn't help notice how tanned he was and although not as muscular as Jez, he had a defined six pack. Why was she looking? Why was she interested?

"What did I say? If you need to come knocking in the middle of the night, it was fine with me."

"I've been awake for most of the night, I just thought I should wait for a more decent hour."

"This sounds serious," he winked at her. "C'mon in, I'll order us some breakfast."

"No, honestly couldn't eat a thing."

"At least a coffee then."

"I had to come and speak to you."

She looked round for somewhere to sit. Scott obviously wasn't particularly tidy, his clothes were strewn over the two chairs in the room. She sat at the foot of the bed, he sat at the other end.

"So, what's so important?" he asked, looking closely at her. She'd been up all night and she still looked amazing. He'd had about three hours sleep and looked like shit.

"I kinda think you have the wrong impression of me. There's stuff you don't know, bad stuff."

She was nervous, she didn't know why she felt the need to confide in him, but if the were going to be friends she didn't want any secrets. She'd had enough to last a life time.

"Did CJ tell you that Jez and I weren't together when he…when he died?"

Scott could only shake his head. If she and Jez had broken up, maybe there was hope for him yet.

"I don't really know where to begin...I suppose at the start would make sense..."

So she began with the car crash and the death of her parent's, telling him all about how she met Jez and how they had fallen in love almost instantly. She then went on to explain about Marcus, who he was and some of the horrible things he'd done. She told him all about the vacation in Colorado and how she'd discovered Marcus' body in the hot tub. Then, finding the strength from somewhere she told him about Jez's confession and Marcus' revelation that Summer and Jez shared the same dad.

"Sick," was all Scott could mutter.

"It wasn't true, we weren't really related. It was all a lie," she protested.

"Not you, this Marcus dude."

She carried on. "Once Jez told me the reason he'd killed Marcus, I didn't see how we could be together. We loved each other so much, but we had no future. Amber and Jackson were suspicious of Marcus' story, knowing what a liar he was. They found evidence to prove that Jez and I weren't half brother and sister. Jez killed him for nothing and our relationship was over for nothing. Jez never got the chance to tell me this, he found out the truth the day he...the day he died. I lost our baby and I lost Jez all because of Marcus. We never got the chance to make up, to say I love you. I know he loved me and he knew I still loved him, but somehow that isn't enough. I really wasn't coping well after he died. I kinda went off the rails a bit. Remember that night at the party when I tried to seduce you and you rejected me?"

"I wanted you, I want you so badly," he whispered. If she heard him she didn't acknowledge what he'd said.

"That was basically what I'd been doing till I met you, sleeping with guys, didn't matter if I knew their name or not. I hate myself for it and Jez would hate me to. I was always his sweet girl next door type that he loved looking after and now I can't even look after myself." The tears slid down her face.

"I'll look after you."

She smiled gratefully.

"I can't believe what you've been through, it's one hell of a nightmare. I don't understand how it took so long for you to find out what Jez did. Didn't the cops investigate properly?"

She'd come this far, she may as well tell him the rest, she took a deep breath.

"This is probably the worst part. I can't believe I'm telling you this."

"You can tell me anything."

"What we did was illegal, we got rid of the body. We protected the killer. We knew it was on of us and we were helping out a friend, who, at the time we didn't know and I never in my wildest dreams thought it could've been Jez. If I'm honest, if the thought ever entered my head I dismissed it straight away. We were and still are guilty of covering up murder."

For the first time in his life Scott was speechless. He'd heard some things in his career, but never something quit like this and never from someone he cared about. No wonder she was in such a mess.

"That's changed things hasn't it? You don't wanna know me anymore. That's ok, I understand. It was important to me to be totally honest with you even though I knew it might mean the end of our friendship..."

She got up off the bed. "Thanks for everything Scott, it's been fun."

She turned to leave and walked towards the door. Once she reached it, she couldn't bring herself to look back, so she let it shut behind her. The sound of the door closing bought Scott back to his senses. Was he gonna let this girl walk out of his life? Was he hell. The past should be well and truly left where it was. He jumped off the bed and ran out of the room, he saw her walking along the corridor, she was almost at the elevator.

"Summer, wait!" He ran down the hall way not caring that all he had on were his boxers. When he got to her he reached out and pulled her to him.

"It changes nothing, there's nothing you can do about the past, just leave it where it is. All I care about is the future and I hope to God my future involves you."

He gently put his finger and thumb against her chin and tilted her face up towards his. He bent down and kissed her lips, their eyes locked together, everything seemed to be going in slow motion and the few seconds they gazed at each other felt like ages. He closed his eyes, kissing her again, her mouth opening underneath his, their tongues teasing each other.

The elevator pinged, breaking the spell. Summer moved wordlessly away from him and got into the elevator. They still held the look between them right up until the doors closed. Scott leant against the wall with his head in his hands, he slid down the wall muttering to himself.

"Shit, shit." What had he done?

Summer sat in the lobby of Scott's hotel. She didn't know where to go or what to do. Her emotions were all over the place, She hadn't expected to feel so sad walking out on Scott, it had suddenly hit her how close they'd become and how much she valued his friendship. She was also relieved that she'd shared the whole Goddamn nightmare with him. She didn't know he was gonna run out after her and she certainly hadn't seen that kiss coming.

She hadn't known how to react, her instincts had been to run away, but maybe she wanted to stop running and besides, it'd been a nice kiss. It hadn't swept her off her feet, not like Jez did every time he kissed her. God she had to stop comparing them, all she knew was she enjoyed Scott's company. He might not be Jez, but he was his own person and she liked the guy. The kiss. She sighed, his lips had been warm and soft and she had felt...God how did she feel?

Part of her felt like it was natural, she and Scott had been growing closer by the day, the rest of her felt like she should've stopped it. What would Jez think? Why did she feel like she'd cheated on him? What was Scott thinking right now? She wished she hadn't got in the elevator. There had never been any awkwardness between them and now she'd walked out on him, twice. She couldn't leave things like this. She got up and headed back towards the elevator. She didn't have a clue what she was going to say to him, but she had to see him.

Scott lay, staring up at the ceiling. He'd been so stupid, kissing her like that. He knew she wasn't ready, he just wanted to make her see that all this Marcus shit didn't matter to him. She was all that he cared about and now he'd ruined any chance he might've had with her. He'd been prepared to wait however long it took, now he'd messed it all up. He'd be a friend for as long as she needed, until she was ready to take it to the next level.

He knew how emotionally scarred she was, all he wanted to do was love her back to life, make her feel alive again. Maybe he could pass the kiss off as a kiss between friends. Only problem was, he couldn't remember ever kissing a friend like that. Why was falling in love never easy? Falling? Who was he kidding? He had already well and truly fallen. There was a knock at the door. Wearily he pulled himself up off the bed. God he needed some sleep.

"Summer," he said in surprise as he opened the door. She stepped closer to him, staring him straight in the eye. He was aware that the space between them was minimal. She wrapped her arms around his neck and pulled him to her, kissing him. He pulled her even closer, his arms encircling her waist as he kissed her deeply. When they moved apart he had a quizzical smile on his face.

"Sorry Scott, it was rude of me to walk out in the middle of our conversation. I hadn't finished what I wanted to say.
"Keep talkin'- anything else you wanna say?"
"Plenty." She shut the door behind her. He took her by the hand and led her to the end of the bed, as soon as they sat down they were kissing again. Scott was running his fingers through her hair. He stopped suddenly.

"What's wrong? Don't you want me?"
He heard the panic in her voice and knew she was thinking about the night they met.
"God Summer, I want you like I've never wanted anyone before. I just don't want to rush you, we'll take it as slow as you like. You don't have to do this, I don't want to push you."
"You're not pushing me."
"I just want you to be sure."
She leaned forward and kissed him. All protests were forgotten.

Amber was making scrambled eggs in the kitchen, well scrambled egg whites, when Matt walked into the kitchen looking serious.

"Seen Summer this morning?"

She shook her head as she scooped the eggs out of the pan.

"She's not in her room," he sighed.

"So?"

"So? So she obviously stayed out all night. Jesus," he ran a hand through his hair. "I thought all this staying out all night had stopped. She's seemed so much better since she met Scott."

"There's probably a perfectly reasonable explanation."

"Why is she going out having all these one night stands again?"

"Just hold it right there buster! Firstly we don't know if she is and secondly you are in danger of doing that overprotective big brother thing again."

"I'm sorry," he sighed. "I just worry."

"And don't we know it."

"Maybe I should call Scott, he might know where she is," he reached for his cell phone. Amber grabbed it.

"I'll talk to Summer when she gets back."

Summer lay in Scott's arms. He was gently stroking her arm and every now and then kissing the top of her head. She could hear his heart beating fast as she rested her head on his chest.

"Whatcha thinkin?"

"I'm thinking I can't believe I'm doing this."

"I knew I shouldn't have pushed you, I'm sorry."

"No, I don't mean that. I mean I can't believe I'm here in your arms and I don't hate myself."

"What?"

"You know, what I said before about those one night stands, how much I hated them and me."

"Ah, but I'm not a one night stand am I?"

"I hope not. Being here with you, in this bed feels strange, but it feels right. Does that make sense?"

"Sure it does. I'm a shrink remember? So I suppose I should feel flattered."

"Stop making fun of me, this is a big deal for me. I feel like I've turned a corner."

"I know and I'm really proud of you. The first time I saw you I wanted to help you and I'm gonna keep doing that, although, I must stress this isn't my normal process."

"Your patients don't know what they're missing out on," she laughed.

Love her back to life? Goddamn right he would.

It was late on in the afternoon when Summer returned to the apartment. Scott was taking her out for a meal so she'd popped home to get changed. She was hoping Amber was around, she needed to talk. She found both Amber and Claudia in the living room.

"The wanderer returns," Amber smiled.

"What?"

"Matt was getting stressed, he didn't know where you were last night."

"Last night? I was here all night. I slipped out early this morning.

"So spill, where have you been?"

"Well, lets just say, I'm glad you're both here 'coz I need to talk."

Amber and Claudia looked at her expectantly as she settled herself down on the leather sofa.

"It's about Scott, we've spent all day together."

"Honey, you've spent all day with him for weeks," Claudia acknowledged.

"No, I mean I've spent all day in bed with him."

Both Amber and Claudia leaned forward.

"You go girl," Amber cheered.

"How did that happen?"

"I'm not sure, it just kind did. It wasn't like all those one night stands, this was different. It felt right but I feel so damn guilty. What would Jez think? D'you think he'd hate me?"

"Don't be stupid, he'd be a helluva lot happier about this that what you were doing. Of course it feels strange, but Jez'd want you to be happy," Claudia replied.

"If it was the other way round, you'd want Jez to be happy wouldn't you?"

Summer nodded. "I wasn't looking for anyone, I wasn't expecting this to happen. I love Jez with all my heart and I always will. I know if the fire hadn't happened, we'd still be together. I'd have forgiven him for Marcus, for the simple fact that I loved him. I feel I've betrayed him by being with Scott, belittled our love. I don't want to be with anyone except Jez and yet I enjoying spending time with Scott. He's a nice guy and he makes me laugh but I haven't got that feeling about him."

"What feeling?" Claudia asked.

"Well, he's an attractive guy and real fun to be with and maybe possibly, eventually I could love him if I was ready to, but I haven't had that feeling of floating on air.

Amber laughed. "We're not all that lucky honey."

"What d'you mean? As soon as I saw Jez when I was in the car, it was like wham bam. Something connected with us straight away, I didn't know what had hit me. He made me feel dizzy with excitement at the thought of being with him. I like Scott, but I don't get that same feeling."

"You and Jez were one of the lucky few who have had that kind of passionate relationship that sends you crazy. You can't eat or sleep with anticipation, they make your heart beat faster just by the way they look at you and you can't think of anything but them," Amber replied.

"If you've never had that feeling, how come you know so much about it?"

"I read too many trashy novels," Amber smiled. "It's only these past few months that I'd say I was in love and it's probably for the first time, but just because Matt doesn't make my heart race it doesn't mean it's wrong. The same is true for you. You don't feel those intense feelings with Scott that you had for Jez, but that only makes what you and Jez had all the more special. You have to stop comparing Scott to Jez though, you hold Jez so high in your expectations that Scott hasn't got a hope in hell of getting any closer to you. Unless you let him.

"Look at me and Leyton, if I'd have said yes the first time he asked me out I'd have saved myself so much misery."

"You'll never forget Jez, but give Scott a chance. You deserve to be happy."

"Amber's right, you've got to move on sooner or later."

"You're forgetting one thing guys,"

"What's that?" They asked in unison.

"Scott goes back to LA in three weeks".

CHAPTER TWENTY THREE

The next two weeks flew past really quickly for Summer and Scott as she
continued to show him the sights of New York. They caught the Knicks playing at Madison Square Garden, they went up the Empire State Building, caught a show on Broadway and ate at her favourite restaurant, the Bridge Street Café in Lower Manhattan. She loved its waterside location and just sitting there watching the world go by.

They also spent a great deal of time in Scott's hotel room, in bed. She was still battling this huge feeling of guilt towards Jez, but she was trying to work through it. She had to, it was slowly starting to dawn on her that Jez was never coming back. She also knew that she cared about Scott more than she probably should. Her body and emotions had become intermingled with his. She supposed on reflection that it was a good thing that she hadn't fallen head over heels for Scott, it would've just led to more heartache, him being in LA and her in New York.

Once he went back to LA she was sure their romance would fizzle out, but she hoped they would always remain good friends, he was a special guy. She hadn't really given much thought about him going home but now it entered her head it made her feel sad. She realised that she wished he wasn't leaving, they'd become so close. Maybe she had to treat the whole thing as a holiday romance. Scott had shown her that she was going to be ok. Maybe that was all she needed from him.

Waving bagels at them, Scott called in to CJ and Jackson's for breakfast.
"Hey guys."

"Hey, how's it goin?" Jackson asked.

"Cool man, cool. It's a beautiful day, the sun is shining and the birds are singing."

"Jeez, you've got it bad," Jackson rolled his eyes.

"I suppose your good mood is down to Summer?" CJ asked.

"I'm from California, I'm always in a good mood but, in answer to your question I am in a particularly good mood and yes it's 'coz of Summer."

"Are you sleeping together?" CJ asked.

"Yes." Scott was surprised by the directness of the question.

"D'you think that's wise?"

"Why not?"

"Summer's very fragile at the moment; she's had a lot to deal with these past few years. Not just Jez, but stuff you don't know about and I just think…"

"You mean Marcus?" he asked innocently interrupting CJ. He saw the worried look pass between CJ and Jackson.

"She told you about that?" CJ asked.

"Yep," Scott nodded.

"Every' ting?" Jackson asked. "She told y'all what happened to him?"

Scott nodded again.

"Jeeeezus, I can't believe she did that." CJ put his hand to his fore head.

"What's the big deal? There's no need to dwell on it anymore. Marcus is dead; Jez is dead so there's no need for anyone to know you covered it up. Draw a line under it. It's gone, it's in the past."

"It's just hung over us for so long," CJ sighed.

"There's no need for it to. Just file it in a box in your mind marked unwanted."

"I thought you were supposed to talk through problems, get

therapy," Jackson said.

"For 400 bucks an hour? Just get over it. The Marcus situation has been dealt with, when Jez confessed it should've given you all closure. The problem is no longer there. That'll be 400 bucks please."

CJ grinned. "Friends should get free advice. Anyway, you've changed the subject; we were talking about you and Summer."

"Why did you wanna know if we're sleeping together?"

"I just don't want her to get hurt anymore. It's obvious how you feel about her and she seems to have gotten close to you. I just don't think she'll cope very well when you go home, she's not strong enough."

"You're wrong, she's stronger than you think. She's come on so much these past few weeks. She wants to come out the other side. She's so special, I've never met anyone like her."

"So what about when you go back to LA?"

"There are such things as planes, cells, email. It'll be fine," Scott smiled.

"Well I reckon it's great. It's about time that girl had something to smile about and there's nothing that puts a smile on your face like sex," Jackson laughed as he high fived Scott.

Despite a full day sight seeing with Scott, Summer found herself wide awake at three am. She'd been asleep but she'd had a dream that had awoken her. It was the reoccurring dream, when she was on the beach trying to catch up with Jez. This time when he stopped, he waved to her. Scott was chasing her and when he caught her up he kissed her. Not a passionate kiss, just softly on the lips. She turned back to Jez; he smiled, blew her a kiss and was gone.

She didn't know whether to ask Scott what it meant after all he was a shrink. Although deep down she knew exactly what it meant. Even in her dreams Jez was slipping away and there was nothing she could do to stop it.

She wondered if after next week she'd ever see Scott again, she hoped so. She absentmindedly fiddled with her engagement ring; she knew it still sparkled, unlike her. It never entered her head to take it off, as long as she wore it Jez would always be a part of her. She rolled over onto her side; she'd spent the last couple of nights with Scott in the hotel room. She'd never let him stay here, not in her and Jez's room. She was surprised how much she was missing having Scott next to her, she felt lonely. She half thought about going over to his hotel, but it wasn't really a good idea to go traipsing across the city in the middle of the night. Besides which, what would she do next week, get on a plane at three am? No, she didn't think so. She closed her eyes, she wanted to go back to sleep and dream about Jez, that they were together and life was uncomplicated.

Scott was also awake, for someone who usually slept like a log he was having major problems since meeting Summer. He was really missing her tonight, he loved turning over and finding her next to him. He imagined her lying in bed asleep, had she missed him tonight or was she dreaming about Jez? He'd never expected to come to New York and fall in love with this amazing woman. He wondered if she knew he was in love with her, she must know he was serious about her. CJ said it was obvious to all of them so surely she must've seen it to. Not that she was thinking clearly at the moment. He knew she was battling with her emotions and the feeling that she was betraying Jez.

His job had taught him how crazy relationships were and if he was advising one of his patients on this particular situation he'd tell them to run a mile. But he couldn't do that; he couldn't walk out on Summer. His attraction to her was too strong, she made him feel amazing. The closer his flight got, the more he didn't want to go. He had to go back, but he didn't want to leave Summer. They had spent practically every moment together since she first came to his hotel over a month ago; she had become such a big part of his life. It was bad enough that she was in bed without him just the other side of the city. How was he gonna feel when it was thousands of miles between them?

An image flashed through his mind, Summer sitting on the veranda at his beach house dressed in one of his shirts, her long legs stretched out over the rail as she watched the ocean, He called out to her, she turned to look at him and threw her head back as she smiled, the smile reaching her green eyes and making them sparkle. She looked so relaxed and at ease, in a place where she felt comfortable. The picture formed so quickly in his mind but he kept replaying it over and over again. She looked so happy sitting there looking out over the Pacific, in stark contrast to when he first saw her looking miserable as she surveyed the New York skyline.

A smile slowly spread across his face, of course! That was the answer. Why didn't he think of it before? She would never be able to get over Jez while she was here in New York, surrounded by memories of him. He could help her make a fresh start in a new place. There was nothing keeping her here, well nothing except a ghost. He could offer her a whole new life in LA. He wanted her in his life so much; he couldn't bear the thought of getting on that plane and not knowing when he'd see her again. It seemed the perfect solution. He closed his eyes and with a smile on his face, fell asleep.

Summer had also succumbed to sleep after taking two sleeping pills. As she hoped, she was dreaming about Jez, unaware of Scott's life changing decision.

Claudia and Leyton met up with Summer and Scott for lunch a few days later. Scott was still waiting for the right moment to ask Summer to move to LA, he had no idea what her response would be. He hoped that she'd fling her arms around him and say she'd been thinking the same thing. Then reality would kick in and he'd remember he was up against Jez the great and the only weapon he had to fight with was his heart.

"So, how have you been enjoying New York, Scott?" Leyton asked.

"It's been beyond my wildest dreams," he replied as he squeezed Summer's hand under the table. She smiled at him.

"It's been great to finally meet you, I'd heard so many stories about your college days from CJ. It's a shame you have to go back West, we're only just beginning to get to know you," Claudia said.

"I know, it's a bummer, but I gotta get back to work. All my patients will be goin even crazier without their usual shrink. Y'know you guys can come visit anytime you want, there's plenty of room at my house," he smiled.

"That'd be cool, we could go star spotting," Leyton said excitedly.

"Did Amber mention Saturday night to you?" Claudia asked.

Summer shook her head.

"We thought we'd do pizza night and have a few drinks, a sort of farewell for Scott." She noticed as she said farewell, both their faces clouded over briefly.

"That'd be great, I was hoping to see you all before I left."

Scott glanced at his watch. "Lunch was great, but we better get going, we've got some serious shopping to do. I need some tacky souvenirs and I wanna treat this little lady as a thank you for looking after me." He put his arm around Summer's shoulders and pulled her close.

"You don't need to get me anything, it's been fun."

He pulled her to her feet. "We'll catch you guys later."

Claudia watched them walk out of the deli hand in hand.

"Have I missed something? Are they together?" Leyton asked.

"Unofficially, yes but I don't think either of them will know how they feel until he gets on that plane home," Claudia sighed.

"I'm so glad you don't live on the other side of the country," he leaned across to kiss her.

"Mmm. Me too," she murmured as she pressed her lips up against his.

By the time Saturday night came round Summer wasn't in a very sociable mood. She appreciated the guys making an effort for Scott, but she had this weird feeling of possessiveness over him. They only had two nights left together and she wanted it to just be the two of them. She sat at her dressing table, applying her make up.

"Summer, it's me. Can I come in?" She heard Scott ask as he knocked on her bedroom door.

"Sure."

"Hey you," he walked over to her, bending down to kiss her as he reached her.

"Looking good Stevens," he grinned.

She was wearing the black off the shoulder top with the pair of DKNY jeans that he got for her on their shopping trip. She looked really sexy, her bare neck and shoulders were just asking to be kissed.

"You spoilt me far too much, but thank you anyway."

"It was cool spending my hard earned cash on you, In fact there's something I forgot to give you."

He pulled out a long velvet box from his jeans pocket and handed it to her. She opened it slowly. Inside was a white gold necklace with an emerald jewel.

"Scott," she whispered. "I can't accept this, it's too much."

"No it's not; let me put it on for you." He draped it around her bare neck and kissed her shoulder as he fixed the clasp.

"I don't know what to say."

She spun round to face him and found herself in his arms.

Her head was spinning. It felt so nice to be in Scott's arms, to feel protected again. Yet over her shoulder she could see Jez smiling at her from the photo on the bedside table. What was she doing? She felt like she was torn between living in the past and finding a future, she really didn't have a clue where she wanted to be.

"C'mon, lets go find the guys." She grabbed his hand and headed out of the room,

After going through a couple of bottles of wine, the laughter and the chatter were getting louder. Summer headed off to the kitchen to get more wine. When she returned she stood by the door watching, unnoticed for a while. She surveyed the group, her eyes resting on Amber and Matt, now there was a couple she never would've put money on working out. However, since Amber had told Matt about the abortion they looked happier than they'd ever been, she wouldn't say they were loved up but they seemed to have turned a corner.

Claudia and Leyton on the other hand had a great relationship, she watched them slouched on the sofa, laughing. Their bodies intertwined, it somehow made them look like one person, like they fitted together perfectly. As happy as she was for Claudia, sometimes seeing her together with Leyton was a painful reminder of the soul mate she'd lost.

She'd turned her gaze to CJ and Jackson, who was sitting on the floor at CJ's feet. Despite CJ coming out nothing much had changed, Jackson still camped it up and CJ was the quiet guy he'd always been. The only slight difference was the occasional looks that passed between them; they were an intensely private couple.

Finally she looked over to Scott who was chatting with CJ, probably reminiscing about old college buddies and stories. How did she really feel about him? All she knew at that moment in time was that she didn't want Monday morning to arrive. Who knew when she'd see him again? She needed some fresh air so she slipped out onto the balcony.

Looking for Summer, Scott had a feeling of déjà vu as he watched her leaning against the wall of the balcony out over the city. He knew she loved that view. Question was, was she willing to trade it for the Pacific? Her hair blew gently in the night air. Was it only just over a month ago that he stood here for the first time. It seemed like only yesterday but it also felt like a lifetime. Well, it was now or never, time to lay his cards on the table. He took a deep breath as he walked up to her. He whispered her name, not wanting to startle her. He put his arms around her waist and turned her round to face him.

"Sorry, was I dragging you away from your thoughts?"
"Perhaps I needed dragging away from them," she smiled sadly.
"I've just been watching you and it was like the first time I saw you but I know when you come out here you have different memories and maybe you don't even think about me."
"I'm sorry, it's just Jez and I…"
"I know, it's ok. I just got to thinking it'd be nice to make our own memories."

"But you're going back to LA on Monday."

"Yeah and the closer it's getting, the more I don't wanna leave you."

"I'll miss you too."

"OK, here's the thing. Summer, I'm totally crazy about you, I've fallen in love with you," he whispered.

All she could do was look at him, she didn't know what to say

"I know you're still hurting over Jez and missing him like hell, but I also think you have feelings for me. I know you're confused but until you're in that place where you're ready to love again, well, I've got enough love for both of us."

"Scott, I do like you, more than I should and maybe we could work but you'll be the other side of the country."

"That's why I'm hoping that when I get on that plane on Monday you'll be with me and not just for a vacation. Come to LA with me."

"I...I...can't." She shook her head.

"Yes you can. There's nothing keeping you here. You'll still be able to visit your friends, they could come out to us. You can get a job, start living again. If you stay here you'll always be living with a ghost, Jez totally surrounds you here."

She was finding it hard to take it in and hold it together. This had come like a bolt out of the blue. "If I leave here, I'll feel like I've left Jez behind."

"You wont, he'll always be in your heart, I'm just hoping there's enough room in there for me and if you come to LA I think we could be happy, I could make you happy. I know I'm not Jez, but I'd never try to be like him. I'm just me, a guy who is in love with you. Please come with me Summer, please," he pleaded.

"I can't give you an answer right now."

"The last thing I wanna do is push you into any decision, but from what you've told me about Jez, he'd want you to be happy..." he placed his hands on her shoulders, she broke away.

"Don't tell me what Jez'd what, you don't know him. He was mine, all mine and what he wanted was me," she screamed at him. Tears sliding down her face, she backed away from him and ran back inside.
"Shit."
He clenched his fist and wrapped his other hand around it. He knew it was too much to hope that she'd come with him. Now what was he going to do?

CHAPTER TWENTY FOUR

Summer ran through the apartment straight into her bedroom, slamming the door behind her. The guys in the living room all exchanged worried looks as they heard her tear through the apartment.

"I'll go and see if she's ok," Amber said.

She found Summer huddled up on the window seat in her room, her legs pulled up close to her chest, her arms wrapped tightly round them. She'd rested her head on her knees and she was visibly shaking as she cried.

"What's the matter honey? Is it Scott?"

Summer nodded her head. Amber went over to her and laid her hand on her back, gently rubbing it.

"You'll still see each other," she consoled.

"He wants me to go with him."

"He wants what?"

Summer lifted her head up and looked into her friend's concerned face. "LA. He wants me to move to LA and be with him…on Monday."

"Jesus, what did you say?"

"Nothing, what could I say? I can't make a decision like that. I just can't pack up and go."

The two girls were quiet for a moment until Amber broke the silence.

"Yes you can. I think you should go."

"What? Are you crazy?"

"Nope, just thinking a helluva lot clearer than you. This is your chance Summer, your chance to be happy. There's nothing keeping you here. Even if things don't work out with you and

Scott you can build a new life. Away from the New York and the ghosts of your past, Marcus and…" she couldn't finish the sentence.

"I can't leave Jez, I won't leave him. Jez is here."

"No Summer, Jez has gone."

"Thought y'all could do with a beer." Scott took the bottle from Jackson.

"Cheers," he took a big gulp. "I've really gone and messed up."

"Happens to the best of us."

"You were right, well CJ was, he always knew me better than I knew myself. It's not gonna be enough to see her every now and then. Just to make do with emails and just hearing her voice on the phone and knowing she's so far away. I don't wanna be without her. I told her I'm in love with her and asked her to come to LA with me, permanently."

"She said no?"

"She didn't say either way."

"So there's a chance she might say yes."

"Not a chance in hell, I crossed a line. I said Jez would want her to be happy, she totally freaked. Said how would I know what he'd want. I tell ya, it's kinda hard trying to get the girl when you know you aint never gonna be good enough."

"Jez would want her to be happy. She's had so much shit to deal with and now finally, things are going in the right direction for her. I know she could be happy with you and don't give me all that shit about not being good enough. That girl needs you and sooner or later she's gonna realize it."

"It's too late now."

"It's never too late. She didn't say no, so part of her must be considering it."

"I'll be back at my beach house in forty eight hours an I gotta hunch that I'll be on my own."

"Don't give up on her. You love her, fight for her."

Jackson had a strange feeling of déjà vu, he remembered being in his apartment with Jez when he told him he was gonna split town. He'd told him not to go, to stick around. Jez had taken his advice and look what happened to him.

"Hell, what do I know?" Jackson shrugged. He recalled something else from that conversation, something he'd put to the back of his mind till now.

Matt was unable to sit with the others, he needed to know what was going on. He'd gone into Summer's room, straight away Amber filled him in on what had gone on.

"No way. No. You can't go, you belong here with me. You know I promised mom and dad I'd take care of you."

"Matt, she's a grown woman she can stand on her own two feet."

"I am here y'know."

"Sorry," they both muttered.

"Look Summer, you know how much I worry about you and I'd miss you if you moved away."

"I don't know what I'm gonna do yet."

"Stay."

"Matt, she needs a fresh start."

"I don't dispute that, but she can do that here. I mean I've got nothing against Scott, but she's only known him five minutes. She isn't in the right frame of mind to make a life changing decision like that and quite frankly I think it was selfish of him to put her in that position."

"Stop talking about me!" Summer shouted. "Scott only wants to help me; he hasn't got a selfish bone in his body. Maybe it's you I need to get away from Matt. You and your big brother over protective thing that you do, it stifles me. You treat me like I'm a kid. You think I'm crazy, deranged, unhinged, whatever. Well I'm not; now both of you leave me alone, you're not helping."

She pushed them both out of the door and as she slammed it shut after them she slid down the door to the floor. She just sat there staring into space, not even knowing what she was thinking. After what seemed like hours she finally crawled into bed. She knew she wouldn't get any sleep, not with a decision like this to make. She was shocked when he'd asked her to go with him and even more shocked that she couldn't say no. Not that she was finding it easy to say yes either.

How could she even contemplate leaving New York, leaving behind everything that had once been so important? She knew she could love Scott, if she let herself. Not like she loved Jez, no one could ever come close to the love she had for Jez, the passion, the intense feeling that was always between them. She had to accept that however much she loved Jez and however much he loved her, he really was gone. If she went to LA wouldn't that be like she'd never loved him? Shouldn't she be grieving forever?

She didn't know what to do. She picked up a photo of Jez.
"Tell me babe, help me. What do I do? What do you want me to do? Please help me," she whispered.
She looked long and hard at his gorgeous face; he would always look like that to her. She would never grow old with him; never know what he'd look like in twenty years time. What would she be doing in twenty years time? Still here in this bed, looking at dog eared photos of the past?

She turned on her side, God she felt lonely. Scott only had two nights left in New York. Once he was gone, if she was still here, she really would be all alone. The need to be with him swept over her like a wave. She didn't want to talk, to try and come to a decision, she just wanted to be in his arms.

Scott lay on his bed with his hands behind his head. Sleep seemed to be evading him also. He didn't know if he'd made things worse for Summer by asking her to be with him, all he knew was he was missing her already. It would be good for her to get away from the City, but he couldn't see how he could persuade her to move. It wasn't fees able for him to relocate. He had never felt so confused in all his life, not good for a shrink to admit. There was a knock at the door, his heart practically leapt through his chest. There would only be one person in the world that would be at his door at twenty past two in the morning. Was she coming to tell him what he wanted to hear or was he about to lose this girl forever?

"I don't wanna talk. I'm sorry for what I said before about Jez," she said.
He moved to one side to let her through the door.
"I haven't made up my mind, I'm tired, so tired. I just need to sleep and I don't wanna sleep alone." She began to take her coat off.
"Summer, I…"
"Sssh." She moved towards him, placing a finger on his lips. "No more talking remember, not tonight anyway."
She kissed him softly on his lips. "I just want you to hold me."

He watched as she got undressed and practically fell into bed, he was only a few seconds behind her. As he lay next to her he pulled her close to him, stroking her hair and it seemed like she fell asleep in an instant. He wanted to commit this moment to memory, the smell of her coconut scented hair, the softness of her skin, the warmth of her body, just incase this was the last time. He was trying to take comfort from her being here, they obviously weren't finished yet. She did want him, she did need him.

"I need you too and I love you," he whispered into her hair and kissed her cheek. He tried to drift off to sleep but he was far too aware of her lying there in his arms. It scared him to think that in a few nights time all he'd have for company were his two Porsches. Sleep must've come eventually because before he knew it the light was streaming through the drapes, burning his eyes as he tried to open them.

Summer was sprawled out next to him, one arm flung across his chest. He reached out and stroked her bare back. She murmured slightly. This time tomorrow he'd be at the airport, would she be with him? He just wished they could stay like this, in bed forever. He watched her sleep for a while longer. Her beauty struck him each time he laid eyes on her. He reached out and drew his finger along the outline of her cheek bone and along to her lips, her eye lids began to flutter and he was greeted by those mesmerizing emerald eyes.

"Good morning."
She smiled slowly and moved back to cuddle him. He held her tight, never wanting to let her go. Neither of them spoke for a while. Where do you start when you haven't got a clue what the end might be? He wanted to kiss her, hold her, and tell her how much he loved her and that he'd take care of her forever. Is that what she wanted to hear?

"When do we start talking?"
"Scott, I don't know where to start."
"OK. I put you on the spot yesterday, you weren't expecting the question. I'll ask you again. Come to LA with me, let me make

you happy."

"I'm scared."

"Of me?"

"No. Of falling in love with you, forgetting Jez. I belong in New York, my heart is here."

He didn't like the way this conversation was going. "Your heart is wherever you take it Summer."

She moved away from him and sat up, hugging the duvet to her.

"So, what are you trying to say? You're staying here?"

She ran a hand through her hair. "I don't know what I'm trying to say."

She turned to look at him, she reached out and held his face in her hand. "I know I could love you if I gave us a chance."

"Goddammit then why won't you do it?" He knew he sounded harsher than he meant. She recoiled from him, suddenly very aware that she was naked underneath the duvet.

"I'm sorry baby, I didn't mean to sound angry. It's just, you are so important to me and I just don't wanna live my life without you."

Tears sprung into her eyes. "It's too soon."

They stared at each other for what seemed like an eternity.

"I'm sorry Scott."

She got up out of the bed, dragging a sheet behind her as she disappeared into the bathroom to get changed.

He rubbed his face with his hands. How could you be so close to someone one minute and a million miles away the next? He was still sitting on the bed, his head in his hands when she emerged a few minutes later. She stood in front of him and ran her fingers through his hair. He looked up and grabbed her hand.

"Don't leave it like this," he pleaded.

He stood up and pulled her to him, kissing her hard, his fingers roaming through her hair. She was breathless as she pushed him away.

"I love you Summer, I love you so Goddamn much."

"Don't, don't do this."

She moved away from him, he still had hold of her hand. "No, don't you do this."

He felt his heart contract as she wrangled free of his grip and headed towards the door, she stood there just looking at him.

"If this is so wrong, why is it so difficult for you to walk away?" he shouted.

She couldn't answer, she turned and left.

She cried the whole way back to her apartment. She couldn't be sure that she'd made the right decision, but the doubt wasn't enough to make her change her mind. Only time would tell if she'd just made one big mistake.

Scott was throwing his clothes into his suitcase, the sooner he got out of this City the better. He couldn't blame her, it was his own fault. He'd let her get to him, let her get under her skin. He wasn't the type of guy who was into serious relationships. It was kinda an occupational hazard; he saw what being in love did to people when it all went wrong. He was damned sure he'd never let that happen to him, but then he'd come to New York and met the girl of his dreams... Why couldn't she see how much she meant to him? Jackson had told him to fight for her, but he knew it was a battle he could never win. Until she was prepared to let Jez go she wouldn't let anyone else in her heart. He slammed the case shut.

CHAPTER TWENTY FIVE

When Summer arrived home she found Jackson waiting for her in the living room.

"I take it you've made your choice?" he asked taking one look at her tear stained face.

She nodded her head slowly.

"I'd say I'm glad you're staying here, if I thought that was what you really wanted."

"You know why I can't leave."

"I've got something here. I don't know what's in it, it might help, it might not."

He handed her a large brown envelope. She immediately recognized Jez's handwriting, she looked up at Jackson.

"He gave it to me, just before he died. He said he was thinking of takin' off and if he did I was to give you this. Circumstances being the way they were I didn't give it to you after he died. Then I kinda forgot about it, until yesterday."

She sat down and stared at the envelope, feeling like she'd just been kicked in the stomach. She hadn't even opened it yet and she was already a mess.

"D'you want me to leave you alone?"

"No Jackson, please stay. I don't think I can do this on my own."

She slowly opened the envelope and pulled out a letter and a CD. She took a deep breath and began to unfold the letter; it was a shock to see the familiar writing after such a long time.

My gorgeous Summer,

"Jackson, I can't do this. Will you read it to me?"

He wasn't sure if he could read it either, but he wasn't about to let her down. She held the letter out to him; he cleared his throat and began to read.

My gorgeous Summer,

Where do I begin? You know how much I love you. It's killing me not being with you, not holding you in my arms, not kissing you and not waking up next to you. Every night you're in my dreams, but when I open my eyes you're gone. I know what I did was wrong but I never meant to hurt you. Please believe that.

If you're reading this letter it means I've gone away, where? I don't know, but I can't bear to see you knowing that you are no longer mine and what's more it'd break my heart watching you fall in love with someone else. I know sooner or later it'll happen, when you finally manage to get your life back together after the mess I've managed to make of it. I hope you do find someone else, someone who will make you laugh again, but I can't stand by and watch it happen. Seeing some other guy kissing you, holding you and loving you - when more than anything I want to be that guy. I know now that we can never be together, I always thought our love would get us through anything...but I guess not even our love is above the law.

I am truly sorry for all the pain I've caused

you. You are the love of my life; I will never love anyone like I love you. We're soul mates; you will always be the only girl for me. I don't know where I'm going, but I want you to promise me one thing, one last thing. Forget about me, I'm not worth your tears. You go and find that guy, the one who will fix your broken smile. BE happy and live the life I thought we'd have...

I love you baby, forever and always...

Jez xxx

Jackson's voice was breaking as he choked back tears. Summer could barely take it all in. He went straight over to her to hug her.

"The CD," she mumbled.

"Sure you wanna hear that honey?"

She nodded as she tried to dry her eyes. Jackson put the CD in and pressed play, stepping back not wanting to intrude on this moment for Summer.

She recognized the opening bars of the song, she'd heard it so many times at Claudia's it was Bon Jovi's Always...

"This Romeo is bleeding..."

She'd never listened to the words before, Romeo - that was Jez.

"...Now I can't sing a love song like the way it's meant to be, I guess I'm not that good anymore, but baby that's just me..."

The tears slid down her cheeks.

"…I'll be there till the stars don't shine, till the heavens burst and the words don't rhyme and when I die, you'll be on my mind and I love you. Always. When you say your prayers, try and understand I've made mistakes I'm just a man…"

The song said it all…

"…When he holds you close, when he pulls you near, when he says the words you've been needin' to hear, I wish I was him coz those words are mine to say to you in till the end of time…"

She cried into her hands.

"…If you told me to cry for you I could, if you told me to die for you I would…"

"He was going to leave me," she sobbed.

"Honey, he didn't know the truth when he wrote that, he thought it was all over for you two."

"Everything is such mess, if only he hadn't died in that fire, we'd be together now."

"Summer look at me,"

She lifted her face to his.

"Jez loved you so much, he loved you enough to let you go, for you to try and find happiness with someone else. I know how much you love Jez, but you've gotta do the same thing here; you've got to let him go. It's the only way," he reached out and stroked her face. "I know it's hard but you gotta do it. You and Jez can't be together, so do what he's telling you to do…move on."

"I can't, I've already told Scott I'm staying here."

"So change your mind."

"We parted on bad terms."

"You'd do anything for Jez, right?"

She nodded her head,

"So do the last thing he asked you to do, go and be happy. Tell Scott you wanna be with him."

Summer re-read the letter over and over again. She could almost hear him say the words. She loved him with all her heart and soul, could she really find room to love Scott, even half as much? Was Amber right, did the love she and Jez shared only happen to a few people? If that was true, shouldn't she be grateful for the time they'd had together? She had spent so much time feeling guilty for enjoying Scott's company, worried that she'd betrayed Jez, now she felt like she had his blessing. Deep down she knew she should go with Scott and give them a shot, but her conscience wouldn't let her leave New York, it was her only tie with Jez. She'd asked him for help, for a sign about what to do. Well he'd responded, it couldn't be any clearer...it was practically in big neon lights.

Scott's last night in New York was spent alone in his hotel room. Well, not quite alone, he had a bottle of JD for company. The TV was on, but he wasn't paying any attention. He'd been hoping against hope that she'd come and see him before he went. He'd never been in a situation like this before and he didn't know what the hell to do. Didn't she know he was totally crazy about her? Of course she did, it wasn't his feelings she doubted, it was her own.

He couldn't believe he was just going to let her walk out of his life, no scratch that, he wasn't going to let her walk away. He wouldn't give up, he'd be back. Maybe all she needed was time. Once he was back in LA it might give her space to think more clearly and if she missed him half as much as he knew he would miss her then he was coming back for her.

One of these nights, she might actually get a proper night's sleep, Summer thought as she tossed and turned. Why was she missing Scott already when he hadn't even gone? They had laughed so much these past few weeks, he had brought her back from the brink of despair. When she thought back to what she'd been like when they first met, it scared the hell out of her. All the guys thought she'd gone crazy after Jez, Scott never made her feel like that. He'd helped her come back to life again. She had changed her mind so many times over the course of the night, yes she'd go... no she'd stay. She still wasn't any clearer.

The one thing she did know was she hated how she'd left things with Scott. Despite what he might think, she cared about him a lot. He had been the only good thing to happen to her since Jez's death. She glanced at the clock. Scott would be leaving for the airport about now. She jumped out of bed and pulled on sweat pants over her PJ's and a FDNY sweater. She quickly brushed her teeth, pulled on a Knicks baseball cap, grabbed her purse and ran out of the apartment. She got into a cab outside of her building and headed for the airport, she had to know he was ok with her.

By now Scott couldn't wait to get on the plane and leave this Goddamn City behind. He had the hangover from hell after finishing off the whole bottle of JD last night. Maybe he'd feel better after some good old LA sunshine. He'd just checked in, ignoring the admiring look from the check-in girl. He was off women at the moment, well all except one. He was just about to go through to departures when he heard someone call his name. He looked around, he must've been hearing things.

"Scott!"

He turned back round and nearly fell over Summer. A million thoughts ran through his mind.

"Have you changed your mind? Come with me please."

"Oh Scott, I've come to make sure we're still friends. I couldn't leave things the way they were. I still wanna keep in touch and I promise I'll come and visit real soon."

"Summer, I love you. Of course I'd still wanna see you and d'you know what? I don't care how long it takes, I'll wait for you."

He pulled her close, she hugged him tight. As she looked up at him the tears in her eyes mirrored his own. He bent down and kissed her, making the most of this final kiss. He moved back from her once they'd stopped kissing, their arms out stretched as they still held hands. He took another step back, towards the departure lounge, their fingers losing their grip on each other and eventually their arms dropped away from each other. They never once broke their gaze, the airport felt empty as they were only aware of each other. She slowly lifted her hand to wave and then he was gone. She turned with a very heavy heart and walked out of the terminal. At least they'd kissed and made up.

Scott sat on a chair in the departure lounge. He finally knew what his patients meant when they said their heart was broken. The first thing he'd do when he got back to LA was arrange another trip back to New York. He promised himself he would love her back to life and he wasn't about to go back on it. He ran his hand through his hair and sighed. Life was shit sometimes.

Summer has jumped a cab right out side the airport and was now headed back home, still unsure if she'd done the right thing. The cab driver was trying to talk, she wasn't in the mood. The feelings she had inside after saying goodbye to Scott took her by surprise, maybe there was room in her heart for him after all. Jez always said he'd look after her and maybe he was still doing that right now. He'd like Scott, he'd know he was good for her and the timing of that letter yesterday couldn't just be a coincidence, could it? Her attention was grabbed by the radio as she heard Jon Bon Jovi's husky voice.

"Can you turn this up please?"

"…It's been raining since you left me, now I'm drowning in the flood, see I've always been a fighter but without you I give up…"

My God this must be fate.

"…The pictures that you've left behind are just memories of a different life, some they made us laugh, some they made us cry, but they made you have to say goodbye…"

She could feel Jez's presence so strongly; it was like he was there in the cab with her.

"…what I'd give to run my fingers through your hair, touch your lips and hold you near…"

It was too much of a coincidence, she'd made a mistake. She leaned forward.

"Can you take me back to the airport please?"

The driver tutted, but nodded.

"Quickly," she said realising there wasn't much time left.

"…We can pack up our old dreams and our old lives and find a place where the sun still shines…"

She settled back in her seat. She did need Scott, needed him more than she realized and it had taken Jez to get it through to her when no one else could.

Jez, wherever you are, thank you, for loving me and for showing me the way forward. I love you so much, but we both know I've got to do this."

"...And I'll be there forever and a day and I love you...always."

Summer ran through the terminal and managed to get a standby ticket, she was just in time. She went straight through to departures and towards the gate. She felt like her heart was on fire. She saw him up ahead at the back of the queue waiting to board. The excitement bubbled up inside her. She snuck up behind him and tapped him on the shoulder. He spun round; the expression on his face told her she'd made the right decision.

"Is a girl allowed to change her mind, if the offers still open?"

He flung his arms around her, picking her up and swinging her round.

"God, Summer yes, yes of course it is."

They couldn't stop kissing and laughing.

"You don't know how happy you've made me."

"I was wrong, I do love you. I just didn't know I loved you."

"What made you change your mind?"

"Let's just say an old friend made me realize I would've been making a mistake."

"Obviously a good friend."

She smiled a sad smile. "The best."

He squeezed her hand.

"I haven't got any luggage, I changed my mind in the cab," she lowered her voice. "I've got my PJ's on under my clothes.

He burst out laughing. "God I love you, don't ever change. I'll but you a whole walk-in wardrobe of clothes when we get to LA."

They walked onto the flight, hand in hand.

"Hey it's not exactly driving off into the sunset, but flying into it is so much cooler."

She grinned at him. She was sure Jez was around somewhere, watching over her. "Thank you," she whispered.

"Hey, what did Matt and the others say about you coming with me?"

"They don't know," she replied and leaned over to kiss him. "It's just you and me now."

EPILOGUE

12 months later... New York City

Summer, Claudia and amber were in a suite at the plaza having stayed there the previous night. They were helping summer into her dress.

"Jeez, I only had my fitting last week, I can't have got that much bigger in such a short space of time," she protested.

"summer, its ok. I've zipped you up, it fits perfectly," Claudia tried to placate her friend.

"I'll be waddling down the aisle."

"You're only just four months pregnant, you can't really tell and besides you look fantastic," Amber said.

Summer turned to look in the mirror. She did love the dress and she felt like a princess in it.

"Scott will think you look a million dollars," Claudia added.

At the mention of his name she couldn't help but smile, she really was happy. She turned back to face her friends.

"You guys have really been there for me. We've all been to hell and back, but this is definitely the start of something new," she took both of their hands. "You both look beautiful."

They hugged each other, being careful not to crease their dresses.

"We better get going, we're running late," Claudia noticed the time on the clock.

"Brides prerogative to be late," Amber grinned as the three girls left the hotel suite.

The church was packed full of people. The organist began playing the wedding march, indicating the arrival of the bride. Scott stood, looking up the aisle to catch his first glimpse of summer. When he saw her she took his breath away, she looked radiant, just like a princess. The beginning of her bump was just about noticeable, she was blooming already. It was so sexy. She smiled at him as she came closer. He held his hand out to guide her into the pew.

Together they watched Amber join Matt at the alter. Scott put his arm around her waist, resting his hand on her swollen stomach.

"How impolite, you've totally upstaged the bride," he whispered into her ear.

She turned and smiled at him.

As she watched the ceremony proceed she was still amazed that she was standing here at Amber and Matt's wedding. Amazed, but glad things had worked out for them. She knew the subject of adoption had come up recently and once they returned from honey moon in Antigua, it was all systems go.

Claudia and Leyton were next to her, still as happy as ever. They had moved in together but were in no rush to get married, they'd both taken a career break and were off travelling after the wedding. Starting in the Bahamas to catch up with Claudia's old boss Doug Harper. Leyton had changed Claudia's life for the better.

Jackson and CJ were joint best men and were up at the alter with Matt. They had split up briefly a few months ago when CJ told Jackson he either committed to their relationship or it was over. Jackson thought he couldn't commit, but a few weeks without CJ made him see otherwise, they were now planning their own wedding.

As for her, her life had totally changed, she'd gotten used to living in la very quickly. She started off helping Scott to run his surgery, but more recently she was in charge of Amber's West Coast office and she was loving every minute of it.

More importantly she was getting her life back together. She and Scott had married at a sunset ceremony on the beach in front of their beach house four months ago. She was pretty sure that the baby she was carrying was conceived later on that evening as they made love by the bonfire as the sun came up.

She had dealt with all her demons, with the help and support of Scott. She very rarely thought of Marcus, but jez was never far from her thoughts. His engagement ring was on her right hand and she could think of him now and smile, she knew he'd kept his promise to look after her. He had led her to a new life and she was gonna take that chance and grab it with both hands.

Scott squeezed her hand; she looked up and met his warm smile with her own.
"You ok Mrs Morgan?" he whispered.
"I am now," she replied. I am now, she repeated silently.

THE END

Lightning Source UK Ltd.
Milton Keynes UK
09 November 2010

162608UK00001B/4/P